FIELD GUIDE

TO THE

SUPERNATURAL UNIVERSE

ALYSON NOËL

FIELD GUIDE TO THE SUPERNATURAL UNIVERSE

MARGARET K. MCELDERRY BOOKS

New York · London · Toronto · Sydney · New Delhi

MARGARET K. McELDERRY BOOKS • An imprint of Simon & Schuster Children's Publishing Division • 1230 Avenue of the Americas, New York, New York 10020 • This book is a work of fiction. Any references to historical events, real people, or real places are used fictitiously. Other names, characters, places, and events are products of the author's imagination, and any resemblance to actual events or places or persons, living or dead, is entirely coincidental. • Text © 2022 by Alyson Noël, LLC • Jacket illustration © 2022 by Maike Plenzke • Jacket design © 2022 by Simon & Schuster, Inc. • All rights reserved, including the right of reproduction in whole or in part in any form. • MARGARET K. McELDERRY BOOKS is a trademark of Simon & Schuster, Inc. • For information about special discounts for bulk purchases, please contact Simon & Schuster Special Sales at 1-866-506-1949 or business@simonandschuster.com. • The Simon & Schuster Speakers Bureau can bring authors to your live event. For more information or to book an event, contact the Simon & Schuster Speakers Bureau at 1-866-248-3049 or visit our website at www.simonspeakers.com. • The text for this book was set in Granjon. • Manufactured in the United States of America • 0322 FFG • First Edition • 10 9 8 7 6 5 4 3 2 1 • Library of Congress Cataloging-in-Publication Data • Names: Noël, Alyson, author. • Title: Field guide to the supernatural universe / Alyson Noël. • Description: New York : Margaret K. McElderry Books, [2022] | Summary: "When 12-year-old Max is sent to live with his eccentric grandfather for the summer, he finds himself on an unlikely quest to uncover an enchanted book that contains the key to defeating an unearthly nemesis."—Provided by publisher. • Identifiers: LCCN 2021015615 (print) | LCCN 2021015616 (ebook) | ISBN 9781534498235 (hardcover) | ISBN 9781534498259 (ebook) • Subjects: CYAC: Supernatural—Fiction. | Books—Fiction. | Magic—Fiction. | Grandfathers—Fiction. | Family secrets—Fiction. • Classification: LCC PZ7.N67185 Fh 2022 (print) | LCC PZ7.N67185 (ebook) | DDC [Fic]—dc23 • LC record available at https://lccn.loc.gov/2021015615 • LC ebook record available at https://lccn.loc.gov/2021015616

For Michael Zoumas

A mind that is stretched by a new experience can never go back to its old dimensions.

—Oliver Wendell Holmes Sr.

Believing is seeing.

—Ramhart Woodbead

L ook, I know this probably isn't the best way to begin a story, considering how pretty much everyone hates a pop quiz, but before you go any further, I need you to answer a question.

If you feel very committed to your answer, you might want to circle it with a pen so everyone will know exactly where you stand.

If you can't find a pen, or if this book doesn't actually belong to you, then it's probably better to just circle the answer in your head.

Ready? Here goes:

Do you believe in ghosts?

YES   **NOT SURE**   **NO**

If you answered YES, you are correct. Feel free to turn the page.

If you answered NO, please keep in mind that just because you don't believe in something doesn't mean it doesn't exist. For further proof, definitely turn the page.

If you're NOT SURE if you believe in ghosts, you should absolutely turn the page so the next time someone asks you that question, you can answer correctly.

1

Boy Meets Bogey

So, you passed the test and made it to the first chapter—well done. Though I'm guessing the real reason you're here is because of the video.

You know, the one of me (allegedly) freaking out on the last day of school?

The one that circled the globe faster than the speed of light and went totally viral?

There's a good chance you may have even helped it go viral by sharing it with your friends so you could laugh even more when you watched it with them. It's not like I blame you. If I wasn't the subject, I would've done the same thing.

But what if I told you the video was a lie?

What if I said that's not at all how it happened? That there are things in this world—terrible, dreadful, invisible things—that were 100 percent responsible but couldn't be captured on film?

Would you believe me?

Or would you roll your eyes and shake your head along with the rest of the minimifidians?

If you haven't seen the video, don't bother looking for it now. You'd only be wasting your time.

If you don't know what a minimifidian is, not to worry: all will be explained.

The absolute true story of what really went down is in the pages that follow. And while there may be times when you'll find yourself questioning if something so outrageous could've actually happened, I'm here to tell you it did.

And I've got the blue streak to prove it.

But before we go any further, here's a few things you should probably know about me:

My name is Maxen (Woodbead) Smith.
I'm twelve and a half years old and completely
normal in every way.
Except for the fact that I can see ghosts.

You may have noticed that part of my name is in parentheses. I think of it like a silent surname—kind of like the *g* in phlegm or the *h* in asthma. Woodbead would've been my real last name if my dad hadn't legally changed his own to Smith.

Unfortunately, what my dad didn't realize is that while you can change a name to protect your identity, you can't change a legacy. And as the grandson of Ramhart Woodbead, world-famous ghost hunter/paranormal explorer, who's widely known as the Indiana Jones of the supernatural world, I'm pretty sure the Woodbead part of me is totally responsible for the ghost-seeing part of me.

I've been seeing ghosts since I was a kid. Long before I understood that most people couldn't see them and hardly anyone believed in them.

You have no idea how much I envied those people.

If you happen to be one of the lucky ones, then congratulations—you are far more fortunate than you can possibly realize. Take it from me: seeing ghosts is an awful burden that can lead to public humiliation, terrifying moments, and repeated visits to the principal's office, where you're forced to explain the unexplainable.

But before you start thinking that will never happen to you, I have some bad news:

> Just because you think you can't see ghosts
> doesn't mean you haven't already seen one.

You see, not all ghosts are the same. They're not always transparent, and they don't always wear raggedy old nightgowns and float around crumbling houses wailing about the horrible things that happened to them. Some ghosts look like completely normal everyday people, and they're the ones you need to watch out for. Problem is, by the time you've identified them, it's usually too late.

Anyway, as I've already mentioned, it was the last day of school, and there were only eleven minutes standing between the end of sixth grade and the beginning of the rest of my life.

My teacher, Ms. Rossi, was at the chalkboard jotting down

a list of fun facts about Hawaii—as soon as the final bell rang, she was headed for the Aloha State. Until then, she instructed us to assume a "chill island vibe," which pretty much translated to *Stay in your seats, keep quiet, and don't even think about starting any nonsense that'll make me late for my flight.*

Sounds easy enough, right? And it was, until the temperature suddenly dropped, and the lights started flickering on and off.

You might think a blast of cold air and flickering lights are no big deal, nothing to get worked up about. But I knew from experience that whenever those fluorescent tubes started buzzing and blinking and my breath fogged up before me, it meant a ghost had just entered the room.

Normally, I'd close my eyes, slump low in my seat, and brace for whatever paranormal prank was headed my way. But when something slammed hard against the back of my chair, I breathed a little easier, figuring it was just Sven—this jerk of a ghost who'd been haunting me forever and was way more annoying than scary.

Years of experience had taught me that the best way to handle Sven was to ignore him. So I yanked my hood up over my head and waited for him to move on. I wasn't about to let some phantom bully get between me and my goal of finishing the school year "incident"-free.

This would probably be a good time to mention how I'm known for having what my teachers and principal refer to as *incidents.*

I've also heard them use the words *disturbing episodes*, *violent outbursts*, and *unsettling behavior*.

For the record, none of those *incidents* were ever my fault. In every case, a ghost was responsible.

Like that time when it looked like I swiped the substitute's wig from his head and flung it across the room like a Frisbee—it was a ghost, not me. I was actually trying to keep that from happening, not that anyone believed me.

Sure, it made me a legend among my classmates. But while they were doubled over in hysterics, I got suspended.

While they went to summer camp, I was sentenced to summer school.

To make matters worse, my dad cut off my internet access.

Do you really think I'd risk all that just to get a few laughs?

According to the principal, who likes to keep track of these things, I've been averaging three or four *incidents* per year. And while I'll spare you the details, the point is, in every one of those cases I was actually trying to stop something way worse from happening.

Some of those times I was successful, which of course no one noticed, and why would they, when they were completely unaware of the danger that lurked right there beside them?

And other times . . . not so much.

In the end, it was just another unfortunate consequence of being the only person in all of Boring Elementary (the actual name of my school, named after the actual name of my town) who could see ghosts.

When Sven slammed my chair a second time, I didn't so much as flinch.

It wasn't until he let out the longest, loudest, most disgusting burp I'd ever heard in my life that I knew something was up.

You see, Sven was part of a small category of ghosts I call Loopers. And the thing with Loopers is, well, *they loop*. They're not into improv, and they never wander off script. They just repeat the same scene over and over until they eventually crash, only to reboot and start up again. And let's just say that disgusting burps weren't part of Sven's loop.

At first I figured it must be some other ghost. Considering how ghosts like to feed off things like big emotions and high energy, most schools are pretty much teeming with them. But that theory failed the second I was hit by a smell so awful, so foul, it can only be described as the scent of some dead, decaying thing left to rot in the sun.

My first reaction was to pull the cord on my hoodie and block it all out. But all I succeeded in doing was to leave a small opening for me to see through and a place for my nose to stick out. As for the smell, it grew worse with each inhale.

I was in the process of freeing myself when this . . . *thing* . . . this hideous *beast* with an enormous head and elongated snout, landed on top of my desk and proceeded to pull what looked like a tiny fish skeleton out the side of its mouth.

If you'd asked me just one day before if monsters were real, I would've laughed in your face. Like most people, the only monsters I'd ever seen were in the super-scary, late-night movies

I usually regretted watching. But one look at this horrible thing and I knew straightaway there was no other word to explain it.

For one thing, ghosts come in only two forms—they're either humans or pets who've passed on.

For another, ghosts don't eat—and yet, according to the drops of water trailing between the newly vacant aquarium and my desk, that thing, that *monster* had devoured our class goldfish like it was some kind of delicacy. And yet despite the horrible scene unfolding before me, my classmates continued scrolling on their screens as Ms. Rossi sketched a bright yellow hibiscus (the Aloha State flower) onto the chalkboard. Everyone acted so oblivious that I was starting to doubt my own eyes when the monster suddenly lunged forward and took a hard swipe at my face. I reeled back in fright, only to lose my balance and crash on the floor.

Last thing I remember before I went down was the sight of that repulsive creature looming above, its creep-show eyes gleaming as it licked a drop of my blood from its claw.

By the time I came to, my classmates were practically falling out of their seats to get a better view as Ms. Rossi knelt beside me and said, "Max? You okay?"

I groaned in response. The tip of my nose was pure agony, but my teacher seemed more concerned with checking for signs of head injury.

"Open your eyes wide," she instructed. "Now follow my finger." She traced a lazy loop before me. "How's your vision— is it blurry? Any nausea? Do you remember what happened?"

That last question made me jolt upright in panic only to find that dreadful humpbacked freak still camped out beside me. The monster was sickening, grotesque, and as I watched it sharpen its claw along a row of rotting black teeth, I knew it was just a matter of time before it turned that sharp, gleaming blade against me again.

"You should see the nurse." Ms. Rossi helped me to my feet. "I'll write you a hall pass."

If I really did have a head injury, taking time to write a hall pass seemed risky. But with escape within reach, I was in no position to argue.

I'd made it halfway to the door when Jasmine Skink whined, "Why does *he* get to leave early?" And just like that, my dream of a speedy exit was over.

One week before, a ballot had been passed all around, and after the votes were counted, I was designated Class Weirdo (not an official category), while Jasmine was given the title of Cutest Smile. Honestly, I had no way of knowing if that was true, seeing as how every time Jasmine looked my way, she wore a scowl on her face.

Ever since I accidentally threw up on her at her fourth-grade birthday party when a ghost tried to serve me its own severed bloody ear instead of a vanilla cupcake, she'd had it out for me. Even after my dad made me spend my hard-earned allowance to replace her vomit-splattered dress, she still made it her mission to terrorize me as much as any ghost ever had.

Seriously, it was so bad that if you'd asked me back then to make a list of my Top Five Terrifying Things, it would've gone something like this:

MAX'S LIST OF TOP FIVE TERRIFYING THINGS
1. Ghosts
2. Jasmine Skink
3. My dad when I try to talk to him about seeing ghosts
4. Public speaking
5. Spiders (the hairy kind)

Which is why I found it pretty hilarious when the monster spread a set of undersized wings I hadn't noticed before and soared clumsily through the air, only to land on Jasmine's head.

Was it possible the monster wasn't entirely bad?

"He's totally faking," Jasmine sneered, and she flicked an irritated hand through her hair, totally unaware of the monster making her bangs stand on end. "He'll do anything for attention. He's completely pathetic."

For a fraction of a second, I could've sworn I saw Jasmine's eyes glow yellow, her tongue flicker blue. But as soon as my teacher spoke up, she was normal again.

"Jasmine, that's enough." Ms. Rossi's chill island vibe was long gone. But it wasn't enough to keep Jasmine from purposely sticking her foot in my path.

"Faker," she hissed, quietly enough for Ms. Rossi to miss, but still loud enough for her friends to join in.

She was baiting me, but I wasn't biting. Nothing she could

do would keep me from getting the heck out of that classroom.

Or at least that was what I thought until I caught sight of Churro, the class hamster, crawling from Jasmine's arm to her shoulder.

This is the part where things got tricky. And despite what you may have heard—despite the jam-packed file in the principal's office detailing my "problematic" history at Boring Elementary—I'm not the sort of kid who goes looking for trouble. If anything, trouble goes looking for me. Unfortunately, on that day, I walked right into its trap.

Normally, if I saw something like that, I'd just mind my own business and pretend not to notice that Jasmine had nicked the hamster from his habitat without asking permission.

But when I saw how the monster's gleaming red eyes tracked Churro's every move—the way its long, spiky tongue quivered in anticipation of yet another class pet to make a meal of—well, clearly something had to be done. Thing was, none of my options were good.

If I made a grab for Churro, Jasmine would make a huge scene, thereby wrecking my chance to finish the school year *incident-free*.

If I kept going, our beloved class hamster would meet the same fate as our beloved class fish—which, despite no one noticing its absence, didn't make it any less tragic.

I gulped, torn between two possible futures.

One where I'd be an accomplice to a hamster murder but could possibly start junior high with a clean slate.

The other where I'd be voted Class Weirdo for the rest of my life.

Before me, Ms. Rossi impatiently waved the hall pass.

Beside me, the monster's tongue rolled toward its prey, as Jasmine, oblivious to everything but me, whined, "Tell Max to stop staring! He's giving me the *creeps*!"

The girl with a hideous monster on her head said *I* was giving *her* the creeps. If the situation weren't so urgent, I would've laughed. But with Churro just one flick of the tongue away from annihilation, I knew I could never live with myself if I didn't at least try to save him.

My arm shot out before me.

My fingers made a grab for Churro's warm, furry belly.

But just as I lifted the squirming hamster to safety, the beast leaped forward, seized hold of my arm, and lobbed Churro clear across the room in a way that made it look like I was responsible.

The room broke into chaos.

People were shouting. Jasmine was crying. And with Churro already on the decline, there was no time to waste.

Some of the comments left on the video swear it's a fake— claiming it's humanly impossible to cross a room in less than a blink. All I can say is adrenaline spiked with horror is a powerful thing, and by the time I reached the other side with a trembling hamster cupped in my hand, I grinned like a superhero. Until I noticed Ms. Rossi standing over me, hands on hips, a murky splotch of red rising to her cheeks, and I realized I was the only one celebrating.

"Max, hand over Churro. *Now!*" Her jaw clenched. Her eyes blazed in a way that would normally scare me. But after years of saving my teachers and classmates from countless catastrophes unknown to them, their lack of appreciation was really wearing thin.

Still, aware that anything I said in my defense would only be held against me, I was just about to surrender the hamster when I noticed a new monster curled around Ms. Rossi's neck, and I instinctively yanked Churro back to protect him.

"Max, this is not a joke." Her voice was tight, strained, and other than the squeal of my sneakers scrambling across the floor in an attempt to get away, it was the only sound to be heard.

I'd never seen her so mad, but I also knew if she could see what I saw, she'd totally understand. Ms. Rossi's monster was grotesque, with an oversized skeletal head and large empty eye sockets that were glowing and red. Its neck consisted of long, skinny vertebrae wrapped in a thin veil of flesh, and the body beneath was deceptively spindly, with gaunt, wasted arms that stretched and unspooled as they proceeded to chase me.

I'd just reached the back wall when I realized the situation was even worse than I'd thought. Everywhere I looked, hideous, monstrous creatures—some with horns, some with tails, some of them winged, but all of them with the same evil glowing red eyes—crept free of the shadows and onto my classmates.

Jason, the kid who wore extra-thick glasses, played unsuspecting host to an alien-like monster with long, pointy fingernails that scratched at his eyeballs.

Shannon, the girl who suffered from a permanent skin rash, carried a beast with a forked tongue and sharp teeth that incessantly gnawed at her flesh.

August, the boy who carried an inhaler wherever he went, had a monster twisted around his chest so tight that it was amazing he could take so much as a single breath.

From chin acne to frizzy hair, there seemed to be a monster responsible for putting it there.

Had it always been like this? Were monsters the reason for all their problems?

And if so, did that explain why I was scheduled for braces next year?

I guess I'd gotten so caught up in the sight, I'd failed to notice that the only reason my classmates were silent was because most of them were recording.

In a move I didn't see coming, Ms. Rossi lunged for the hamster just as her monster sprang free from her neck and aimed straight for my head.

If you've seen the video, you probably think you know what happened next, but the video doesn't look anything like what I experienced.

Just as Ms. Rossi pried Churro from my fingers, her monster, along with all the others, descended on me in a frenzy of gnashing fangs and jagged claws so sharp that all I could do was close my eyes and prepare for the end.

You know how they say that just before you die, your entire life flashes before you? Well, all I saw was an endless stream of ghosts.

Ghosts were the reason I was repeatedly sent to the principal's office.

It was because of ghosts that I didn't have any friends and my parents argued so much that my mom left.

And then, just when I was finally getting a handle on them—an army of monsters had taken their place.

Maybe it was a decade's worth of pent-up frustration that drove me.

Maybe hours of playing video games and watching superhero movies on repeat had finally kicked in.

All I know for sure is that one moment I was spiraling into an abyss, and the next I was back on my feet, landing the sort of solid left hooks and ninja-style airborne kicks I'd only seen in movies as one by one, the monsters fell around me.

My fist cut through the air like a plastic spoon through a soft-serve ice cream, laying waste to a trio of skull-faced monsters.

My right foot thrummed with a life all its own as it kicked out from behind me and took down a snake-bodied beast—as my left leg swung around to the front and demolished a three-headed freak.

After years of being victimized by supernaturals, I'd somehow miraculously transformed from a skinny, somewhat uncoordinated kid into the ultimate monster-destroying machine. And now that the tables were turned, I vowed to rid my life of ghosts, monsters, and whatever other creepy things dared to come near.

What felt like hours of battle turned out to be only one

minute and thirty-seven seconds on video. I'd just pulverized a pulpy, skinless freak, and was about to do serious damage to a horned two-legged fiend that towered well above me, when the end-of-day school bell shrilled so loudly it was like an alarm going off in the middle of a dream.

And much like waking from a dream, it took me a few dazed beats to adjust to my surroundings.

A stream of cold sweat slipped down my face as a deep, throbbing pain radiated from my neck to my wrist. My legs felt wobbly, my knees uncertain as the adrenaline that had once fueled me vanished as quickly as the last remaining trace of the monsters.

Wearily, I took in my surroundings, moving from the mess of toppled desks to the overturned chairs to the jeering looks on my classmates' faces—all of them unaware of the fact that I'd just slayed the heck out of an army of monsters.

For one startled inhale, the class was the quietest it had been all year.

By the time I exhaled, school security had arrived and swiftly escorted me out of the room.

2

The Man with the Monkey-Tooth Medallion

By the time I made it out of the principal's office and over to the parking lot, my dad was the only parent left, and from the unhappy look on his face, I assumed he'd heard the whole story.

"Max." He pinched the bridge of his nose and regarded me with a sigh. "You've truly outdone yourself this time."

Normally when someone says that, a modest *thank you* is the correct response. This was not one of those times.

"What on earth were you thinking?"

I slid onto the passenger seat and stared at my knees. I mean, what else could I do? Use the excuse when it's never worked before?

"Not a great way to end the school year." He shook his head wearily. "I thought you were past this sort of thing."

He turned his phone toward me and pushed play so I could watch the video one of my classmates had made. When it reached the part where I went full-on action hero, punching and kicking at . . . well, according to the video, *nothing*, I cleared my throat and looked away.

"You're a good kid, Max. But you can't continue with these kinds of stunts. You've got to get a grip on yourself." He gave me this sort of imploring look, like he expected me to commit right then and there to a complete personality overhaul. Knowing it was easier to go along with him, I nodded as though I were totally on board.

As though the *stunts* he referred to were mine to control.

As though I hadn't just single-handedly rid the school of evil class-pet-eating monsters and there was no obligation to thank me.

"You know, you don't have to act outrageous to get people to notice you."

I nearly fell out of the car. Seriously, I could hardly believe that after all these years, he still didn't get it. Seeking attention was never the goal. Sure, I had a reputation for being hilarious in an unexpectedly zany sort of way, but I never saw any of my so-called friends after school.

Whether it was because the parents didn't want their kid to hang out with someone *unhinged* (I'd once overheard one of them say that), or they were afraid of me (I'd heard that one too), I couldn't say for sure. All I knew was I hadn't been invited to a single party or sleepover since the time I tried to stop a ghost from taking the mom's minivan for a joyride, only to be caught behind the wheel fighting with a car thief no one could see.

Without another word, my dad heaved a deep sigh and pulled out of the lot and onto the road. At first I was glad for the silence, but it wasn't long before I sensed it had nothing to do with me—that something much bigger was brewing, and going by the set of deep lines etched onto his face, it was taking a toll.

My mom always claimed I looked exactly like my dad did when he was my age. But even after she presented the evidence, holding an old class picture of his next to mine like two unlikely suspects in a police lineup, I still couldn't see how a head of brown hair, a pair of brown eyes, a square of chin, line of mouth, and jut of nose somehow meant we were clones.

But now he looked nothing like the kid in those pictures. The whites of his eyes were shot with red streaks, and his mouth twisted into what seemed like a permanent grimace. He was tired. Beaten. Like a man on the brink of irreversible defeat. And the way he stared through the windshield, his gaze dull and empty, gave the impression he had no idea where he was, despite having lived in Boring since before I was born.

"Max," he said, "I've been thinking . . ."

Something about his tone had me digging my heels into the floor mat, bracing for whatever came next. I had no idea where it was leading, but I was sure it wasn't anywhere good.

"Since I don't know where this new job search will land us, and with your mom—"

"In Australia." I cut him off before he could finish. "She's in *Australia*." I leveled a challenging gaze his way, leaving no doubt that I wasn't open to alternative theories.

Sydney had been my mom's last known address. She'd even sent me a postcard from the zoo with a couple of koalas pictured on the front. Just because some official from the consulate had called bearing terrible news didn't mean that the news was true.

My dad drew a slow, measured breath. On the exhale, he said, "Look—I know it's been hard for you. It's been hard for me too. But you have to stop this. It's time to face facts. She's gone, Max, and she's never coming back. You need to accept that."

That's pretty much when I flat-out stopped listening, reducing his voice to a jumble of consonants and vowels that didn't make any sense. If my mom really was gone, surely I'd be the first to know. My proof: I'd been seeing ghosts my whole life, but I'd never seen hers. Which only proves that consulate official had gotten it wrong.

I figured my mom was probably somewhere deep in the outback, exploring in some faraway place with no cell service. As soon as she found her way out, she'd give me a call, and we'd share a good laugh at how everyone had been gullible enough to believe the sad news except me.

I'm not sure when, but at some point my dad gave up and surrendered to silence. When we finally turned into our driveway, I bounded out of the car and into the house, only to discover that all our furniture was gone.

Over the past few weeks, I'd watched as our belongings began to gradually disappear, either put into storage or sold off to strangers. It started with the kind of stuff we rarely used, like the formal dining room table and the wooden cabinet where my mom kept the fancy dishes she saved for special occasions. Then on to smaller things like side tables, decorative pillows, and lamps. But even though I knew it was coming, seeing the house I grew up in stripped of everything familiar left me feeling pretty shook.

I glanced between the empty space where the couch once sat and then over to the collection of boxes and suitcases piled up in the hall.

"It really is happening," I said, sounding as deflated as I felt. Somehow I'd managed to trick myself into believing my dad wouldn't actually go through with the move.

"Last day of school, last night in this house. It's a big day for both of us." My dad placed a hand on my shoulder. And though I knew he meant well, seeing all that vacant space left me so angry I felt like I was about to explode.

"How is Mom supposed to find us if we no longer live here?" I ducked out from under his hand and spun around to face him. "What if she shows up only to find another family has taken our place?"

My dad stood before me, his jaw slack, eyes narrowed so tightly I could just barely make out the whites. "Max . . . ," he started, but I turned my back and stormed to my room—only to discover that my posters had been ripped from the walls and my bed, nightstand, and drawers were gone too. The only sign I'd ever lived there was the lone T-shirt and jeans left hanging in my closet.

"Where am I supposed to sleep?" I gestured around the hollow box of a room. There was not so much as a pillow or blanket in sight.

"I was thinking we could set up camp in the backyard." My dad stood in the doorway and attempted a grin. "You used to love that."

"Yeah, when I was, like, eight." I folded my arms over my chest. My day had just gone from really bad to epically worse.

I watched as my dad heaved a sigh of defeat and slid down the wall to the floor, where he landed with his knees awkwardly turned out to each side.

For the longest time, he didn't speak, and with nowhere else to sit and nothing else to do, I eventually plopped myself on the floor too.

"I feel like I'm failing you." My dad held his head in his hands, which left the words sort of muffled, though the meaning was clear. "Between your denial over your mom and now this latest . . . *incident* . . . on your last day of school. You're lucky they didn't expel you or charge you with animal cruelty."

Animal *cruelty*? I'm the one who'd saved Churro! It's not my fault the real villain was invisible to everyone but me. I was just about to shout out in my defense, but another look at my dad and the fight seeped right out of me.

It wasn't the first time I'd seen him so upset. The whole thing with my mom—first the separation and then the phone call—left him pretty much wrecked. Still, knowing I was the cause this time around made me feel really bad.

"I don't know how to reach you," he said. "We don't connect the way we once did. And this obsession with ghosts, it's not . . ."

In my head, I finished the sentence for him:

It's not normal.

It's not healthy.

It's not how a sane person acts.

But what he said was, "You'd been doing so well this past year. I thought you'd outgrown all of that."

I just sat there, leaning against the wall across from my dad where my dresser once stood, not entirely sure what he expected me to do.

"But now . . ." He lifted his head and settled his eyes onto mine. "I'm thinking you'd be better off spending time with someone who might be able to help you in a way that I can't. And because of that . . ."

It was the pause that nearly did me in as a zillion wild scenarios played out in my head, and yet not one of them turned out to be nearly as wild as what he said next.

"I've decided to send you to stay with your grandfather for a bit while I get our life sorted." He blinked, tried to stretch his lips into a grin. But from where I sat, he looked like a person who had just eaten something truly disgusting and was forcing me to have a taste too.

"You can't be serious!" I cried. "You mean Ramhart? Ramhart *Woodbead*?" The name felt strange on my tongue. Since my dad and his dad didn't speak all that often, I'd only met my grandfather once, back when my mom, determined to make peace between my dad and my granddad, drove us all out to Ramhart's house so he could meet his new grandson. Needless to say, I was too young to remember, so I wasn't sure what I was supposed to call him. Grandpa Woodbead would probably be the appropriate choice, but somehow it didn't seem right. From what I'd been told and the few pictures I'd seen of his bizarre clothes, blue-streaked hair, and the monkey-tooth medallion that hung from his neck, Ramhart was no ordinary grandpa.

According to my dad, his earliest childhood memories are of being left alone with his mom (my grandma) while Ramhart was away on some sketchy supernatural adventure. Then one day, when my dad was eight, Ramhart left and never came back. Even after his mom died two years later and my dad was sent to live in foster homes, Ramhart still didn't return. It wasn't until years later, when my dad was already an adult, that Ramhart bothered to find him. And even then, his only excuse was that he'd spent over a decade trapped in a time slip, which is probably the worst excuse a person could use.

Anyway, the whole thing left my dad really bitter to the point where I distinctly remember him referring to Ramhart as *a misfit, a fraud, and a cautionary tale of just how risky it is to live on the wrong side of normal.* It was right after one of my earlier incidents, when I blamed the ghost that haunted my kindergarten classroom (who was also named Max) for painting my name all over the walls.

Even though I was just a little kid, I still understood the true message behind my dad's words: every time I talked about seeing ghosts, I risked becoming a weirdo like Ramhart.

That was also when I began to understand that most people couldn't see what I saw. At first I worried there was something wrong with me—like, maybe my eyesight was broken, or even my brain. But since I was 100 percent certain I wasn't responsible for putting my name on those walls, I figured it was just easier for people to convince themselves that what they couldn't see couldn't possibly exist. From that point on, I was a lot more careful.

Except for the times when I slipped.

Seeing as how my dad blames his whole lousy childhood on his dad, I couldn't understand why he'd send me to live with the very cause of his misery.

"Since when is Ramhart considered an appropriate summer guardian?" I crossed my arms and glared. I knew I was pushing it, and when my dad sighed heavy and deep, I felt bad for asking. Still, I was desperately in need of some answers.

"Listen, Max. I've got a string of job interviews lined up, and they all require an overnight stay. And since I can't exactly bring you along or leave you to sit in a motel room all day—"

"But that was the plan!" I cried. "You said you trusted me. You said I'd proved I was mature enough to handle myself, and that—"

"That was before . . ." My dad paused, his face looking pained.

"Before *what?*" I demanded. For some reason I wanted him to say it, even though I was sure neither of us wanted to hear it.

"Before I got the call from your principal." He frowned in a way that left me wondering why I'd pushed it. "I can't take the risk of leaving you on your own. Not after today."

His words left me momentarily speechless. Once again, what happened at school wasn't my fault. Here I'd done something heroic, brave even, and instead of being rewarded, I was headed for what would surely turn out to be the worst summer of my life.

"But you said Ramhart was a freak!" It was the best defense

I could think of, but it didn't help that my voice cracked at the end.

My dad flinched. "He's a bit odd, it's true. But he's not dangerous," he insisted. "Besides, it's only for the summer. Or until I can get our lives sorted. Whichever comes first. And more importantly, I think he can help you."

"How can a summer spent with the world's biggest weirdo possibly help me? You're the one who said the best decision you ever made was to legally change your name from Woodbead to Smith."

I remembered the moment so clearly. At the time, I had no reason not to believe him. But now, sitting across from my dad in that empty shell of a room, I couldn't help but think how he'd dedicated his entire life to becoming the opposite of Ramhart, and still his life had fallen apart.

"Look—" My dad raked a hand through his hair in a way that left it standing on end. But I was so annoyed, I decided not to tell him. "I was never like you. I never experienced the sort of things that you see, and maybe that's why it's so hard for me to understand. And yet you've been like this for so long, I can't help but wonder if there might be something more to it."

I stared at him wide-eyed, not trusting what I'd heard. "Does that mean you believe me?" I asked. It was the first time my dad had even so much as considered I might be telling the truth. "Because back in the car, you pretty much accused me of attention seeking." I watched in satisfaction as my dad winced at the memory.

"I'm sorry if I haven't handled this well," he said. "It all feels so out of my league—"

"But do you *believe me?*" I cried. My cheeks were beginning to heat, and my ears roared with the sound of my own heartbeat. It was the first time I'd ever asked him point-blank. Probably because I was always too afraid of what he might say.

After a moment's hesitation, he spoke. "I believe that *you* believe it's real. And who am I to deny your experience?" He stretched his legs out before him and studied the dull shine of his shoes. "I can't help thinking you might benefit by spending time with someone who can understand what you're going through. And since Ramhart's familiar with that sort of thing, he seems like the obvious choice."

On the surface, it made sense. But the longer I sat with it, the more questions I had. "How did this even happen?" I asked. "I mean, since when do you even talk to him?" I searched my dad's face, looking for clues.

"We've spoken a few times." His fingers nervously picked at the carpet. "He reached out after hearing the news about your mother, and—"

Immediately, I dropped my head to my knees and covered my ears. I didn't want to hear any more—didn't want to see my sad, empty room. All I wanted was to block out the world and rewind to a better time before my mom left and there was no talk of sending me away to live with some oddball grandfather I hadn't seen in years.

Turns out, my dad was much better at things like patience

and waiting out a prolonged silence. So when I did finally lift my head, he just looked at me and said, "It's settled, Max." Effectively putting an end to any and all attempts at negotiation.

"Where does he even live?" I frowned, assuming it must be in some horrible place.

"At Woodbead Mansion, in the town of Glimmerville," my dad said.

Mansion? That got my attention. Did that mean Ramhart Woodbead was rich? "You never said anything about a *mansion*!"

My dad shrugged, then leaned his head against the wall. "I didn't live there for long. After your grandmother died, I was sent to a foster family in another town. Besides, it was hardly a mansion back then. The important thing is, Ramhart's getting older, slowing down, and he really wants to get to know you before . . . well, before it's too late. And I can't help thinking, who am I to rob you both of that chance?"

It wasn't the sort of question that required an answer, which was good, since I had no idea what to say. I just watched as my dad slowly got to his feet, came to stand before me, and offered a hand to help me to mine.

"Got the tent set up out back." He jabbed a thumb in the general direction. "What do you say we go grill ourselves a couple of cheeseburgers and maybe some s'mores for dessert?" His eyebrows rose, his mouth tugging up at the side. Clearly he was trying to make the best of a bad situation. The least I could do was try too.

"Did you pack the telescope?" I asked, following him into the hall.

"You kidding?" He reached back and ruffled the top of my head, probably making my hair stand on end just like his. "How are we supposed to see Mars without it?"

As we made our way to the kitchen, I trailed a hand along the wall where our family pictures had once hung. The faded, empty squares left in their place reminded me of ghosts from a time that would never return.

3

Why Did the Ghost Girl Cross the Road?

We didn't talk much on the long drive to Ramhart's. My dad mostly listened to some motivational audiobook where the narrator kept repeating things like *You don't have to be great to start— but you have to start to be great!* while I stared out the passenger window at an endless smudge of green forest.

When we finally exited the highway, and a blue sign with white letters burst through the fog and popped into view, reading

WELCOME TO GLIMMERVILLE
WHERE EVERYTHING SHINES JUST A
LITTLE BIT BRIGHTER!

the reality of the situation hit me anew.

"Listen—" My dad lowered the volume as he navigated his old hometown's streets. "I should probably warn you, Ramhart's a collector of . . . artifacts."

I stared at my dad.

"He has a lot of strange and bizarre objects that he pretends are real, but don't let any of that nonsense scare you. Also, if he tries to show you his book—"

"Ramhart wrote a book?" I frowned, wondering why he'd never mentioned that before. "Is it about ghosts? Do we own a copy?" I'd already convinced myself that it was, we did, and my dad had purposely kept me from reading exactly the sort of book that I was desperately in need of.

"It's not that kind of book. It's . . ." He squinted, tapping a thumb against the steering wheel. "Honestly, it's ridiculous. Forget I even mentioned it." He waved a hand in dismissal and tried to change the subject. But if he expected me to spend the summer with a grandpa I barely knew, the least he could do was answer my question.

"Is that what made Ramhart world-famous?" I asked. "The book?"

After my dad had fallen asleep in the tent the night before, I'd hunkered down in my sleeping bag and used my phone to scour the internet for whatever I could find on my grandfather. I was amazed to discover there were tens of thousands of search results—a seemingly never-ending scroll of articles, pictures, and fan sites all about Ramhart. And honestly, seeing all that left me feeling kind of torn. Like, part of me was angry at my dad for dumping me at some strange mansion so I could spend the summer locked up with a weirdo, while the other part was sort of excited to think I was related to someone the internet considered a legend.

"It's not the sort of book you find in a bookstore," my dad said, drawing me away from my thoughts and back to the present.

"*Field Guide to the Supernatural Universe* is just something Ramhart threw together, like a cross between a diary, a scrapbook, and a paranormal encyclopedia."

My dad's tone was dismissive, but I was lit with possibility. I mean, *Field Guide to the Supernatural Universe?* Come on! The title alone was filled with promise.

"Ramhart used to claim it had magical powers." My dad shook his head. "But I'm sure that's all in the past. He's living a normal life now, and I really believe he can help." He tore his eyes away from the road to glance at me. "I know you're probably nervous, but this is all for the best. Remember—just be yourself, and all will be well."

That last part left me frowning. The true me was a normal kid who could see ghosts and apparently monsters, too. But since no one was willing to accept the real me, I was forced to pretend I was somebody else.

But what if my summer with Ramhart really was what I needed to change all that?

Unlike my dad, I wasn't convinced Ramhart would be willing to help me overcome my ghost-seeing abilities. Considering how he became world-famous and lived in a mansion because of his pursuit of the supernatural, it seemed more likely he'd try to mold me into a younger version of him.

But what if I didn't even have to ask Ramhart for help?

What if that book, the *Field Guide*, could help put an end to all the things that made me a freak?

I mean, if it really was a paranormal encyclopedia, then it

was entirely possible it contained a chapter that could teach me how to stop seeing supernaturals so I could start junior high like any other seventh grader.

I stared out the window, imagining a ghost-free future, while taking in a fog-drenched view that offered an occasional glimpse of a cobblestone road or colorful storefront, when, from out of nowhere, a girl ran into the road, seemingly unaware of our car barreling toward her.

"Stop!" I shouted. Instinctively grabbing the dashboard, I squeezed my eyes shut and braced for the worst.

My dad slammed the brakes hard, making the wheels screech on the pavement as the car lurched forward, then back, before finally coming to rest.

With my heart slapping hard against my ribs and my nostrils jammed with the scent of scorched rubber, I sneaked an eye open to survey the damage.

What I saw was a blond-haired, blue-eyed girl probably around my age, and she was laughing as though the near miss was . . . funny?

When she rose onto her toes and twirled in a way that made her curls lift from her shoulders and the skirt of her white dress balloon all around, I realized that what appeared entirely real to me was completely invisible to my dad.

"Max!" My dad peered hard through the windshield, unable to see the ghost girl smiling and waving at us as she skipped on toward the large iron gate that led to Glimmerville Graveyard. "What the heck?"

If there was a single word that could sum up an expression that was simultaneously frustrated, angry, confused, and worried—well, that's the word I'd use to describe my dad at that moment.

I cleared my throat nervously. I had no idea what to say. But one thing was sure: the truth was the last thing he wanted to hear.

"I guess—I thought I saw something. Must've been a rabbit or, um, m-maybe a squirrel," I stammered.

My dad studied me, wearing the same expression he'd worn the day I'd told him Great-Aunt Lucy had died moments before the phone call confirming her passing.

Just when I was sure I couldn't take another second, he moved his foot from the brake to the gas, pulled into the next driveway, and said, "Never mind, Max. We're here."

"He lives across from the cemetery?"

I shot a worried look over my shoulder, wondering why I'd failed to remember that detail. Then again, last time (the only time) I visited, I was basically a pudgy, drooling blob whose biggest achievements were pooping my diaper and sleeping through the night. I wasn't big on making memories.

I twisted around in my seat, searching for any sign of the ghost girl. Was she my new neighbor? And if so, how was I supposed to survive an entire summer living so close to such a horrible, mocking dead thing?

My dad stopped before a tall, black iron gate and lowered the window to confront an eerie sculpture of a large black raven. After pushing a finger against one of the raven's gleaming red eyeballs, the raven's beak sprang wide open and a disembodied voice drifted through a hidden speaker. "Welcome to Woodbead Mansion," it croaked. "We are currently closed to visitors but will resume normal operating hours on . . ."

Before the recording could finish, my dad repeatedly jabbed at the eyeball and yelled, "Ramhart—we're here. Open up already!"

"Visiting hours?" I shrank back in my seat, wondering what exactly I was getting into.

Slowly, the gate creaked open, and my dad drove up a long, winding stretch of stone driveway that eventually yielded to a wide, rambling sprawl of a house with so many levels, layers, turrets, and towers it was impossible to take it all in at one glance. Was it two stories, three, or possibly more? I blinked as I peered through the windshield, then climbed out of the car and blinked some more.

I tried to focus on the more normal bits, things I could relate to that didn't leave me feeling so off-balance. The house was painted white with black shutters—nothing unusual there. But there was also a large window way up high on the third floor that was shaped like an octagon and seemed to flash with what looked like a bolt of lightning—on the inside—every few seconds. A collection of four menacing gray gargoyles perched along the edge of the first-story roof—their wings ready to take flight, their sharp teeth ready to take a bite. The only thing that seemed to hold them in place were the thick silver chains clamped to their necks.

My dad grunted as he heaved my duffel bag onto his shoulder, then nudged me up the front steps. "Best to think of it like a movie set," he said. "Everything you see is just another of Ramhart's props."

I gaped at the large snake statues guarding either side of the door, both coiled and ready to strike at whatever unfortunate visitor they deemed unworthy of entry. Like the raven at the gate, their eyes were also made of red glass, and I swear I saw one of them blink as I passed.

Before I had a chance to react, or beg to go home, the black door swung open, and the grandfather I hadn't seen in eleven years and eight months stood before us. "David, Max, so good to see you again. Won't you come in?"

I stood frozen, like my knees had forgotten how to bend. My grandfather, with his cropped gray hair, khaki pants, and pale blue cardigan buttoned over a starched white shirt, was pretty much the opposite of the wild-haired man I'd seen pictured all over the internet.

Ramhart ushered us inside, and I stumbled over the threshold and into a house that, like Ramhart himself, seemed disappointingly normal.

The internet search described the place as overflowing with skeletons, crystal skulls, dragon eggs, alien X-rays, and other oddities Ramhart claimed to have collected during his journeys. But the view from the foyer revealed a house that wasn't much different from anywhere else.

While the outside of the house was undeniably weird, the

inside was like a museum of boring furniture. There were woven rugs hugging wood floors, thick velvet drapes covering large windows, stacks of hardcover books practically spilling off the shelves, and an ugly flowered couch with an assortment of needlepoint pillows that clashed. And the man at the center of it all, the subject of too many dire warnings to count, looked like an older version of my dad. Not a silk tunic, velvet cape, or monkey-tooth medallion in sight.

I watched as my dad ran a suspicious gaze over Ramhart's clothing, as though his mundane appearance were some sort of illusion he could easily debunk if he just studied him hard enough.

If Ramhart noticed, he didn't let on. He just stood calmly before us and said, "It's been a long time, son." When he grinned, his eyes had a way of crinkling up at the sides. "And I assume this is Max." He gave me the sort of deeply appraising look that immediately had me shifting nervously from foot to foot. "Looks like you and I have a lot of catching up to do."

He chucked me lightly on the shoulder in a way that was probably meant to seem friendly, but before I had a chance to respond, my dad said, "What's this about house tours? You still running those?"

Ramhart glanced between us, his face blank.

"The raven at the gate—" My dad hooked a thumb over his shoulder.

"Oh, that!" Ramhart laughed. "Recording's just a fun bit of nostalgia, is all. Kept the gargoyles and the snakes because the neighborhood kids get a kick out of 'em, and it saves me the hassle of having to decorate for Halloween every year. If I didn't know better, I'd think you were disappointed." He cracked a wry grin my dad failed to return.

I stood awkwardly watching as my dad peeked his head into the nearby rooms. I guessed he was looking for skeletons, or blurry photos of Bigfoot sightings. When he came away with his face arranged in a frown, I couldn't help but wonder if he was as annoyed as me to discover that nothing stood out. After all the outrageous stories my dad had told me through the years and all the articles I'd read online, seeing Ramhart in person looking so ordinary felt like a letdown.

"You're welcome to stay overnight," Ramhart offered. "Plenty of room."

He sounded sincere, and I was hoping my dad might consider it, but he seemed pretty eager to go.

"Please, Dad," he said as he made his way back to the porch. "I'm counting on you. So no nonsense, okay? Don't try to turn Max into something he's not meant to be."

Ramhart glanced between me and my dad. "Wouldn't dream of it," he said, moving in for a hug, or maybe even just a pat on the shoulder. But before he could make contact, my dad was leaning toward me.

"Listen—" He lowered his voice so Ramhart couldn't hear, though I sensed he still did. "It's just for the summer. And if I hit a run of good luck and can sort things out sooner, I'll be right back to get you, okay? In the meantime, try to make the best of it."

I followed him to the door and watched him climb into his car. After he drove away, Ramhart turned to me and said, "I suppose I should show you to your room so you can get settled."

I nodded slowly, then grabbed my bag and followed him up the curved staircase.

"So you go by Max, not Maxen?"

Again, I nodded. Then, realizing he couldn't see me, I answered, "Yes."

"And what would you like to call me? It's entirely up to you, though I will say I've never liked the sound of 'grandpa.' It's too musty and dull. Though G-Man is always an option." We'd reached the second-floor landing, which, from what I could see, looked every bit as dreary as the downstairs. My grandfather stood before me, waiting for an answer, and since I couldn't see myself ever calling anyone G-Man and had mostly always thought of him as more of a Ramhart than a grandpa, I said, "What if we just stick to a first-name basis?"

He grinned in agreement, then whisked me down a long hall and into a room that was, once again, disappointingly ordinary.

I dropped my bag on the floor beside the bed and took a good look around. There was a desk, a chair, a closet, and a window with a view of the cemetery, which didn't exactly thrill me, especially after my encounter with the ghost girl, but compared to what I'd thought I was in for, it was nothing I couldn't handle for a summer.

Ramhart must've noticed my frown, because he was quick to say, "This was your dad's old room. But if it's not to your liking, there are plenty of others to choose from. Why don't you settle in here for tonight? Then tomorrow, after I give you the grand tour, you can pick the room you like best."

I glanced around the room. Everything looked so new I couldn't find a single item that once might've belonged to my dad. The shelves were overflowing with comic books and paperbacks, but no sign of *Field Guide to the Supernatural Universe*. On the far wall, across from the bed, was a poster of a movie I'd once watched three times in one night.

The room was so normal it seemed almost . . . weird. Like it wasn't quite real. My dad had told me to think of Ramhart's house like a movie set filled with props. Well, that was exactly how the room felt—like it was staged for a movie about some boring, small-town family.

"You can unpack if you want, or if you're hungry, I've got pizza and a pie from Miss Petunia's World Famous waiting downstairs."

It really wasn't much of a decision. Even in Glimmerville, pizza and pie would always win over unpacking. Besides, why bother shoving my clothes into drawers when I'd probably end up changing rooms anyway?

Following Ramhart downstairs, I asked, "What kind of pie?"

That was the last normal night of my life.

The Mystery of the Rare White Rhoven

Morning came quickly, but surprisingly, I slept great.

It was surprising because normally whenever I stayed some-place new, I had a hard time relaxing. But after we'd settled into the den, where we shared a pepperoni pizza and a couple of slices of warm cherry pie with vanilla ice cream, it became clear that despite my dad's warnings, there was no need to worry. Ramhart was as normal as any other granddad.

The view out the window revealed a gloomy, gray day, and I guessed it would probably stay that way, since, according to Ramhart, Glimmerville was known for its terrible weather.

"People come for the pies, not the sunshine," he'd said the night before, drinking from his glass of weird-looking blue juice as he slid another slice of pizza onto my plate.

He also told me how the town was named after a type of mer-maid supposedly found in the lake in the graveyard. "They're known as Glimmers because of their sparkling fins and irides-cent sheen, or so the legend claims."

Other than the mermaid story (which I definitely didn't

believe), he talked about Glimmerville as though it was the world's most charming, if not completely ordinary, place. Though I couldn't help but notice how he failed to make a single mention of the haunted cemetery. For a supposedly celebrated ghost hunter, it struck me as not only strange but disappointing in a way. Apparently, his supernatural days really were well behind him, which didn't bode well for getting my hands on the *Field Guide*.

A light tap sounded from the other side of my door, and then someone called out, "Sorry to disturb—just wanted you to know breakfast will be served in the dining hall downstairs."

"Um, okay," I said, as surprised to hear there was a hall for dining as I was to be greeted by someone other than Ramhart. "I'll be down soon."

"As you wish. It is ready when you are, sir."

Sir?

I continued staring at the door long after the person's footsteps had faded. Normally, I'd just trudge downstairs in my pj's and dig in. Then again, I didn't normally enjoy breakfast in a dining hall where people referred to me as *sir*.

So after splashing some water onto my face and doing a quick brush of my teeth, I pulled the least wrinkled tee I could find over my head, dragged on the same pair of jeans I'd arrived in, retrieved my sneakers from under the bed, and shoved them, along with a fresh pair of socks, onto my feet, then headed downstairs with a great deal of curiosity.

Locating the dining hall wasn't easy. Especially since the only clue I had to go on was that it was downstairs. I was convinced

I'd gone the wrong way when I happened upon a room with an enormously long table, where Ramhart sat waiting.

In one fluid motion, he rose to his feet and self-consciously gestured toward a seemingly endless spread of food that ran the full length of a very long table. "I wasn't sure what you liked, so I arranged for a bit of everything."

There were baskets overflowing with glazed pastries and donuts; large woven trays piled high with steaming mounds of freshly baked biscuits and small boats of gravy; dizzying towers of pancakes and waffles that rose precariously from round silver platters, as dozens of fried eggs and thick slabs of bacon sizzled on multiple griddles. Just the sight of it all made me realize I was hungrier than I'd thought. So I claimed the seat across from Ramhart's and started filling my plate.

"I was thinking," he said. "After I give you the grand tour, we could—"

He didn't make it any further before a bird—a stark white bird with a matching beak and piercing blue eyes—appeared from out of nowhere and landed on Ramhart's shoulder.

I dropped the sprinkled donut I was about to bite into and gaped in astonishment. The bird hadn't exactly appeared out of nowhere. I'd witnessed its arrival. Problem was, when I replayed the scene in my head, what I saw didn't make any sense.

It was like one moment I was anticipating a mouthful of rainbow sprinkles, and the next, right before my eyes, the air grew blurry—like it was distorted or something—and a white bird burst into view.

"Oh dear," Ramhart muttered. Neatly folding his napkin, he placed it beside his plate and glanced between the bird on his shoulder and my openmouthed stare. "I was hoping to at least make it past noon. Allow us more time to get to know each other better. Guess I should've anticipated this. After all, you know what they say: 'Glitches happen!'" He let out an awkward chuckle, then quickly lifted his napkin to his lips as though to erase it.

"What is that thing? What is happening?" I sounded way less cool and collected than I intended.

"This is Rhoven. He's a rare white raven. Rhoven, meet Max—Max, Rhoven."

"But . . . I thought ravens only came in black."

"I thought Rhovens only came in black!" the bird mimicked, followed by a fit of laughter that stopped only when Ramhart shushed him.

"Apparently, not all of them." Ramhart flashed me a tentative grin. "Also, as you probably noticed, he can talk. So be careful what you say around him. He's guaranteed to find the most inopportune time to repeat it."

With nervous fingers I picked at my donut, struggling to put it all in perspective. So Ramhart had a rare bird. Not a big deal. Especially for someone who'd spent a lifetime traveling the world. And as for that part about the atmosphere blurring, it was probably nothing more than stress—a consequence of my life being so abruptly upended.

I'd nearly convinced myself when, right before my eyes, the

newspaper Ramhart was reading morphed into an oversized, leather-bound book with a bunch of deep purple crystals embedded on the front.

My gaze lit upon it. It had to be the *Field Guide*. I was sure of it. But just as I was about to ask, I watched as his blue button-down shirt and pressed khakis dissolved, revealing the blue silk tunic and faded jeans he truly wore. His clean-shaven face sprouted into a scraggly mustache and beard, and his short gray hair grew into a wild and wavy mane of blue-streaked hair and . . . feathers?

Elaborate markings crawled up his wrists and snaked under his sleeves, as his once bare fingers were suddenly stacked to the knuckles with rings. And there, hanging from his neck, was the monkey-tooth medallion my dad had long ago told me about.

"Max, please, I can explain—" Ramhart started, but it was too late.

I was already up.

Already knocking over my chair.

Already making my escape.

I had to reach the door. If I could just make it outside, I could scream until someone came to help me.

Surely someone would come to help me?

I'd just reached the end of the table when the whole house began to rumble and roar. It was like being in an earthquake, not that I'd actually ever been in an earthquake, but I guessed it was the same, especially the part about struggling to stay upright during the shaking.

I stumbled forward and fell to my knees, but not before stubbing my toe on a cabinet that appeared out of nowhere. Deciding to stay low rather than risk another fall, I started crawling, nearly reaching the door when a long, lanky skeleton materialized before me.

I screamed.

I couldn't help it.

I was way beyond caring what anyone thought. It was like being trapped in the world's scariest haunted house.

"Max, please—*stop!*" Ramhart lunged toward me while I struggled to find my way out of a room that kept changing wherever I looked.

"What is happening?" I shouted. I was boxed in on all sides, surrounded by strange curiosities I couldn't begin to identify. "What the heck is going on?"

Ramhart stood breathless before me. "I'm so sorry," he wheezed. "I never meant to scare you. Never meant to scare your father, either. And yet it seems like that's always how it ends up."

I cowered on the floor, wondering when—and if—the nightmare would end.

"Almost over now," Ramhart said, his voice sounding weary.

"What's almost over? I don't understand."

"The glamour—it's wearing off. It will only hold for so long before the truth insists on revealing itself."

"Glamour? What the heck is a glamour?"

"I thought if you could first learn to trust me, then I—"

"You wanted to gain my trust by *lying* to me?"

"Well, when you put it like that..." He winced. Even Rhoven tucked his beak against his breast and turned away.

A moment later the roar began to fade, the house settled and stilled, and I slowly rose to my feet and took in my peculiar new surroundings. It was everything my dad had warned me about—times a zillion.

"Nothing in here can harm you," Ramhart said.

Still perched on Ramhart's shoulder, Rhoven mimicked the sound of a human clearing their throat.

"Nothing in the immediate vicinity can harm you," he corrected.

I swiped a hand through my hair and took another look around. My toe throbbed from when I'd stubbed it. My head hurt from everything I'd witnessed. My heart hurt knowing that despite the overwhelming urge to flee, I couldn't become one more item on my dad's long list of things to worry about.

My dad was downsized. My mom was down under. And I was trapped in a terrifying haunted house for the summer.

Three months. That was it. How hard could it be?

I gazed around the transformed space, reminding myself that somewhere among all the horrors was the book that might possibly change my life. I was more determined than ever to find it.

My grandfather was wild, unhinged, and I knew in that moment I couldn't count on him to help me with my supernatural problem.

"Anything else you need to tell me?" I asked, trying hard to keep it together.

He paused a few beats. "Nothing that can't wait."

"Promise, no more lies."

Ramhart folded his little finger and thumb toward the center of his palm, then placed his hand over his heart and said, "Scout's honor."

"Okay." I nodded. "Then answer me this: On a scale of one to ten, how scary is the room you put me in?"

Ramhart took a moment to consider. "Four," he said. Then, after a quick recalculation, he added, "Maybe six if you accidentally look on the top shelf of the closet. Pretty sure that's where I stashed my collection of cyclops heads. But honestly, they only look scary. It's a funny story, really. See, there's this group I lived with over in . . ."

With Ramhart still talking, I walked out of the dining hall, calling over my shoulder, "If you don't mind, I think I'll take breakfast in my room after all."

Max's List of Top Five Terrifying Things

1. Glamour glitches
2. Skeletons that come to life
3. Monsters
4. Ghosts
5. Jasmine Skink

5
Call Me Crowther

With the glamour spell broken, rooms that had appeared nearly empty before were suddenly overflowing with all kinds of weirdness. There were strange, unidentifiable bits floating in jars, flesh-eating houseplants with snapping leaves, and framed portraits of people whose painted eyes squinted and blinked.

By the time I made it back to my room, I was braced for just about anything. If Ramhart rated it between a four and a six on the scary scale (depending on whether or not I looked in the closet), I assumed it was worse.

Cautiously, I opened the door and peered inside, only to find that while nothing had moved—the bed was still against the wall, the desk was still under the window—there were a few notable additions that hadn't been there before.

The books on the shelves were no longer bestselling paperbacks, but rather thick hardcover tales of true encounters with witches, Bigfoot, flying saucers, but still no sign of *Field Guide to the Supernatural Universe*. The movie poster had transformed into a glass shadow box with a set of eyes mounted in the center that seemed to watch me wherever I went. The plaque under-neath claimed they were the deactivated eyes of a basilisk—a legendary creature that can kill with a glance. The hook where I'd hung my hoodie was actually the bony hand of a skeleton. And yet, as long as I avoided the closet, it seemed safer inside that room than anywhere else.

My first instinct was to hole up in there for the rest of the summer until my dad came to get me. But if I wanted to get my hands on the *Field Guide*, I'd have to venture outside. Besides, despite what Ramhart said, according to the internet busloads of tourists still paid to visit the place, which meant it was entirely possible that the house just took some getting used to. Like when you watch a scary movie so many times you start laughing at all the parts that once made you scream.

Before I could talk myself out of it, I marched out of my room and into the hall, where I ran smack into a tall white man with jet-black hair, a thin mustache, and a short, pointy beard. He was standing before a very large oil painting in a fancy gold frame.

"Normally, this place would be swarming with ticket-holding, selfie-posing gawkers looking to me to provide the sort of mildly supernatural scares promised on the brochure."

I recognized his voice as the one who'd called me *sir* when he knocked on my door.

"Because of your visit, the tours have been paused, and I'm not sure whether to thank you or blame you for sparing me that. After all, some of them do tip rather nicely." His icy blue gaze slid from the top of my head to the toes of my sneakers. "Anyway, it's nice to finally meet you, Max. I'm Crowther Graves, Ramhart's assistant."

Though he was much younger than Ramhart, his clothes were just as eccentric. His white long-sleeved shirt was paired with a blue silk scarf, a matching printed vest, and a black velvet jacket with silver buttons that ran down the front. His pants were slim cut with sharp creases. His freshly polished black boots were the kind that lace up.

I wasn't sure if it was how he always dressed or if it was some kind of costume Ramhart made him wear for the tourists. Either way, he reminded me of one of the actors in my mom's favorite movies—the ones where people talk in crisp English accents, drink loads of tea, and perform weird group dances at parties.

Still, if he worked for Ramhart, then he could probably direct me to the *Field Guide*. But before I could ask, he started talking again.

"I was beginning to wonder if you truly existed or if you were some sort of imaginary grandson Ramhart invented." His thin lips pulled to the side as he continued to study me. "Tell me, do you go by Woodbead or Smith?" Not giving me a chance to reply, he gave me another once-over and said, "I'm guessing Smith. So anyway, what has Ramhart shown you? Have you tried the spirit spotters?"

I had no idea what he was talking about, but I didn't like the sound of it.

"The glasses he invented that enable one to see ghosts."

"Oh. Uh, no." I immediately decided I wanted no part of that.

"How about the soul phone?" Seeing my blank look, he added, "Like a cell phone, only it dials the dead. Have you called a long-deceased relative yet?" Crowther's tone, like his face, was outwardly friendly, but something about his gaze left me feeling off-balance.

Tentatively, I shook my head.

"Just as well." He shrugged. "The reception is lousy, loaded with static. And even when you do hear them clearly, they mostly go on about how much they love you and how proud you've made them. Not a single one of 'em seems the least bit interested in divulging the winning lottery numbers. It's like they forgot how things work over here."

The laugh that followed was so contagious, I found myself joining in.

"Doesn't sound like he's gotten very far with your training."

I stared blankly.

"Has he shown you the future viewfinder, or the proper usage of the toe compass?"

It was like he was speaking another language. I had no idea what the words meant.

"No trips to the Wunderkammer, then?"

"Uh, the Wunder—" I started to ask what a Wunderkammer was, but he cut me off before I could finish.

"I must say I'm surprised." With black-painted nails, he stroked the pointy end of his beard, reminding me of a cartoon villain plotting revenge. "Ramhart's inordinately proud of his discoveries. I was sure he would've at least shown you the toe compass. Well, all in due time, I suppose."

"I just got here yesterday." For some strange reason I felt the need to defend Ramhart.

"You know who this is?" The way Crowther jumped from one subject to the next made it hard to keep up. "That's your great-great-grandfather, Magnus Woodbead, and his faithful companion, Scout." He bent his head toward the portrait before him of an older man wearing a safari jacket and pith helmet that had seen better days.

I'd never even heard of my great-great-grandfather (though I'd of course assumed I had one somewhere in the Woodbead family tree), so I inched closer to get a better look.

The artist had painted a man with a sharp beak of a nose, a bushy mustache that drooped down around the corners of his mouth, and even more blue in his hair than Ramhart. Behind his wire-rimmed frames were a set of squinty dark eyes that reminded me vaguely of my dad's. In his right fist he clutched a three-headed cyclops by the neck, probably the same one that ended up in my closet. Beside him sat a bloodhound with deeply sunken eyes, long floppy ears, loose saggy jowls, and a dignified tilt to his head.

"He was a celebrated monster hunter," Crowther said. "Later, after he retired, he purchased most of Glimmerville and designed and built Woodbead Mansion from the ground up. Of course, the house wasn't nearly as large back then. Ramhart added on quite a bit through the years."

I glanced between Crowther and the guy in the picture. There were so many things I was desperately curious about. I led with the obvious. "Did you say *monster hunter?*"

"Said to be one of the best. Though you can judge for yourself when you meet him."

I blinked at the painting. If great-great-grandfather Magnus Woodbead was still alive, he'd have to be well over one hundred years old. But before I could ask, Crowther moved on.

"You know, Max, all this will be yours someday."

I gulped, unsure how to respond. I guess that would qualify as exciting news to some. From my perspective, it felt like the floor had dropped right out from under me. "You mean, like, *all of Glimmerville?*" A wave of panic rolled through me.

"Well, not *all* of it," he said, as though that somehow made the news easier to swallow. "Just the mansion, the cemetery, the mineral rights, and a few other things. They were forced to sell the rest during the lean times."

"Lean times?" I screwed up my face.

"Back when Ramhart was caught in the time slip, he lost a lot of years and a lot of income. Which is one of the main reasons he opened the mansion to tourists now."

Although I couldn't actually see myself, it felt like my eyes were about to pop out of their sockets. I never expected anyone to mention the time slip. And I certainly never expected anyone to mention it so casually, as though I were fully expected to believe such a ridiculous story.

I sank my hands into my pockets and shrugged. Truth was,

I had no interest in inheriting a cemetery, a toe compass, or anything else. I was only there for the summer. As soon as it was over, my life would return to normal.

"I think Ramhart views you as a second chance. After what happened with your dad—" Abruptly, he stopped and shook his head. "Anyway, that's all in the past. Hardly worth the rehash when a toe compass demonstration is in order."

Even though I was sure I'd end up regretting it, I couldn't pass up a chance to see something like that. "What is it?"

"Are you familiar with the Hand of Glory?"

I screwed up my gaze. I had no idea what he was talking about.

"It's the pickled hand of a felon that was removed while the body was still hanging from the gallows. It's said to hold supernatural powers. There's one in the Whitby Museum in England."

"Okay . . ." I dragged out the word, wishing he'd just get on with it so I'd know whether to pretend to go along with his story.

"Well, the toe compass is just what it sounds like. It's a big toe that came from a giant and holds the power to locate lost objects."

"You mean someone actually cut off a giant's big toe just so they could find some misplaced keys?" It sounded incredibly cruel.

"Would it help to know it was a very evil giant?" His eyebrows rose in a challenge, but I opted for silence. To answer would require me to believe in giants—which, of course, I didn't. "Trust me, you've never seen anything like it," he said. "There's nothing it can't find. In fact, why don't you give me something of yours so we can purposely lose it, and then I'll show you how it works?"

Not having anything else on me, I handed him a quarter.

Crowther shot me a withering look. "Something more valuable, perhaps?"

I made a show of patting my pockets. I was light on valuable accessories. Or at least that was what I thought, until Crowther gestured at the watch my mom had given me just before she left for Australia.

I shifted nervously, trying to drum up a good excuse for why I couldn't hand it over. It wasn't like he'd done anything wrong. Up to that point he'd seemed friendly enough. And yet, for some reason I couldn't quite name, I was reluctant to play along.

We stood before each other. Him wiggling his fingers impatiently. Me hesitating. After a few awkward moments, I blew a deep exhale, worked the watch from my wrist, and handed it over.

"So, what you want to do is—" Crowther rubbed his fingers over the watch face, then flipped it over and stopped cold. "Oh," he muttered. "I do apologize." He returned the watch with a frown. "I wasn't trying to pry. I can see how much you miss her."

"Wait—what?" I glanced between Crowther and my watch, wondering how he could possibly know about me missing my mom.

"It's called psychometry," he told me. "The items we carry every day are imprinted with our memories, emotions, and energy. Those who are attuned can receive certain messages. It's similar to how the memory video camera works." He looked at me expectantly. "I suppose Ramhart hasn't shown you that, either?"

I really wanted to know what he'd seen, but I couldn't bring myself to ask.

"There's no message," he assured me. "I just felt your sadness over her absence. So tell me, has Ramhart shown you the Winter Room yet?"

I remembered the window I'd noticed when I first arrived— the one that flashed with brilliant bolts of lightning—and wondered if that was what he was talking about.

"Trust me." He urged me toward a hidden set of spiraling stairs. "You haven't lived until you've enjoyed your own personal on-demand winter storm."

Reaching the Winter Room took longer than expected, and when we finally arrived, I was pretty much crying with laughter after listening to Crowther's stories. At the time, I had no way of knowing he was entirely serious about his confrontations with lizard-faced men, running into alternate dimension versions of himself, and being chased by a beautiful fairy who claimed she only wanted to invite him into her world for tea, despite the very sharp, though very tiny, sword she brandished.

"Have you ever visited the Louvre?" Crowther stopped before a polished wood door. "It's a museum in Paris. It's where the *Mona Lisa*—which, by the way, is surprisingly small—lives. Imagine a very tiny painting stored in a very big museum and you get the picture. But not really an accurate picture, as there are loads of other paintings, sculptures, and artifacts housed there as well. Anyway, my point is, you should think of Woodbead Mansion like the Louvre."

I had no idea what he was getting at.

"By which I mean, it will take a very long time to see all the wonders. And even then, you can be sure you've missed several things. Certain areas are deemed strictly off-limits. Though I'm not entirely sure that applies to you, considering your special status."

Special status?

Before I could ask, he grasped the knob and swung the door open to reveal a wondrous room that resembled the inside of a cozy log cabin. There was a stone fireplace against the far wall, a colorful braided rug covering most of the wood floor, and a carved wooden desk that sat before a large window caught in a perpetual rainstorm.

I stood mesmerized, watching as a jagged bolt of lightning streaked across the pane and fat droplets of water continued to stream.

A moment later the rain halted, and a flurry of snow began to fall in its place. It was only when I turned away from the window that I noticed it was also snowing inside.

I thrust my palms before me, eager to collect a handful of flakes and maybe make a snowball or something, but the ice quickly evaporated.

"So, what do you think?" Crowther asked.

"It's amazing!" I exclaimed, my words drowned by a drumroll

of thunder when the snow switched back to rain, which appeared to pelt the window from the outside as a light wind gusted inside. "But I'm not sure what the point is, other than to be weird."

Slowly, Crowther cocked his head in study. "But isn't the pursuit of weirdness an honorable enough endeavor in and of itself? Tell me, how many people do you know with such a room?"

I rocked back on my heels. Clearly, we both knew the answer.

"And how many people do you think would actually enjoy having such a room if they'd only allow themselves to think outside the minuscule box where they store their starved imaginations?"

I dropped onto the desk chair and tapped a few keys on an old manual typewriter.

"What are you writing, Max? 'All serious and no weirdness makes Max a dull boy'?" Crowther laughed.

He was making fun of me, but I refused to react. I stopped typing and settled for swiveling the chair back and forth.

"An Oscar-winning movie director once rented this room. He sat in that very chair, at that very desk, and used that very typewriter to craft his screenplay. Turned out to be his most successful film to date."

"Is that true? Which movie?" I swung the chair in Crowther's direction, wondering if it was a movie I'd seen.

"For the record, all my stories are true."

"Including the lizard men?" I said with a smirk.

With a sober expression, he said, "Yes, Max, including the Reptilians. You decide what you believe, and what you reject as impossible." He leaned against a bookshelf. Crossing his legs at the ankle and folding his arms, he regarded me with such intense scrutiny that I felt like a specimen under a high-powered lens. "Anyway, I'm glad you like the room. I'm also glad to finally meet you after hearing so much about you."

"I only met him once, you know." I had no idea what Ramhart might've said about me, but I wanted Crowther to know that as far as I was concerned, my grandfather and I were pretty much strangers. Or maybe I was making excuses for why his world was so foreign to me. It's hard to say for sure. "It was back when I was a baby," I added. "I was still wearing a diaper."

Honestly, I have no idea why I mentioned the part about the diaper. I do know I regretted it the second it was out.

Crowther continued to study me from beneath a lowered brow. "You know, Ramhart has high hopes for you, but I'm not so sure." He fiddled with the snake ring he wore on his right index finger. The way he twisted it back and forth caused the iridescent purple stone eyes to flicker and blink. "You don't strike me as having any real capability, much less any interest in supernatural phenomena. If you ask me, his hopes are misplaced."

It's weird how annoyed his words made me. I mean, on the one hand, it was exactly what I wanted him to think, and yet, considering how we'd just met, it wasn't like he knew the first thing about me.

Before I could respond, he dipped his head and said, "Anyway, it was nice meeting you, Max. Though I'm sure we'll be seeing a lot more of each other."

Since I had no idea how to find my way back, I followed him out. When we reached the front porch, I cringed as the twin serpents guarding the door bared their fangs and hissed, but Crowther just laughed and strode down the driveway. Within seconds, he'd vanished into the mist.

6
Let Them Eat Mood Pie

With Crowther gone, I wandered across the garden toward a bright orange tennis ball left lying on the lawn, which seemed oddly out of place among the gargoyles, serpents, and ravens and the overall haunted house vibe. I'd just picked up the ball and hurled it down the drive, when a red-headed girl rode up on a bike.

"You've got to be kidding me!" She swerved hard to the right and skidded to a stop. "Did you seriously just chuck a ball at my head?"

"I wasn't throwing it at you. I—" I watched nervously as she flipped down the kickstand and came to stand before me. She was short, with white freckled skin and bony limbs. But the way her green eyes glinted as she stared me down, I knew I'd be a fool to underestimate her based solely on her size.

"You look really familiar." She tilted her head and peered closely at my entire face. "Have we met?"

"Ramhart's my granddad," I explained, all the while trying not to stare at the glowing green orb that was hovering just beyond her right shoulder.

"So, it's true then. . . ." After an uneasy pause, she glanced back toward the open gate and gave a thumbs-up to two kids I hadn't noticed before who were watching from the end of the drive. "That's Jools and Krish," she said, as my gaze darted between a Latina girl with long brown hair and an Indian guy with black hair wearing a hoodie the same shade of blue as mine. "They'd totally come up to meet you if it wasn't for company policy."

"Company policy?" I screwed up my face.

"Only employees may interact with the customer during the course of a delivery." She spoke as though reading the words from a manual. "Anyway," she went on, "I'm Bexley—Bexley Harris. But everyone calls me Bex." She stuck out a small, pale hand with nails that were painted dark blue.

"Um, I'm Maxen. Maxen Smith. But everyone calls me Max." I gripped her hand briefly. It felt oddly delicate. Then again, I wasn't really used to shaking hands with girls my own age.

"Why don't you go by Woodbead?" she asked.

I shrugged. "It's a long story."

She crossed her arms over the front of her baggy pink sweatshirt and tapped an impatient foot, as though debating whether to believe me. "So if you're related to Ramhart, then what's your specialty?"

"My what?" I shifted uncertainly.

"Magnus was a celebrated monster hunter. Ramhart is the Indiana Jones of the supernatural world. What's your unique thing?"

"Oh . . . Um . . ." My face went slack, my jaw unhinged in

a way that made me look like a fool. Still, there was no way I'd admit being a ghost-seeing monster slayer to some girl I'd just met who'd probably only use it against me.

"Whatever." She waved an impatient hand and turned toward her bike. "There's plenty of time for that later. For now, this is the Protection pie that Ramhart ordered." She pulled a square pink box from the wire basket and handed it to me.

I squinted at the box. I'd never heard of such a thing. "Protection pie?"

"Miss Petunia's pies are no ordinary pies, they're mood pies."

I shot her a skeptical look. No way was that true.

"Yesterday I delivered a Sweet Dreams pie to Ramhart." She planted her hands on her hips. "Did it work?"

I remembered how solidly I'd slept through the night and how much that'd surprised me. Still, I chalked it up to coincidence.

"So is this your job, then?" I asked. "Delivering pies?"

She smiled proudly. "Tons of kids applied."

"What's so great about delivering pies?" Despite how it may have sounded, I wasn't trying to be rude. She seemed kind of smug about the whole thing, and it left me confused.

"I get to keep the ones I drop. I mean, they're still in the box. It's not like I scrape the pieces off the street or anything." She rolled her eyes. "If you're lucky, I might drop one at some point today, which means you'll get to enjoy a slice at our next meeting. If you're still here, that is."

It was like waking up in the middle of a conversation. I had no idea what she was talking about.

After a quick peek at her friends, she lowered her voice and said, "It's a secret society kind of thing. But that's all I can say until you're fully initiated. Which, by the way, requires a unanimous vote, even if you are Ramhart's grandson."

"What sort of secret society?" My gaze wandered to Krish and Jools. Were they members too?

She swung her long, flame-colored ponytail over her shoulder and climbed onto her bike. "The next scheduled meeting is tomorrow." She turned around on the driveway. "We'll see you then."

While I wasn't entirely sure I wanted any part of it, I figured it couldn't hurt to make a few friends. "Where do you meet?"

She looked back at me. "We'll find you." She was about to ride away when she turned to say, "Oh, and I just realized how I know you—you're the kid from the video!"

With a flash of red hair and spinning wheels, she and the green orb were gone, leaving me with the horrible realization that I'd unwittingly marked my last day of sixth grade by becoming a viral video star.

I was on my way back to the house when I was startled by the sound of something crashing through the hedges, and I turned to see a werewolf with blazing yellow eyes barreling toward me.

Max's List of Top Five Terrifying Things

1. Werewolves
2. Glamour glitches
3. Skeletons that come to life
4. Monsters
5. Ghosts

7
Demon Dog

I was this close to being eaten alive by a werewolf when I caught sight of Ramhart leaning against the porch railing. With one hand sunk in his pocket while the other toyed with his monkey-tooth medallion, he seemed only mildly interested in the outcome.

I screamed in terror and held the Protection pie before me like some kind of shield, thinking that if it really was enchanted or whatever Bex claimed, then it might work to save me. But when the beast's yellow eyes fixed on mine, I tossed the box and ran for my life.

The wolf was gaining on me. I could feel its heated breath scorching the back of my neck, and yet Ramhart remained rooted in place.

"You're just wasting your energy." He lifted his shoulders in a casual shrug. "You'll never outrun him."

It wasn't until I'd reached the first step that he lazily pulled a hand from his pocket and tossed me something so soft, squishy, and disgusting, I nearly dropped it on contact.

"It's a treat," he said, as I gaped in confusion. It looked just like an eyeball plucked from something nonhuman. "A treat for him—not *you!*" He laughed.

With shaking knees and a rattling heart, I turned my back on my grandfather and came face-to-muzzle with a terrifying creature that, upon closer inspection, seemed less like a werewolf and more like a hellhound.

Its flesh was blue-tinged, leathery, and speckled in random spots with mange-ridden fur. Its face was definitely canine, with a long snout and powerful jaw. In addition to its glowing yellow eyes, it bore a bristly sandpaper tongue and a set of razor-sharp fangs that protruded so aggressively it made for the world's most terrifying overbite.

I watched as the beast rose up on its hind legs until it towered well above me. Then, gulping past the lump in my throat, I did as Ramhart instructed and held up the disgusting treat like it was some kind of peace offering.

"Uh . . . who's a g-g-good boy?" I stammered, shifting nervously as the hound dropped an orange tennis ball at my feet and let out a menacing growl.

"Now, tell him to sit," Ramhart called. "He needs to earn it."

Rivers of sweat poured from my armpits as I watched the hound drop to all fours, clip back its ears, and dip its head so low it revealed the long spiky ridged line of its back. "You tell him!" I shot an angry look over my shoulder, furious with Ramhart for not coming to my rescue when the beast was clearly displaying all the known signs of aggression.

"I'm not the one in danger," he sang, and at that moment I despised my grandfather more than all the ghosts, monsters, hellhounds, and Jasmine Skinks combined.

I stared into the eyes of the beast, but when I tried to speak, my mouth went so dry the words stuck to my tongue. "Uh . . ." I sputtered and tried again. "Do you think maybe you could . . . *sit?*" Just after I said it, I shielded my face with my arm and braced for the worst, fully convinced there was no way to survive this.

"You're not asking a girl to dance, Max!" Ramhart heckled from his safe place near the door. "Say it like you mean it. If you don't master him, he'll master you!"

I shut my eyes in defeat and silently cursed my grandfather. Just because I was technically a Woodbead didn't mean I carried some strange mutant gene that would enable me to master what was clearly a hound spawned in hell.

But just as quickly, I remembered how I'd successfully kicked some serious monster butt just one day before, and hoping that power was still with me, I opened my eyes wide and yelled, *"SIT!"* so loudly that the hound whimpered in fear and immediately plopped its rear on the ground.

"Now, let him sniff your fingers so he'll know you're a friend," Ramhart coached.

I stared uneasily at the creature before me. Sure, he seemed obedient, but that could change any second. "What if I don't want to be friends?"

"Then you can be his next meal. Up to you." Without another

word, my grandfather retreated inside, leaving me to sort it out on my own.

Every fiber of my being told me to drop the eyeball and run. But knowing I hadn't gotten any faster since the last time I tried, I nervously surrendered my fingers to the hound's twitchy black nose, fully convinced I was about to lose one, possibly two, when he took a perfunctory sniff, then plucked the "treat" off my palm and gulped it right down. After a satisfied lick of his snout, he nudged the orange tennis ball toward my toes.

I gave him a suspicious once-over, convinced it was some kind of trap. But when he gazed up at me with eyes that instantly switched from a fierce yellow to a friendlier gold and nudged the ball again, I figured it was as good a way as any to be rid of him. So I hurled it as far as I could and made a mad dash for the house, where Ramhart was waiting without a trace of concern.

"Shame about the pie." He forced a glass of water into my hand. "Still, we've wasted enough time already, and we have a big day ahead. Down the hatch." He motioned impatiently. "You need to stay hydrated."

My fingers squeezed the glass so hard I was surprised it didn't shatter. I was furious. Seething. Seriously so steaming mad I half expected puffs of smoke to blow from my ears. "Uh, for your information, I almost died out there!" I hooked a thumb in the general direction of where the near mauling went down, since clearly he needed a reminder. "And all you care about is the Protection pie? Which, by the way, completely failed to protect me!"

For a few tense beats, Ramhart regarded me coolly. When he did finally speak, it was pretty much the opposite of an apology.

"First of all," he said, "the pie merely invokes a *feeling* of being protected. It's not a shield. Second, you were never truly in danger. You just thought you were, and there's a very big difference. In my experience, the terrors we meet in our heads are much scarier than the ones we meet in real life." He followed with the kind of look that was supposed to convey deeper meaning, but I just tipped the glass to my lips and used the moment to decide how I was going to find a way out of this mess.

Ramhart was unlike any grandfather I'd ever met, which meant I had no idea how to handle him. Not only did he look strange with his long, blue-streaked hair, elaborate tattoos, the skull ring carved from bone, and the faint, anchor-shaped scar that curved from his ear to his lip, but the kinds of things that would bother most people (like watching a grandson get chased by a hellhound) didn't even faze him, and it left me curious about the rest of his life.

I mean, I got that he'd inherited Woodbead Mansion, but where did he get the money to keep it all going? Did the tour groups really cover the costs? Or did he actually get paid to travel the globe in search of the sort of mythical creatures no sane person would ever believe in? Was there really such a job?

As my gaze drifted down to his clothes, I noticed how the blue silk tunic he'd worn earlier had been swapped for an olive-green shirt and a pair of matching cargo pants with overstuffed pockets, which, judging by the eyeball he'd retrieved from there earlier, probably contained the kinds of things I'd rather not know about. But it was the monkey-tooth medallion that really captured my attention.

It was bigger than you might think, with a ring of dull, yellowing teeth surrounding a jade carving of a monkey wearing an elaborate jeweled crown. It reminded me of the kind of thing you'd see on a class trip to a museum, and I couldn't help but wonder if he might've pulled off some kind of heist during one of his exotic adventures.

Turns out, Ramhart had an even less believable explanation for how he came to possess it. When he caught me looking, he said, "A gift from the monkey king himself!"

Honestly, it was all I could do not to roll my eyes.

He traced a finger along its slim leather cord and regarded me shrewdly. "I take it you don't believe me."

I drained the rest of the water and placed the glass on the table beside me. "Outside of books and movies, I'm pretty sure there's no such thing as a monkey king." I needed him to know I wasn't some gullible fool who'd believe anything he said just because some people deemed him a legend.

His gaze intensified. His cheeks puffed with air. Just when I was sure he was about to really let me have it, he rubbed his hands together and said, "Well, okay then. If you're *pretty sure*, then I guess that settles it." Abruptly, he turned on his heel and motioned for me to follow. Not knowing what else to do, I grudgingly obeyed. "Don't waste another second worrying about the pie," he said.

"I wasn't," I grumbled, frowning at the back of his head. "And I won't."

"Miss Petunia and I are old friends," he went on. "I'm sure she'll understand."

"Why would you even tell her?" I was truly perplexed.

"Because there are no small secrets in Glimmerville." He glanced at me from over his shoulder. "Only big secrets." His eyes glinted in a way I couldn't quite read. "Now, what do you say you and I head over to the cemetery?"

The mention of the word *cemetery* was enough to make me halt in my tracks. After my encounter with the ghost girl, I was determined to avoid the Glimmerville Graveyard at all costs. "Uh, I'm not really up for it," I told him. "I don't really like cemeteries."

Ramhart turned. His eyes widened. His nostrils flared like a bull. It was the same expression my dad always wore whenever I tested his patience. "All of Glimmerville is built around the graveyard." His voice boomed. "No matter where you go in this town, passing the cemetery is the long route, the short route, and the only route. Which also explains the town motto: 'All roads lead to the dead.'"

I frowned. "I thought it was: 'Where everything shines just a little bit brighter.' Like on the welcome sign?"

Ramhart waved a hand in dismissal. "If it's ghosts you're worried about, I can assure you, they're all friendly." He flashed me a deeply knowing look that left me uneasy and got me wondering just how much my dad might've told him. "Now, that's not to say the spirits don't get a bit mischievous from time to time." His mouth tugged at one side. "Though I guess you can't blame 'em. They're free to go where they want, do what they want, see what they want, and sometimes they abuse it. And yet, despite a few very unfortunate encounters with undeniably tragic outcomes, I'm quite sure not a single one ever intended to harm anyone."

Unfortunate encounters?

Undeniably tragic outcomes?

What exactly was he hinting at?

He pushed me further into the hallway. "Not to worry. As long as you're with me, no ghosts will bother you."

"I'm not worried." After spending most of my life denying my ghost-seeing abilities, the lie came easily. For extra emphasis, I added, "Mostly because I don't believe in any of that."

I realize it was an irrational thing to say for someone desperately in need of a supernatural intervention. But considering what Crowther had said about me inheriting the mansion and Ramhart pinning his hopes on me, admitting I could see ghosts was a slippery slope—just a few steps shy of owning a crystal skull collection, having a headful of blue-streaked hair, and becoming a full-fledged Woodbead.

Unlike Ramhart, I'd yet to have a single positive supernatural experience, and I wasn't about to volunteer for a lifetime of being scared out of my wits. Glimmerville wasn't my future. And if I had any hope of ending my reign as Class Weirdo, then I needed to stay as far away from monsters and ghosts as humanly possible.

While I was busy thinking all that, Ramhart stood quietly observing. When my guilty eyes met his, he spoke pointedly. "Just because you don't believe in a thing doesn't stop the thing from existing." The appraising look that followed left me uneasy.

"Listen," I said, hoping to take the focus off me and return it to him. "If I'm going to be here all summer, then I need you to be straight with me, just like you promised."

He nodded solemnly.

"Like that, for instance." I pointed to a random item sitting on top of the cabinet beside us. "Am I really supposed to believe that's real?" I shot a suspicious glance at the sparkly, spiral-shaped horn displayed under a glass bell jar with a plaque that read GENUINE ALICORN HORN.

I remembered from a book I'd once read about fairy tales, fables, and other made-up things that alicorn was a fancy name for a winged unicorn, which meant Ramhart had no choice but to fess up to the lie, since everyone knew unicorns were a myth.

Ramhart passed a respectful hand over the domed lid, as though shielding it from the stinging burn of my skepticism. "What you choose to believe is up to you. Though I assure you it's not only genuine but also a sought-after remedy for curing a multitude of illnesses and neutralizing poison. I would let you handle it, but the tip is extremely sharp, and I'd hate for you to cut yourself."

"What happens if I cut myself?" I sank my hands deep into my pockets and waited to see what sort of excuse he'd drum up.

"You would die." His gaze darkened, and his lips flatlined as though to better illustrate the point. "Depending on the wound, you'd either go quickly or slowly, but you'd be dead either way."

I glanced between the glittery horn and my grandfather. It seemed like a pretty convenient excuse to keep me from seeing the MADE IN CHINA stamp that was probably fixed to the bottom.

"It's an interesting piece, and quite contradictory as well. On the one hand, if you cut yourself with the tip, there's no way to close the wound. Which means you will either bleed out or die a slow, agonizing death from a festering infection. On the other hand, a tea made with carefully grated shavings from the tip has the power to cure just about anything. Anything, I should say, except for the type of wound that results from mishandling the tip. A bit of a paradox, for sure."

I lifted another jar from the table and studied the contents, which looked disturbingly like the eyeball I'd fed to the hellhound that nearly killed me.

Ramhart tapped a finger against it, his long, pointy nail with a single black stripe clicking softly on the glass. "Snake eyes," he said. "Plucked from a nest of eight-headed vipers I happened upon during my travels through Borneo."

"You *stole* their *eyes?*" My first instinct was not to believe it. Like cutting off a giant's big toe, it seemed exceptionally cruel. When I took a closer look and noticed the pupils were slit, I knew everything he said was at least partially true. Those were snake eyes for sure.

He laughed. "They were in the process of regenerating. Right after we claimed them, they grew new ones."

"But why do you keep them? Are they just for show, or are they useful in some way?" The question could've easily applied to any of Ramhart's belongings.

"They're for Shadow. He can get a little overprotective. I apologize for that."

"Wait—" I blinked in confusion. "You mean to say that hellhound *is your pet*?"

Normal people got golden retrievers, labradoodles, or rescue mutts. Ramhart got a bloodthirsty beast.

"Shadow's what's known as a chupacabra."

"A chu—?" I couldn't remember past the first syllable.

"The literal translation is 'goat sucker,' but don't ever let him hear you say that." He shot a nervous glance down the hall, as though worried the beast might overhear. "You should probably grab a handful in case we run into him on our grave-minding rounds."

Grave minding?

As Ramhart rooted around in one of the cabinet's drawers, searching for what, I didn't know, I debated whether to ask just what the heck grave minding was, because it definitely sounded like something I wanted no part of.

And yet, what better way to back up my lie about not believing in ghosts than to visit a haunted graveyard and refuse to react whenever I saw one?

I shook two of the eyeballs onto my palm and quickly discovered they were every bit as slimy and squishy as the last one.

"This should have everything you need: rope, duct tape, Swiss

Army knife, wooden stake, and a single everlasting match that lights an infinite number of times." He presented me with a brown leather bag that looked a lot like the one he had just strapped across his chest.

"A wooden stake?" I frowned. I definitely wasn't up for wearing a purse, especially one loaded with vampire kill tools.

"Vamps are real, and they're not cute and sparkly like you see in certain movies. You need to be prepared in the event you should meet one."

He rooted around in a different drawer, where he found a small blue tin. "Hopefully, you won't need this, but one can never be too careful. . . ." He pressed the container into my palm, then reached for a khaki-colored safari-style jacket that reminded me of the one Magnus wore in his portrait. It hung from what looked like a withered old claw, with sharp, jagged nails and bits of mangy fur still attached. "My first yeti, also known as the Abominable Snowman."

I tapped my foot and waited for the punch line. When more than enough time had passed, I looked at him and said, "You seriously expect me to believe that?"

Ramhart turned with a deadly serious expression. "Yetis are fiercely powerful creatures and are not to be messed with. Even the Reptilians are afraid of them. And believe me, they're not afraid of anything—except for yetis, of course."

"So . . . yetis *and* lizard people," I said, not even trying to keep a straight face. Crowther had tried to sell me on the concept as well, but I still wasn't buying it.

"You'd be wise not to laugh," Ramhart snapped. "Aside from humans, Reptilians are one of the greatest known threats to humanity. After destroying their own dimension due to their complete disregard for anything outside of themselves, they set their sights on claiming ours and were able to infiltrate with very little notice, thanks to the hybrid program they'd started."

"Hybrid program?"

"They mated with humans, which allowed them to shift to a human form that helped them blend in. Fortunately, I was able to expel them before it progressed very far, and it's all because of one yeti. Without Yeti, I wouldn't be standing here now. Also, if it wasn't for Yeti, the Reptilians would be running our world."

I studied my grandfather, searching for the joke, but he seemed to believe every word.

"Ever hear the old saying, 'Never get between a yeti and a Reptilian'?" He paused long enough for me to shake my head. "Turns out to be true. They're mortal enemies. Saw it with my own eyes. The yeti lost a claw. The Reptilian lost its life. And I got this scar." He pointed toward the anchor-shaped mark that bisected his right cheek. "I survived a yeti attack, and all I got was this lousy scar and a claw!"

He threw his head back and laughed so hard it turned into a coughing fit. With his face flushed, he pointed to the second safari jacket beside the yeti hook, and in a hoarse voice said, "Jacket's loaded with everything you'll need, and it should fit, so . . ."

I eyeballed the jacket. If I wore it, I'd look like a Ramhart

Mini-Me. If I didn't, I risked offending him, but at least I wouldn't feel embarrassed to be seen. "I'll stick with my hoodie."

His lips tightened in disapproval, but then he shrugged and steered me toward the end of the hall, where he stopped before a blue-green wall. "To be clear, while everything you see is authentic and nothing is random, it's important to remember that all is not what it seems."

Once again, he was speaking in riddles. I waited for him to explain.

He gestured toward the wall. "Looks like an ordinary wall, but don't be fooled by appearances. Also, the color was specifically chosen for this part of the house."

I glanced between the wall and my grandfather, noting the way his face lit with excitement, unable to imagine why he was so worked up about a paint job. "Isn't it the same color as the porch ceiling outside?"

"Exactly!" he cried, as though I'd aced a difficult test. "The color is known as haint blue, and, well, obviously it works to repel haints." Reading my blank expression, he added, "Also known as evil spirits or ghosts."

I stared slack-jawed and speechless, wondering if I should maybe get a haint-blue hoodie and wear it every day.

"The color mimics water. And, as everyone knows, ghosts can't cross water."

I'd been seeing ghosts my whole life and never once realized that. Then again, it wasn't like I lived near an ocean or lake.

"If you look closely, you'll see a slim white squiggle of paint just outside the door. It allows the invited to enter." He knocked his knuckles against the wall, and a hidden door sprang open to reveal a long, winding tunnel with no discernable end. "Hurry!" he called as the door began to slide shut. "You have ten seconds to get through before it cuts you in half!"

I peered into the tunnel. It looked like the kind of place where a kid could easily disappear and never return. I shook my head firmly, about to walk away, when Ramhart grabbed hold of my sleeve and pulled me inside with him.

A second later, the secret door slammed shut behind me.

8
Killer Queen

I blinked into a shadowy stone passageway with a smooth, rounded ceiling and a dank, musty smell. Jutting from the wall was a set of large black dragon heads, each with a flaming torch clutched between its teeth. Ramhart pointed to one and told me to take it, but one look at those flickering flames left me uncertain.

Back in Boring, I wasn't even allowed to light the gas fireplace, and that was operated by a switch on the wall. Preferring to play it safe, I slid my phone from my pocket and tapped on the flashlight app, only to watch as a slim beam of light barely flickered before my battery drained down to empty.

"It's a tech-free zone." Ramhart forced the torch into my hand and started down a pathway so worn the stones gleamed beneath our feet.

"Why do you have a tunnel to the graveyard?" I watched as he methodically covered the ground with some strange herbal flakes he pulled from his pocket. "Isn't it easier to just go outside and cross the street?"

"There's more to a journey than the destination." He glanced over his shoulder in a way that made his torch cast an eerie shadow over his face. When he handed me a dried gourd he'd made into a rattle and instructed me to shake it every few steps as he waved a bundle of burning leaves all around, I seriously began to question his sanity.

We ambled along like that for a while until we finally came across what appeared to be a dead end. But like he'd already mentioned, nothing was ever what it seemed. So I stood back and waited for what looked like a solid rock wall to morph in some way.

This time, instead of knocking, Ramhart pressed his skull ring against a small indentation that marked the wall's center. The wall groaned loudly as it rose into the ceiling, allowing just enough room for us to crawl under.

I guess he didn't trust me to follow, because next thing I knew, he yanked hard on my sleeve and dragged me through. A second later, the rock slammed down with such force, the ground juddered beneath us.

First thing I noticed was how much hotter it was in that part of the tunnel. Also, the ceiling was lower and cracked in places where tree roots had insistently shoved their way through like twisted, gnarled fingers.

As I followed, I trailed a hand along the glimmering walls. When a chunk of iridescent purple stone broke off, I stuffed it in my back pocket and continued on.

"What is that?" I watched as Ramhart tossed a clump of herbs onto the ground, tapped it with his torch, then stood back and watched a great silver flame shoot high above our heads, causing the crystal walls to crackle and flare before it quickly died out.

"Bit of insurance to keep the dimensions intact. Otherwise, they risk spilling into each other." He took a deep breath and squared his gaze on mine. "The Glimmerville graveyard is a window. Which is to say it acts as a doorway to other dimensions."

In any other circumstance, I would've burst out laughing. But one look at Ramhart told me he was entirely serious. Then again, he was serious about yetis and Reptilians too, and I still wasn't sure I could truly get behind that.

"The task is laborious, but it must be completed once a week without fail."

"You do this *once a week*?" I could hardly imagine what a chore that must be. Heck, I resented when my dad made me clean my room every Sunday.

"When I'm away, Crowther takes over, though he does only the minimum." Ramhart's tone was as serious as I'd ever heard him. "Max, you must understand, Glimmerville is more than just an enchanted pie shop and a haunted graveyard—the very ground that it's built on contains the stuff of legends."

I arched a skeptical brow. I mean, I got that he was proud of his town, but the stuff of legends? Really?

"Are you familiar with galactrite?"

I shook my head.

"It's a very rare, extremely powerful crystal found in these walls as well as the soil Glimmerville is built upon. Its energy is so powerful that it acts as a vortex—a sort of portal, if you will—for interdimensional beings to come and go as they please."

He paused as though to make sure I was following. I was, though I didn't necessarily believe him.

"And that's where grave minding comes in. It's the reason for the tunnel. The reason your great-great-grandfather Magnus moved here. The reason I live here. I'm the Minder. Which means I mind the spirits, the graves, and the veil between worlds."

He paused to let the words settle. But honestly, it seemed like he'd created a bunch of unnecessary work for himself. I mean, portals? Interdimensional beings? Did he really expect me to believe in all that?

What I said was, "Wouldn't it be better to just get rid of all the galactrite so you wouldn't have to bother with this?"

Ramhart exhaled a long, drawn-out breath as though trying to center himself. "The problem isn't the crystal. The problem is those, both human and nonhuman—and trust me, the non-humans extend far beyond the creatures you've learned about so far—who are intent on using the power of galactrite for their own nefarious reasons. If that should happen, Glimmerville risks falling into chaos. And once Glimmerville goes, the rest of our world would soon follow."

My breath hitched. The answer to my *what is grave minding* question turned out to be way worse than I'd imagined. Back in Boring, there was only one world to worry about, and up until my last day of school, my biggest problem had been ghosts. But now, according to Ramhart, ghosts were the least of my concerns.

In fact, you could even say they were at the bottom of the super-natural food chain.

But the worst part was that it was becoming clear Ramhart was training *me* to take over. Along with Woodbead Mansion, the graveyard, and the mineral rights (whatever that meant), I'd also inherit the weekly grave-minding rounds. It would be up to *me* to keep the various worlds from colliding.

The thought alone left me queasy. While I had no clear idea what I wanted to be in the future, a career as a grave minder wasn't even a remote possibility.

"It's not my intention to push you into anything." Ramhart had obviously guessed the direction of my thoughts. "You're free to choose your own life adventure. I'm merely trying to show you there are many faces of reality. And while some shadow worlds are benign, others are decidedly *not*. It's those worlds that must never be allowed to bleed into ours."

We walked along in silence. It was a lot to take in, and I didn't like the sound of it.

"Also," he continued, "if you happen to find a loose piece of galactrite lying around, leave it be. It's far too powerful for one with no training."

I pulled my hood up over my head and hid my guilty face. I guess I should've gotten rid of the crystal right then and there, but his warning just made me curious to see what the rock might actually do. It wasn't like I believed it could open a portal that would swallow me whole, much less tip the world into chaos. So clearly there was nothing to worry about.

Ramhart droned on, but I mostly tuned him out. I guess I lost track of where I was going, because as soon as we reached a fork in the tunnel, he started to head one way while I went another. It wasn't until he shouted at me to stop that I noticed the air had turned a deep, radiant blue, while the ceiling above glimmered like stars.

"What is that?" I gaped in wonder as Ramhart raised his torch to illuminate what looked like thousands of long, silky threads with tiny droplets of water attached. They reminded me of a constellation of stars I once saw on a camping trip with my dad.

"Mutant glowworms," he whispered. "But don't be fooled, they're only pretty from a distance. And unfortunately, you've just invaded their territory."

I turned toward Ramhart, wondering what he could possibly be so worried about if it was just a bunch of worms, when I accidentally swung my arm right into a mass of strands that immediately attached to my sleeve. Next thing I knew, the torch and rattle slipped from my fingers as those same strands hauled me up toward the ceiling.

It all happened so fast, I barely had time to react. With my legs dangling, I swung my arms wildly, punching the strands in a desperate attempt to break free. But the more I fought, the more the mutant worms began to multiply in both number and size, until an entire army of them was coming at me from all sides. Their slimy, snakelike bodies slid down the strings as their round, luminous eyes fixed upon me.

"Your zipper!" Ramhart cried. "Lose the jacket, Max!" He

leaped toward me and grabbed hold of the bottom half of my jacket, only to rip the hem and crash to the ground in a heap.

I fumbled for the slider and struggled to pull it loose. Managed to lower it a few inches before the fabric jammed in the teeth.

"Whatever you do, don't breathe!" Ramhart shouted.

Through wild, fear-stricken eyes, I looked down at him and shrieked, "Don't breathe?" My voice boomed against the walls and came speeding back at me. "Are you serious? How am I supposed to—"

Before I could finish, Ramhart cut in. "The queen lets off a fume you'll find hard to resist, but you must. Otherwise, she'll completely immobilize you!"

The queen?

And that was when I saw it. That was when I discovered where the glowworms were taking me.

I was on a straight shot toward a giant, gummy mess of a nest, and the hideous thing lying in wait at its center.

Her eyes bulged.

Her slimy lump of a body writhed in anticipation of the meal to come.

Part worm, part python, I guessed her to be at least twenty feet long.

Just as Ramhart had warned, the stale air was suddenly infused with the scent of campfires, melted chocolate, toasted marshmallows, and graham cracker squares—a scent that instantly transported me to a happier time. The last camping trip with my family, back when my mom was still a—

"She will paralyze you!" Ramhart shouted, wrenching me from the comfort of memory and back to the terrifying present. "She will render you useless and turn your insides to liquid!"

He was right about the paralyze part.

My throat had already constricted.

My tongue had turned useless.

And my body fell numb inch by inch, turning me into a hopeless, helpless mass of flesh and bone, unable to do anything but watch as her mouth split wide open, revealing a dark, oily passage from which I'd never return.

As the army of glowworms creepy-crawled up my arms, the queen stretched and unfurled, preparing to swallow me whole.

From somewhere below, I could vaguely make out the sound of Ramhart shouting, but whatever he said didn't matter.

I was limp. Pathetic. Weak.

Hers to command and destroy.

The queen completely controlled me.

I watched as she reared up like a cobra, ready to strike. Her powerful jaw was grinding and snapping as a ghastly, venomous mist sprayed from her depths, inflaming my flesh.

All around me, the glowworms jerked and twitched in a frenzy as they carried me toward the most hideous thing I'd ever seen in real life.

Then, just as she swooped down to strike, she let out a horrible shriek and jolted back in surprise.

And that was when I noticed the rope squeezing her neck.

She thrashed wildly, hissing, biting, and spewing venom at

everything in her path. It took me a few seconds to notice that my free will was back.

Squishing my fingers into my slime-covered hoodie, I frantically tore at the fabric until it started to yield. With one final shred, it gave way, sending me plummeting to the ground, where I crashed hard at my grandfather's feet.

Above me, the queen flailed as the army of glowworms slid down the rope and went after Ramhart.

"The blue tin!" he shouted, struggling to pull the queen from her nest. "Quick—open it, aim the contents at her head, then hit the rope with your torch!"

I shoved my hand in my bag and fumbled past the set of eyeballs until I found what he wanted.

"Max—*now!*" Ramhart yanked the rope so hard the queen's large, bulbous tube of a body was pulled right out of her nest as I emptied the tin and set my torch to the twine at her neck.

Within seconds, the powder sparked and flared, and I watched as the queen's head burst into flames, rendering her a fiery ball of sizzle and slime as Ramhart and I stood back and watched her loyal army shrivel and die.

9
The Soul Eater

"What the heck was that?" I stared at the putrid remains of the thing that had nearly devoured me. My body spiked with adrenaline. My face burned where the queen had sprayed me.

"Are your eyes still stinging?" Ramhart returned an undamaged bit of rope to his bag.

"Pretty sure my pupils are on fire," I snapped, seeing no reason to hide my annoyance.

He reached into one of many pockets and tossed me a packet of something brown, mushy, and potentially disgusting. "Vulture excrement," he explained. "It's a sanitizer. Rub a bit on your face. It'll lessen the burning."

I gaped at the bag of dung. "You seriously want me to rub vulture poop all over my face?" I shook my head and gave it right back.

"You're the boss." He shrugged a little too casually for my liking. "Not to worry," he added. "The sensation should wear off in an hour or so."

Not to worry? I whirled on him, practically spitting the

words. "I almost died up there!" I picked up my torch and swung my flame toward the ceiling, determined to make Ramhart acknowledge the seriousness of what'd nearly become of me.

"It's true that you *almost* died," he said. "But, as it turns out, you didn't. And that's what really matters."

I stared in stunned disbelief. He was unlike any other adult I'd ever met, but not in a good way.

"Besides," he continued, "you've got only yourself to blame. You lost focus. And, as you see, the price of distraction is high." The grin that followed was so wide, I spotted a gold molar gleaming from somewhere deep inside, and it was enough to make me call it quits.

"I'm gone." I swung around, aiming a kick at the gourd rattle I'd dropped. I watched it careen into the wall as I started to head out. I couldn't believe how reckless he was acting about my personal safety.

"You can't go back," he called. "You can only go forward."

"Nice one, *G-Man*." Yep, I called him G-Man. But not in a cool way like he wanted.

"Not a cliché. It's a fact. The doors don't work from this side of the tunnel."

I paused. That couldn't possibly be true. He'd stop at nothing to make me finish the job.

"It's an added protection in the fight against the otherworlds. There are creatures who remain stuck here from the last time the portal opened—back when I was lost in the time slip. And since they're far too dangerous to risk letting 'em loose, I'm forced to keep 'em contained. Which is my way of telling you there's one more . . . situation . . . still to get through."

That was the moment I collapsed to the ground in defeat. I was trapped in a tunnel with a grave-minding clown disguised as my grandfather, and all I wanted was to wake up from the nightmare.

"I'll coach you through it," he said. "Trust me. You'll be fine."

"Trust you?" In a flash, I was back on my feet. "You're supposed to be my guardian—my caregiver! It's your job to keep me from harm!"

He stood before me, fingering his scraggle of beard. "You're the one who refused to wear the vest that contained all the tools you would've needed to survive the queen on your own. But you wanted to look cool in your hoodie, which, if you'll notice, is now gone."

I was speechless. Stunned. He was the most irresponsible adult I'd ever met. No wonder my dad changed his name from Woodbead to Smith. As soon as I was out of here (assuming I made it out of here), I'd never identify as part Woodbead again.

He took a step toward me. "You know what your problem is?"

"Me?" Outraged, I jabbed a thumb toward my chest. "*I'm* the one with the problem?"

"You're too soft." He shook his head sadly. "Let me guess—your dad drives you to and from school every day."

I shrugged. All the parents did that for their kids. It wasn't like it was any big deal.

"On the weekends, he organizes and supervises all your

activities. But mostly, you choose to play video games at home, where the couch is comfortable and the snacks plentiful."

"That's what good parents *do*!" I argued. "They provide a safe environment for their kids! Not that you'd know anything about that!" I knew it was harsh, but I didn't feel bad. As far as I was concerned, he deserved that and worse.

"Maybe you're right. Maybe I wasn't the right kind of dad, and maybe I'm not the right kind of granddad, either. But when's the last time you played outside, far from prying eyes? When's the last time you had a true adventure away from your TV or computer? If you ask me, it sounds like you've spent the last twelve years living like a house cat."

"A *house cat*?" My voice shook with rage. There were so many things I wanted to say, but the words piled up in my throat.

"Name one time you had a better adventure than the one you just lived."

I didn't have to think about it. The answer was clear, but that didn't make it okay.

"Just so you know, I never would've let the queen eat you. Though in the end, I believe you learned the importance of never letting your guard down when the stakes are so high. When you're dealing with the supernatural, distraction is deadly."

"So . . . that was a lesson?"

"*Everything* is a lesson. Your entire life is a lesson, and you'd do well to remember that. Now, are you ready to move on? Because we have one final monster's lair still to get through that'll make the mutant glowworms look like the last day of preschool."

Left with no other choice, I walked alongside him in a state of deeply alarmed silence. It really was a case where the only way out was through.

"Listen." Ramhart glanced over his shoulder. "We're going to descend a deep set of steps, which is easy enough as long as you take your time and don't rush. There's a river running beneath Glimmerville that serves as a conduit to the otherworlds. This next bit is the only place where the water is exposed, which allows us to keep an eye on things, though I don't mean that literally."

Literally or not, I had no idea what he was talking about.

"Once we reach the bridge, you must *never* look down. No matter what happens, no matter what you think you see or hear, not even for a second. Understand?"

I shrugged. Don't look down. After the encounter with the queen, it sounded easy enough. "What's under the bridge?"

"Water," he said.

"And what's in the water?"

"Nothing," he replied. "And it'll remain that way as long as you don't so much as peek."

Once again, his words made no sense.

"Are you familiar with the observer effect?" Without waiting for a response, he went on, "Essentially, it's the theory that by someone simply observing a thing, the thing being observed changes. Or, in this case, *awakens*. There's power in the observation."

I can't say I fully understood, and yet what I did grasp filled me with dread.

"Just follow my example, and you'll get through without a hitch."

The stairway was steep, humid, and shrouded in darkness. By the time we arrived at the rope bridge, my limbs were unsteady, and my T-shirt and jeans were clinging from sweat.

"You need to leave an offering," he said.

I looked at him with blank eyes.

"Nothing too valuable. It's merely a gesture of appeasement. Obviously."

Obviously? None of it was obvious. Or at least not to a normal person.

"Forget it," I told him, defiantly folding my arms over my chest. "I already donated my hoodie to the glowworms, and it was my favorite."

From inside his jacket, he retrieved two small branches I recognized as having come from the flesh-eating plant in his hallway (mainly because the leaves were still yapping) and placed them near the start of the bridge. "There," he said. "One from you, one from me." When he started across, the bridge rocked so precariously I was sure he'd tip over and I'd lose him forever.

The second he was on the other side, I reluctantly followed. And though I tried to mirror his steps, nothing could've prepared me for the way the planks wobbled beneath me.

The farther I went, the worse it became, until I found myself longing for a simpler time when all I had to fear was an army of mutant glowworms.

"Trust me!" Ramhart's voice bounced against the stone walls. "You got this!"

I glanced between my grandfather and the gaping space that remained, knowing one thing for sure: I couldn't trust him with much of anything.

This was a man who had abandoned his family, then blamed it on a time slip.

A man who insisted that his cheap plastic medallion was a gift from a monkey king, which despite all I'd been through still seemed like a stretch.

This was a man who'd led me straight into danger because he thought my life was lacking adventure.

I mean, seriously—what kind of person does any of those things, much less all three?

It wasn't like I was an expert on grandparents, since Ramhart was the only one of mine still living, but I knew enough to know it was not at all normal to make a kid cross an abyss—which might or might not contain a monster—in order to visit a haunted cemetery and do something yet to be determined that would keep evil from seeping into our world.

From his side of the gap, Ramhart urged me to keep moving forward. And though he assured me he knew what he was doing, he looked like someone you'd be wise *not* to follow across a flimsy rope bridge that spanned a bottomless chasm.

I grunted in annoyance and took my next step, only to have my foot slide out from under me, hurling me sideways into the rope as my torch slipped from my fingers and spiraled into the watery void.

It wasn't until Ramhart's voice thundered, "Max—*nooooo!*"

that I realized I'd forgotten his earlier warning. I was staring straight into the void.

Beneath my feet, the bridge jerked violently, resulting in an earsplitting screech of rope grating on wood that cut straight through my bones.

At the time, I would've sworn there was no worse sound than the snapping shriek a rope makes when it's pushed beyond its limits. But that was before I heard the ravenous growl of something ancient and unknown roaring from below.

My gut churned. My heart vaulted into my throat. And though I tried to stop looking, I couldn't break free of the trance-like hold.

"Max!" Ramhart shouted. "You're doing fine!" he claimed, despite all evidence to the contrary. "One foot in front of the other—that's all it takes."

He held his torch high in an effort to guide me, and I'd nearly reached the end when a deafening growl echoed all around, and I instinctively turned to see a hideous beast rise from the water until it towered well above me.

If you took all your worst nightmares and mashed 'em together, I guarantee the result wouldn't be nearly as horrifying as the thing that loomed large before me.

It was massive.

A hulking colossus of a beast made of flesh so translucent, I could see the complicated network of dark pulsating veins and twisted organs that throbbed underneath.

Vertical strips of long, hairy, spiderlike legs jutted out from each side, but my attention was soon claimed by its misshapen head and the single eyeball that bulged from its center. As the pupil faded to white, I watched spellbound as it inexplicably displayed scenes from my life.

Like a compilation reel of my very worst moments, my biggest, most shameful secrets were replayed before me. It knew my deepest fear—that I'd always be the weird kid with no friends and no mom who never fit in. And it taunted me by repeating that loop again and again.

I have no idea how long it lasted. All I know for sure is that when the images finally faded, the eye cracked wide open to reveal a black void of a mouth crammed with zigzagging rows of razor-sharp teeth and a spiky forked tongue that flicked in and out.

As the beast tossed its head back and let out a terrible shriek, Ramhart leaped forward onto the bridge and slapped a bandanna over my face. "Close your eyes!" he shouted.

Without asking questions, I did. And as my grandfather dragged me to safety, the beast whimpered and moaned as though pleading for the recognition that would resurrect it once more before it finally gave up and surrendered to the depths.

The second it was over, I tossed the bandanna and cried, "What the heck? Why would you make me go through that?"

"I warned you not to look." He swiped the bandanna off the ground and placed it beside the bridge. "A final offering," he explained.

"But what *was* it? How did it know so much about me?"

He moved forward. His steps were hurried. "You just met the Soul Eater." He spoke over his shoulder. "No two people experience it the same way. Though I'm guessing it looked like a collection of all your worst fears?" He glanced at me. "Think of it as a long-dormant entity that dwells in the water and feeds off souls."

"I thought you said spirits couldn't be in the water." I raced to catch up.

"That's no spirit, Max. And, because you didn't follow my instructions, you're now connected to it. You know, I can only help you if you're willing to help yourself first."

I was shaking, fuming. He was way past reckless. He was a menace to society. "You seriously think this is *my* fault?" I could hardly believe it. Twice I'd nearly died—both times because of him!

He stopped and spun toward me. "I *told you* not to look, but you just couldn't resist." He quirked a brow and lifted his shoulders in the grandpa version of *duh!*

He was impossible. Totally immune to logic and reason.

"It's not like I *wanted* to come here!" I shouted. "And for the record, I'm *not* a house cat. I'm just a normal kid. Not that you'd know anything about that."

"Oh, I know plenty about normal." He shot me a pitying look. "Normal is boring—it's the default of unimaginative cowards. It's for those who refuse to say yes to the mysteries of life. What you just experienced is called *freedom*. Which, by the way, is the best gift I could ever give you. So, you know, you're welcome."

How do you even respond to something like that? You don't. Which is why I just shook my head and said, "What did you mean when you said the Soul Eater and I were 'connected'?"

Ramhart's shoulders stiffened, the lines in his forehead deepened. "The Soul Eater knows you now. It's feasted on your memories and fears. Which means it knows just how to manipulate you next time you pass through the tunnel."

"Wait—so you're saying that the next time you force me to go grave minding, I'm going to have to reexperience *that*?" I decided then and there I'd never step foot in that tunnel again.

"No one's forcing anyone, Max. I'm merely showing you the ropes. But to answer your question: no."

I exhaled a deep sigh of relief.

"On second thought, make that a tentative no."

I stared at my grandfather, my heart drumming a frantic beat.

"All I can say for sure is that you will experience *something*. What that something might be is YTBD."

I stared at him.

"Yet to be determined." He grinned. Then, clamping a hand on my shoulder, he steered me forward. "The good news is, you survived, and that's what really matters. There are plenty of others who weren't so lucky." His grin grew wider, as though the whole matter was over and done with. And while technically I guess it was, I was shaken in a way I might never recover from.

After trudging up a final flight of stairs, Ramhart reached into his pocket and offered me an old-timey skeleton key made to look like an actual skeleton, with a skull at the top and a barrel that resembled a spine. "It's a key to the entire property," he said. "It holds a bit of magick that allows it to open all the doors that are open to you."

I lifted my gaze to meet his. "So there are rooms I'm not allowed to enter?" I wondered if the room that housed the *Field Guide* was among them.

His expression shifted in a way I couldn't quite read. Motioning toward a solid wood door, he said, "You may do the honors."

I slipped the key into the lock, but it took a good bit of jiggling to get any traction. In a burst of frustration, I kicked the door as hard as I could, only to find it opened onto an elaborate stone chamber with an arched ceiling, loads of columns, and at the center, a large platform displaying a cluster of coffins.

My heart sank.

My toe throbbed.

It was, without a doubt, the worst, most terrifying day of my life.

"Welcome to the Woodbead family mausoleum!" Ramhart gestured toward the caskets like it was some kind of prized classic car collection. "That's Magnus near the center, his faithful hound Scout to the left, and Roscoe—my father, your great-grandfather—to the right."

"Magnus. The one I'm supposed to meet, at least according to Crowther?"

Ramhart nodded as though it could happen any second.

"And Roscoe? Will I be meeting him, too?"

"Absolutely not!" Ramhart motioned toward the dust-covered coffin and the DO NOT DISTURB sign fixed to the side like it was some sort of afterlife hotel room.

"And the big, shiny blue one?" I asked. "Who does that belong to?"

"That's mine," Ramhart replied.

Startled, I swung around. *Was Ramhart a ghost?*

But he just laughed. "Not to worry, I plan to stick around for many more years. I just like to plan ahead. Now, come."

He hung his torch by the other door and was just about to open it when I said, "Who's that?"

From over his shoulder, he shot me a curious look.

I motioned toward the far side of the room. "Over there, standing by the pillar."

Cautiously, he moved to where I was pointing. "Tell me exactly what you see." His words were slow, precise, as though he'd chosen each one carefully. "Leave nothing out."

"Uh . . ." The words stuck to my tongue. The thing was so obvious, it seemed strange he couldn't see it.

"Max?" Ramhart's jaw twitched, but otherwise he remained perfectly still.

"I can't make out the face, but it's tall with broad shoulders and it's wearing a black hooded robe with a rope tied around the waist." While it wasn't nearly as scary as the Soul Eater, it was still pretty creepy. And the fact that Ramhart couldn't see it made it even more alarming.

Ramhart's eyes went wide. His face paled. "The Watcher,"

he said. The words that echoed through the chamber held an audible tremble. "It's an omen."

"What sort of omen?" The quiver in my own voice was no match for his. And the way he looked at me made it clear he was weighing just how much to tell me, which only served to encourage my fear.

"Last time I saw it, I was trekking through the Amazon on a cryptobotany expedition when my guide and I were snatched off the trail by a vampire vine. It nearly drained us of every last drop of blood. If it wasn't for the local shaman, I wouldn't be here today. Turned out, my guide wasn't so lucky."

"So what you're saying is . . . *one of us is going to die?*" At that moment, I seriously thought I might faint.

"I told you I'd keep you safe, and I will." He spoke with conviction, but I wasn't so sure. The nervous twitch of his lips hinted at something much darker he kept to himself. "Now come, we have much to accomplish, and we're running behind."

He propelled me through the door, and when I turned back for one last look, the Watcher was gone.

Max's List of Top Five Terrifying Things

1. The Soul Eater
2. Mutant glowworms
3. The Watcher
4. Glamour glitches
5. Skeletons that come to life

10
Grave Minding

The final door led to the fog-drenched Glimmerville graveyard.

Why I had to risk my life to get there when I could've just as easily gone outside and crossed the street was beyond me.

Though Ramhart said there was more to a journey than a destination, all I knew was that I'd nearly died (twice!) only to end up in some crummy cemetery. It hardly seemed worth all the trauma.

I stared glumly ahead as Ramhart strode down the dirt path. When he glanced over his shoulder and grinned, I didn't grin back. As long as I was under my grandfather's care, I was not in good hands.

I was seriously considering heading back to the house when Shadow burst through the fog and dropped a green tennis ball at the toe of my shoe. Without hesitation, I plucked the ball from the ground and tossed it as far as I could. After everything I'd been through, the beast no longer scared me.

"Funny how we met." Ramhart watched as the hound gave chase. "I was filming a documentary in Puerto Rico about a rash of chupacabra sightings, but despite round-the-clock surveillance, we hadn't managed to find one. It was well past midnight on the final night when we decided to quit. The crew went back to the hotel, but I wasn't ready to sleep, so I strolled around a local graveyard with a reputation for malevolent spirits, and that's where I came across Shadow."

"Wait," I cut in. "You're saying you couldn't sleep so you decided to *take a midnight stroll through a cemetery filled with evil ghosts?*" My voice rang with suspicion, though it wasn't long before I realized it was actually the most believable of all his stories.

"In my experience, it's often the living who're far more frightening than the dead." With a hand at my elbow, he steered me through a patch of fog so thick I could barely see more than a few inches ahead. "Up until the moment I spotted him lurking beside an old crypt, I'd never seen a genuine chupacabra. Most reported cases turned out to be a coyote with mange, so I wasn't entirely convinced there was any truth to the legend. But when he stared at me with those glowing yellow eyes, I knew he was the real deal. I also knew if I managed to capture him, he'd end up in a lab, where he'd be subjected to all manner of tests, and I just couldn't bear that. So I kept the sighting to myself. Two days later I was back in Glimmerville when I stepped out to fetch the morning paper and found him on the front porch. That was over twenty years ago." He grinned. "And I'll be danged if he doesn't look the same as the day I found him. Sometimes I wonder if he might be immortal." At that, Ramhart laughed, but I couldn't bring myself to join in.

"An immortal chupacabra. Doesn't that seem like supernatural overkill?" I shot him a sideways glance. "Also, how do you suppose he made the trip from Puerto Rico to Glimmerville? Did he swim? Buy a ticket on a no-frills airline?" My face took on a satisfied smirk as I waited to see how he'd squirm out of that one.

"For someone who just survived a mutant glowworm attack, not to mention a near-fatal encounter with the Soul Eater, you should know by now that when it comes to the supernatural, there's no such thing as 'overkill.'"

My smirk faded. He made a good point.

"As for how he made the trip?" Ramhart stopped and looked directly at me. "He has a way of traveling through time and space that isn't readily available to the rest of us." After a few silent beats, he added, "I know this must seem like a lot to process. It's been a rocky first day, and I'm sorry for that."

Maybe it was the unexpected apology.

Maybe it was the aftereffect of having faced my own mortality.

All I know is one minute I was having major doubts about Ramhart, and the next, words were lobbing off my tongue like fast-pitch balls at a batting cage.

"I lied," I blurted, totally mortified by what I was doing, but strangely compelled to dump the whole ugly truth on the one person who was sure to believe me. "Before. When I said I didn't believe in ghosts . . . Truth is, for as long as I can remember, I've been able to see them."

Ramhart placed a hand on my shoulder and gave it a reassuring squeeze. "It must've been very difficult to handle your gift when you've spent your whole life surrounded by minimifidians."

I squinted. "Mini-what?" I couldn't pronounce the word, much less use it in a sentence.

"It means 'those of little faith.' A skeptic, a scoffer, a minimifidian—it all amounts to the same thing. I prefer 'minimifidian' because it's more fun to say. I'm afraid it's part of being a Woodbead. Like a supernatural inheritance."

"But what about my dad? How come he didn't inherit the . . . 'gift'?" I hesitated to call it that. Most of the time it felt like a curse.

Ramhart stroked his beard. "Every now and again it skips a generation. My own dad, Roscoe, didn't have it either. No telling why. Just one of those things. It's tough being raised by someone who doesn't understand, and I'm sorry I wasn't there for you, Max. But I'm here now. And though you may not believe it, you're one of the lucky ones."

I remembered all the times I'd been laughed at, ridiculed, and sent to the principal's office. The pain and disappointment I'd caused my parents—all the arguments they had about me, which resulted in my mom leaving. Never mind my complete lack of friends. None of which seemed the least bit lucky.

"It's like getting a backstage pass to the mysteries of life," my grandfather said. "And as long as you're in Glimmerville, you're surrounded by friends." He spread his arms wide as though to include all the buried and dead. "No one will ever judge you for being your true self."

In theory, it sounded good. But soon I'd be moving to a new

town, a new school—and in a world where nearly everyone was a confirmed minimifidian, choosing normal seemed the safest way to go.

"A word of caution, though . . ."

I held my breath. I couldn't imagine what a man like Ramhart might caution me about.

"Whichever path you choose, be very careful about the ideas and beliefs you claim as your personal mythology."

I kicked at a moss-covered stone. As usual, I had no idea what he was talking about.

"A personal mythology is the story people tell themselves about themselves, and then they cling to it like it's some kind of life preserver, afraid of letting go and discovering who they're truly meant to become." Seeing my confused look, he went on, "For example, you like donuts and hoodies, and even though you've had a glimpse of a bigger world, you long to return to the comfort of your old life as soon as possible." He nodded with a look of understanding. "But none of those things have anything to do with *you*. And by that, I mean they have nothing to do with who you truly are and what you're capable of. For example, when you get nervous, you gnaw the inside of your cheek."

Caught in the act, I immediately settled my teeth.

"But one day that may change, and when that day comes, does that mean you're no longer you? Does it mean that a substantial part of who you've always known yourself to be somehow disappeared?"

"I don't think I'm following," I said, feeling completely lost in his maze of words.

"The movies you like, the friends you hang out with, all of that will shift and change with time. What remains true is the one part that can never be touched. And that, Max, is not a mythology—that part is known as your destiny."

"So everyone has a destiny?" I found myself warming to the idea.

"Sure, but that's not to say that everyone discovers what their destiny is. Most people are so stuck in the mythology of their lives that they never realize there was something better out there just waiting to be discovered."

We walked along a row of grave markers as I mulled over his words. "So I guess that means Magnus's destiny was to be a great monster hunter." Ramhart confirmed it with a nod. "And according to the internet, you're the Indiana Jones of the supernatural world." His lips pulled into a grin. "But . . ." This was the part where I stalled. I needed to make clear, in a non-insulting kind of way, that I had no interest in following in the family footsteps. "Well, I guess what I need to know is, is it dangerous to ignore your destiny?"

Ramhart traced a finger along the scar on his cheek. "I think what you're really asking is if you have a choice in all this."

When he looked at me, a rush of blood rose to my cheeks.

"Of course you do!" he said. "That's what's meant by free will. As for whether it's dangerous to ignore your destiny . . . guess that depends on the destiny. It could be dangerous for one, dangerous for many, or of no real consequence whatsoever. The only way you'll ever know is to see where you stand when the final credits roll." Ramhart's features sharpened, but his gaze was kind. "I know you probably haven't heard this a lot, but it's okay to be extraordinary—there's no need to make yourself small. Great minds are always feared by narrow minds, which is why you can't—you *mustn't* allow the minimifidians to define you. Understand?"

I stared down the path ahead, feeling more confused than ever. On my first day in Glimmerville I'd already experienced more than most people do in a lifetime. And while it was undeniably exciting, I couldn't help but wonder what the point was when outside of Ramhart, there was no one to share it with—no one to believe me.

"Why not give it a chance?" He regarded me carefully. "Why not let your summer here help you discover exactly what you're truly capable of?"

"But what if I can't go back?" I asked. "What if I become so weird—so out there—I can't even pretend to be normal again?"

"Would that be so bad?" Ramhart asked.

In my head, I imagined myself in the junior high cafeteria, surrounded by friends—not a single one of them dead. By choosing to go along with Ramhart's suggestion, there was a really good chance that dream would never happen.

"It's not just ghosts," I said, my voice nearly a whisper. "The other day, I saw monsters, too." I turned just in time to watch the blood drain from my grandfather's face, leaving a mere specter of a man with hollowed eyes and a scraggly beard. And though he rebounded quickly, it was too late. My confession had forced us down a new road from which we'd never return.

"What do you mean by 'monsters'?" he asked, so I went on to describe my epic battle on the last day of school. When I finished, he said, "Those weren't monsters, Max. Mainly because there's no such thing. Or, to put it more succinctly, that's really more of a blanket term used to describe a wide variety of otherworldly creatures. Not to mention, for one to go from seeing ghosts to seeing monstrous creatures is basically unheard of. There's a natural progression to these things. What you're suggesting is too big a leap."

I'm not sure who he was trying to convince—him or me. Clearly he'd forgotten how I was the one who saw the Watcher back in the mausoleum, but I chose not to remind him. The idea of it still gave me the creeps.

"So if they weren't monsters, then what were they?" I asked. In my mind's eye I could see them so clearly—their glowing red eyes, the menacing rows of sharp, jagged teeth. "Are you saying they were demons?" My voice shook.

Ramhart took a moment to consider, then quickly dismissed the idea. "Seeing as how I wasn't there to witness, I can't say for sure. But in my experience, demons are often paired with Reptilians—they treat the demons like pets. And since I expelled the Reptilians long ago, I'm guessing what you saw might've been bogeys."

"Bogeys?" I blinked. "Like, the bogeyman? The invisible,

make-believe monster that supposedly lives under the bed?" I started to laugh, but the look Ramhart gave me brought it to a quick end.

"Traditionally, the idea of the bogeyman was created by parents to scare their children into behaving. Unfortunately, fear is a powerful force. And children, because of their vivid imaginations, are powerful creators. When you put the two together . . . well, there are those who believe that over the years bogeys have morphed from a scary idea into actual entities created by the power of fear."

"So . . . you're saying they were *feared* into being?" I tried to imagine such a thing, but it made zero sense.

"You've heard the saying 'mind over matter'?" Ramhart asked. "Well, this is creating matter from mind. In other words, when someone concentrates very intently on an idea, the idea itself can become so real it takes on a physical life of its own."

"But pretty much everyone had one—including my teacher!"

"What you saw was their collective fears made manifest. Everyone's afraid of something—problem is, if you feed it enough, your fear becomes real."

It was an interesting idea, but I was less concerned with how they came into being and more concerned with how to stop seeing them.

"During your struggle," he asked, "did any of the bogeys manage to draw blood? Your blood?"

I remembered that the first one took a swipe at my face, and how, just after, I watched as it licked my blood from its claw.

When I relayed the scene, Ramhart shut his eyes and blew a long, deep exhale that was pretty much the opposite of reassuring.

"I didn't see my first bogey until I was nearly sixteen." With a thoughtful expression, he combed his fingers through his scraggle of beard. "Seems like you're progressing much quicker than I did. And the way you fought them off . . ." He let out a low whistle. "You've got a great power, Max. I must say, I'm impressed."

"But I don't want you to be impressed! And I don't want to progress quicker than you!" I cried, my shoes sinking into the damp earth as I stumbled through the mist alongside him. "I don't want bogey-slaying superpowers—I don't want any of this! Supernaturals just show up in my space, and they've pretty much wrecked my whole life."

The look Ramhart gave me was grave.

"I'm not like you," I said, pleading with him to understand. "I live in the normal world, which is why I need you to show me how to make it stop."

Ramhart turned to me, eyes gleaming. "I'll let you in on a secret," he said. "There is no 'normal' world. Only people who refuse to see the truth." He paused to let that sink in before he continued. "I'm afraid there's no stopping it, Max. You can try to ignore them, which I'm sure you've already attempted, with varying degrees of success. But once you've discovered the gift, there's no going back. The most you can hope for is not to prog-ress any further."

To be fair, he did sound sorry. He also sounded sincere. Still, it was the opposite of what I wanted to hear.

"But what about the *Field Guide*?" I spun toward him, watching as, once again, his face grew ashen.

"What do you know about that?" He regarded me with such scrutiny I couldn't help but cringe. Still, his reaction was all I needed to know I was definitely onto something.

"You had it at the breakfast table. I saw it right after the glitch." I waited for him to admit or deny, but his face was a blank. "According to my dad, it's a sort of supernatural encyclopedia."

"I assure you it's much more than that," Ramhart scoffed. "It's also very dangerous in the wrong hands."

"But not in your hands." I paused, needing to play it just right. Interested but not overly eager—cool but not to the point of blasé. "I mean, since you're the one who wrote it and all. If it's as powerful as you claim, then there must be some kind of spell or something that could help me to stop seeing—"

"The *Field Guide* is not a wish book, a spell book, or anything of the sort, and I don't want you anywhere near it!" His voice rasped. He crossed his arms firmly over his chest. But there was too much at stake, and I would not be deterred.

"Okay." I freed my hands from my pockets and flashed my palms in surrender. "But you should probably tell me where you keep it. You know, so I don't accidentally stumble upon it, and—"

Before I could finish, he was shaking his head. "The *Field Guide* is in a secure location. There's no chance of you or anyone else 'accidentally' stumbling upon it. Now come. Enough of this nonsense. There's still much to do."

He strode deeper into the cemetery, where he stopped before

a very old grave and retrieved a saltshaker from his worn leather bag. A moment later, when Shadow reappeared, the chupacabra gripped the shaker between his teeth and salted a cluster of graves, then bypassed a number of other burials before starting in on the next one.

"Salt keeps the spirits from rising," Ramhart explained, as we followed along at a much slower pace.

"But why is he only doing some graves and skipping others?" I gestured toward the ones Shadow had missed.

"Some ghosts are harmless, some are hungry. Harmless ghosts are free to roam as they please. Hungry ghosts have an agenda—one that benefits no one but them. They need to rest a bit longer and gain some perspective."

I strained to see the date engraved on one of the headstones Shadow had salted. "It says he died in 1888. How much perspective could he possibly need?"

"You'd be surprised." Ramhart laughed. "Before you arrived, I salted all the graves. I needed everyone to stay in their place, so I wouldn't risk scaring you before I had a chance to explain. But once the glamour failed, all bets were off."

I remembered the ghost girl that ran in front of our car. "Pretty sure you missed one," I said.

A sly grin spread across Ramhart's face. "I hadn't realized you'd met. Not to worry, young Miss Wilson and I have an agreement."

"I'm pretty sure she bailed on her end."

His head shook with laughter, sending blue streaks and feathers fluttering down his back. "Point is, there are loads of ghosts who are dying to meet you!" He stopped to search through his bag. "And this will help them to rise again."

He displayed a jar containing some sort of red sparkly liquid, then sprinkled it across a grassy mound. Next thing I knew, a twirling wisp of smoke rose from the earth as a ghost began to stretch and grow until it fully materialized before me.

The spirit was tall and slender and wore a crisp black suit, driving gloves, and a cap, which he tipped as he bowed. "Dear sir! I am very pleased to make your acquaintance," the ghost said. "I am Barnabas, the trusted chauffeur to the great Magnus Woodbead." He bowed once again, and though I knew it was rude, that was the moment I turned on my heel and made for the gate.

I wasn't up for meeting a bunch of dead people, and I certainly had no interest in continuing a grave-minding lesson, since it wasn't exactly a skill I planned to use in the future.

I needed some time alone, some space to think. If my first day in Glimmerville was any indication, then there was a very good chance I'd either die a tragic, premature death, be horribly maimed, or be possessed by an evil spirit well before the summer could end. And it wasn't like I could count on my grandfather to step in to save me.

I mean, I didn't actually believe he was out to harm me (even though it sometimes seemed like it). I guess he'd just grown used to living among so much weirdness that he couldn't understand my need to fit in with all the other minimifidians.

Which made me even more determined to get my hands on the *Field Guide*.

Although he tried to stay neutral, it was clear he wanted me to claim my destiny as the next great bogey-slaying grave minder. And the fact that he didn't want me to get ahold of that book only proved it could help me.

I plowed through the fog, accompanied by the squish of my sneakers moving across the damp lawn and the high-pitched squeals of the spirits that, thanks to Ramhart, were left to float freely. Some of the graves were plain, nothing more than a small plaque and a mound of dirt; others were more elaborate, with large sculptures of angels, cherubs, and other fantastical creatures. Though they all shrank in comparison to the one that loomed at the end.

Surrounded by a tall black iron gate intended to keep trespassers away, a life-sized statue of a young girl sat at its center, with a semicircle of rosebushes at her back and a collection of toys at her feet.

The plaque at the bottom read:

CHERISHED DAUGHTER—BELOVED BY ALL
ROSIE GRACE WILSON
1877–1890
MAY SHE FOREVER REST IN OUR HEARTS

"People travel from all over the world just so they can leave presents at my grave. They say my statue cries tears of blood whenever the toys are taken away."

Slowly, I turned. I'd been so engrossed in reading that I'd

failed to notice the overwhelming scent of roses. Instantly, I recognized the ghost who'd tricked me the day before.

"It's a bit of fun I have with the tourists." Rosie Grace hovered before me. "And in case you're wondering, it was pneumonia that took me, and it really was a shame. I had such a wonderful life. My parents were extremely wealthy and loved nothing more than to dote on me. As their only child, I got everything my heart desired. One Christmas, they even—"

At that moment, Shadow ran up beside me, and while Rosie Grace was talking (there seemed to be no end to it), I tugged the saltshaker from between his teeth and began sprinkling.

"It was the cutest pony you've ever seen! I named her Sparkles, and—Hey! I beg your pardon, but what in tarnation are you doing?" She shrieked with outrage, but more importantly, she began to fade.

"Oh, you mean this?" I continued shaking the salt when Ramhart raced toward me, snatched the shaker, and furiously scooped the salt into his palm. "I heard she cries tears of blood!" I watched Ramhart swipe and gather as the ghost girl hovered nearby, desperate with worry. "I figured that should be put to a stop."

Wiping his hands down the front of his pants, Ramhart rose to his feet. "Max, Rosie Grace is not only a friend but a town favorite. People travel from all over hoping to see her. Do you really want to disappoint them? Much less silence such an important part of Glimmerville lore?"

Rosie Grace returned to her full ghostly self and shook a finger at me as she hovered just beyond Ramhart's shoulder.

"Now please refrain from wandering off," Ramhart scolded. "We've wasted more time than we can afford."

I glanced between my grandfather and the army of ghosts he'd unleashed. They stared back with wide, hollow eyes. After what I'd done to Rosie Grace, they seemed as wary of me as I was of them.

"Ease up," Ramhart said. "She could really use a friend her own age." He slipped an arm around my shoulder and led me away just as Rosie Grace stuck out her tongue and waved.

11

Saved by the Ghost

I didn't follow Ramhart.

The moment he tried to lead me to a bottomless lake, claiming the Glimmer mermaids lived at the bottom, I ditched my bag and made my escape.

How could mermaids (which didn't exist) live at the bottom of a lake he claimed to be bottomless?

"Where are you going?" my grandfather shouted as Shadow gave chase.

"Away," I muttered. "And please, call off your goat sucker." I glared at the chupacabra before plowing into a blur of fog so dense it was hard to see clearly.

As soon as I reached the cemetery gate, the mist began to lift, allowing for a view of a charming neighborhood of tidy, pastel-colored houses with matching mailboxes, freshly mowed lawns, and well-tended gardens.

It was the sort of place where you'd expect to find a friendly neighbor with a basket full of kittens and home-baked cookies cooling on the counter.

The sort of place where nothing bad could ever happen.

Or at least that was how it seemed until I caught sight of Woodbead Mansion looming on the corner.

With the gargoyles perched on the roof, the red-eyed door serpents, and squawk-box raven, I couldn't help but wonder what the neighbors must think of my grandfather.

Did they scoff at the spectacle?

Did they resent the busloads of tourists who came to gawk at the strangeness?

As I headed for the main part of town, I must've been lost in my thoughts, since it's the only way to explain how I failed to notice I was being stalked by that awful Rosie Grace.

The first two times she materialized before me, I darted around her.

The third time she appeared in my path, glaring at me with a hand on each hip, I took a deep breath and made a decision that surprised even me. I plowed right through her—only to pop out the other side completely incapacitated by a sudden blast of crippling cold as a dizzying floral scent shot up my nose.

"You'll think twice before you try that again!" She hovered nearby as I doubled over from a combination of nausea and frostbite.

"Stop!" I pleaded. "Stop with the cold and the . . . *god-awful smell!*"

"You don't fancy the scent of roses in bloom?" Her blue ghost eyes went wide, her blond curls shook. "Well, that's truly a pity, considering how it's my signature scent and you, my new friend, are going to be smelling *a lot* of it."

New friend? How clueless could she possibly be? I'd just tried to salt her, and I would've gladly completed the job if Ramhart hadn't stopped me.

"We're *not* friends." I took a step forward, relieved to find some of the feeling returning to my limbs.

"I beg to disagree!" She hovered alongside me. "If for no other reason than you can see me and I can see you. I'm sure there are plenty of friendships that started with less."

"Look—" I kept my voice low. I knew better than to risk getting caught talking to someone who was clinically dead. "I'd really appreciate it if you'd just leave me alone. There must be loads of other people you can haunt."

"But you're the one who saved me from getting run over by a car!" She bounced onto her toes and burst into loud peals of laughter.

With my legs back to functioning, I did my best to escape. But she turned out to be a pretty fast floater, which made her impossible to outpace.

"You should have seen your face when you yelled at that old man to stop—it was hilarious!"

"My dad." I spoke through gritted teeth. "The 'old man' was my dad."

"He did seem rather peeved. Tell me, did he add on extra chores, make you go without supper, or was it something much worse?" At the thought of my punishment being much worse, her eyes gleamed with delight, but I was too focused on her use of the words *peeved* and *supper* to care.

I stole a sideways glance at her outdated white dress and the blue bow in her hair, probably the same clothes she'd been buried in. "You should really find someone your own age," I told her.

"I'll have you know I'm thirteen." She sounded proud of herself, like she'd achieved something grand.

"In human years—of which yours ended more than a century ago."

Her expression soured. She seemed a lot less proud of that.

"Remember my name," she shouted, but I was on the move and pretended not to hear. "All you have to do is call my name three times! Say 'Rosie Grace, Rosie Grace, Rosie Grace' and I'll be there!"

"Hey, Rosie Grace," I called over my shoulder. "Have a nice afterlife!"

I'd just started to relax, just started to breathe in a normal rhythm, when a group of kids rode up on their skateboards and purposely blocked my path.

The kid on the right was short, with a mean look in his eye. The kid on the left was skinny and tall with a patch of acne that covered his chin. The one in the middle, who I guessed to be the brains of the group (which isn't saying much), tugged on his beanie and said, "Were you just talking to Rosie Grace?"

Knowing better than to admit to the truth, I squinted in a way I hoped would pass for confusion while still managing to look effortlessly cool. "I don't know what you're talking about," I told them.

Beanie Boy consulted his friends. "What do you think?"

"I think I heard him say the name Rosie Grace," Mean Eyes said.

"Same," said the tall, skinny kid with acne on his chin.

"See, I *know* I heard him tell her to have a nice afterlife." Beanie Boy stared me dead in the eyes. "Looks like that makes three against one. So why are you lying about the thing we all know you did?"

The way they spread out before me, there was no way to get past without making a scene that would only end up being even more embarrassing.

"Yeah, what's up with that?" Mean Eyes drove his board against my sneakers, stopping just short of slamming into my toes.

I stood frozen. Mute. Trying not to flinch while silently reminding myself to stay cool. Ramhart had claimed that as long as I was in Glimmerville, I was surrounded by friends, but clearly he was mistaken. Which left me wondering just what else he might've been wrong about.

Was there actually a way to rid myself of my supernatural abilities?

And did the *Field Guide* hold the key?

"We saw you, man," Acne Chin said.

"We recognize you from the video." Beanie Boy smirked. "Who you trying to play?"

My stomach clenched. My heart took a nosedive. That made three more kids who'd seen the video. Clearly, what happened in Boring did not stay in Boring.

"My favorite part is when you did that midair scissor kick!" Acne Chin said as his friends laughed alongside him.

I stared mutely, unable to think of a single way out of this mess. It wasn't like I could explain why I'd been caught talking to a dead girl only to lie about it a few seconds later.

I was just about to do something extremely uncool like make a run for it when, from out of nowhere, a gust of wind kicked up, and the boys' skateboards slid out from under them, sending them sprawling, arms windmilling wildly, before all three crashed in a heap on the pavement.

"Are you sure you don't want to be friends?" I looked up to find Rosie Grace hovering nearby. Unfortunately, I was the only one who could see her.

I glanced between the ghost girl and the three bullies she'd taken down on my behalf. It didn't take a psychic to know they blamed me for what happened.

"You broke my elbow!" Mean Eyes howled in pain as he hugged his arm to his chest.

Instantly, I held up my palms and started backing away.

"You're dead!" Beanie Boy shouted as he struggled to stand. "You hear me? Dead!"

Before he could finish, I was running faster than I ever had in my life. Driven by a combination of mind-numbing fear and a spike of adrenaline, I was so bent on escape that I lost track of where I was going.

All I knew for sure was that one minute my knees were pumping, my soles pounding, and the next, something that can only be described as a strange vaporous tunnel rose like a dome until it swallowed me whole.

The atmosphere grew unnaturally quiet and still. My own labored breath was the only sound to be heard. In my desperation to flee, I'd gotten lost. When I tried to turn back, it was like some unseen force kept driving me forward until the vapor cleared and I found myself in a place that reminded me of a set from an old-time movie.

The streets were dusty and unpaved. The few people moving about wore outdated clothing.

"Watch it—watch it, I said!" an angry male voice roared from behind as I turned to find a horse-drawn carriage barreling toward me.

I froze, unable to do anything more than stare in shock as the driver jerked the reins hard, sending the horses into an eye-rolling, snorting frenzy as they veered to avoid me.

From out of nowhere, a hand grasped my wrist and yanked me safely out of the coach's path. When I turned, it took a moment to realize it was Rosie Grace who had saved me.

Unlike all the other times I'd seen her, she was no longer translucent. With her blond hair sparkling with mist, her blue eyes shining, and her cheeks flushed bright pink, she looked just like any other three-dimensional thirteen-year-old girl. You could even say she looked . . . uh . . . kind of pretty.

"Max, I need you to listen." Her tone was urgent. Her grip unbearably tight. "I'm going to borrow your energy. It won't take long, but you have to trust me."

Though I understood the words, I had no idea what they meant. When I finally caught on that the reason she looked so real was because she was stealing my life force, it was too late to stop it. The world dimmed down to nothing.

She must've dragged me back through the tunnel, because the second we burst through the other side, I sprang back to life.

"What the heck?" I jerked free of her grip, struggling to make sense of what'd just happened. Three times in one day I'd nearly died. The odds of making it to the end of the summer were definitely not in my favor.

Also, the sun hung lower in the sky, my watch was stuck at 3:33, and my phone was melted beyond repair, which was probably the worst news of all, since I wouldn't get to replace it anytime soon.

"Seriously," I said. "What the—"

She cut me off before I could finish. "The first rule of visiting an alternate dimension, which is also known as dimension hopping or time-slip tourism, is don't eat or drink anything unless you want to be stuck there forever."

"I wasn't a tourist," I snapped. "I have no idea how I got there, but it wasn't on purpose."

Her eyes narrowed. Her lips pursed. "The first rule for avoiding unintentional time slip, time warp, and/or alternate dimension tourism is to always be on the lookout for the following elements: electronic fog, electrical storm manifestations, and or the Oz Effect, which is when the atmosphere turns unnaturally silent and still. These are all indicators that a supernatural event is about to occur."

I sank my head in my hands, only half listening.

"Which one did you experience?"

I blinked at her. "Uh . . . the Oz Effect, I guess? And fog. There was definitely fog." I squinted into the distance as though that might help me recall. "Then again, Glimmerville always has fog, and I'm not sure it's electronic."

Rosie Grace looked on with concern. "I'm surprised Ramhart didn't warn you, considering his own tragic history with getting stuck in a time slip."

"So it's true, then?" I know it might seem like an odd thing to say after all I'd gone through, but after years of believing Ramhart had made up the world's worst excuse for abandoning his family, it took some time to adjust to the extraordinary truth.

"You think ghosts like me are the end of the supernatural story?" Rosie Grace frowned. "You've got a lot to learn, Max Woodbead."

"Smith," I mumbled. "I go by Smith." Though, after a day of glamour glitches, mutant glowworms, a Soul Eater, the Watcher, grave minding, and an unintentional visit to an alternate dimension, I felt a lot more like a Woodbead than ever before. And that kind of worried me.

"You're lucky I followed you," she said. "I wasn't going to, but when I watched you run away only to vanish into thin air, I thought you might be in need of some help." She glanced back toward the place where the world as I knew it had melted away. "Though I do wonder what triggered it." Her head cocked to the side, sending a cascade of blond curls spilling over her shoulder.

"Glimmerville is a very peculiar town, but there hasn't been any otherworld bleed-through for . . . well, since Ramhart discovered a way to reverse the polarity of the galactrite and cut off all interdimensional travel. Did you see anything strange when you guys were out grave minding?"

"Everything was strange." I shook my head and breathed an exhausted sigh. Never before had I packed so much into one day, and according to Ramhart, I could expect the rest of the summer to unfold in a similar way.

When I looked at Rosie Grace, I noticed a trail of black sludge streaming from the inner corner of each eye. "You okay?" I pointed at her face, reminded of the legend of her statue crying tears of blood whenever her toys were taken away. Only the stuff streaming from Rosie Grace's eyes didn't seem very bloodlike to me.

Her hand flew to her cheek, and when she saw the mess on her fingers, she began wiping furiously. "I beg your pardon," she said, abruptly turning away.

I stared awkwardly at her back, knowing I should thank her for saving me, but I was so used to ghosts going out of their way to make trouble, the words wouldn't come.

As if reading my mind, she tossed a casual wave over her shoulder and said, "I'm not a tramp soul, if that's what you're thinking."

"Tramp soul?" I'd never heard of such a thing.

"Low-level spirits that are so attached to the earthly plane that they refuse to move on. They carry a very different energy. Mainly because they're strictly out for themselves."

"Oh, so like pretty much every ghost I ever met," I said.

"Not all ghosts are bad, Max. Anyway, truce? We are friends, yes?"

She didn't stick around for an answer. And honestly, I'm not sure what I would've said if she had. Sure, she'd saved my life, but I also remembered how helpless I'd felt when she'd stolen my energy and how easily she could've killed me.

The fact that she didn't—did it mean I could trust her?

Or, like every other ghost I'd ever met, was Rosie Grace luring me into her own kind of trap?

Max's List of Top Five Terrifying Things

1. Time slips
2. The Soul Eater
3. Mutant glowworms
4. The Watcher
5. Skeletons that come to life

12

A Brief History of Time Slips

"And so, the prodigal grandson returns."

I looked up to find Crowther leaning against the porch railing, his sharp blue gaze seeming to slice right through me, leaving a shivering trail in its wake. "And to think I bet against you," he said.

I trudged up the front steps, painfully aware of the frenzied beat of my own thudding heart and the way the hair stood up on my arms as I passed. I had no idea what Crowther meant, but one look at his arched brow and tilted chin had me determined not to ask.

When I reached the top, he gestured toward my hair. "Despite your myriad adventures, it's interesting to note that the lack of blue streaks persists."

Although I didn't fully understand the significance of blue streaks (other than that they served as some sort of supernatural merit badge), I knew my dad would totally flip if he saw me with blue hair, so I didn't feel all that bad.

"Ramhart's waiting inside." Crowther turned on his heel to

better follow my progress. "Seems you got the old man in a bit of a panic."

I paused before the door. After all the danger Ramhart had put me through, I seriously doubted that was true. "I wasn't gone all that long," I said, not even bothering to hide my annoyance.

Crowther tossed back his head and laughed, a low, hollow sound. When he righted himself, he fixed his gaze on mine. "On the contrary, Max. You lost an entire day."

The words hung suspended between us as I studied his face, trying to determine whether to believe him. Crowther seemed to enjoy making me squirm, so I wasn't sure I could trust him to tell me the truth.

"Don't be fooled by that tough exterior," Crowther went on. "I've been working for your grandfather for nearly a decade. And I'm sorry to say it, but the past few years have taken a toll. He doesn't recover as quickly as he once did. Which means every time you give him a reason to worry, you put him at risk. And I'm sure that's not your intention now, is it?" The way he looked at me felt like an injection of ice water straight into my veins.

When I realized he was waiting for me to respond, I dutifully shook my head no.

"Good—glad we're on the same page." He nodded. "Now, if you're looking for a way to make it up to him, you can start by giving him this." He reached into his inside coat pocket and retrieved a small glass bottle he then gave to me. "I know it wasn't your choice to come here, Max. And frankly, you've not gotten off to a very good start. So may I suggest that from this point forward, you come to me with your questions instead of bothering Ramhart?"

The only question I had was about the location of the *Field Guide*. But I couldn't imagine asking Crowther to help me with that. So I shrugged and turned my focus to the jar of blue liquid. It reminded me of the stuff I saw Ramhart drink with his pizza.

"That's what keeps his hair blue." Crowther broke into what might normally be considered a grin. But from where I stood, it was more a menacing display of stretched lips and white teeth. "Now go." He waved me toward the door. "And don't mind the serpents. It takes years to win their approval. Still working on it myself."

I scooted past the twin snakes, wanting nothing more than to grab a snack and hole up in my room. But just as Crowther had warned, Ramhart really was waiting, and he called out to me the moment I walked through the door.

I followed his voice into the kitchen, where I found him leaning against the counter. With Rhoven perched on his shoulder, Shadow sitting obediently by his side, and the monkey-tooth medallion hanging from his neck, he reminded me of a supernatural Dr. Doolittle, and despite Crowther's claims, he didn't appear all that stressed.

"Heard about your close call with the time slip." Ramhart motioned toward a place he'd set at the table. "Go on." He pulled out the empty chair, clapped his hand on my shoulder, and pretty much forced me to sit. "Hope you like ham and Swiss."

I did like ham. And Swiss. But the truth is, I was so hungry,

I probably would've eaten just about anything. As I dug into my sandwich, Ramhart reached for the small bottle, added the strange blue liquid to his water, and took a long, thirsty swig. "You're lucky Rosie Grace was there to save you." He claimed the seat opposite mine.

In an instant, my sandwich threw itself in reverse, and I found myself choking as much on the crust as I had on his words. How could he possibly know about that, considering how I'd just gotten back?

"Did—" I covered my mouth to cough, took a desperate sip from the glass of water Ramhart nudged toward me, and tried again. "Did Rosie Grace tell you—" I started, but before I could finish, Ramhart was shaking his head.

"I asked her to follow you." He polished off the rest of his drink, then dabbed the corners of his mouth, leaving splotches of blue on his napkin. "You can't go charging off by yourself when you don't know the lay of the land." He slid his elbows across the table and peered at me in a way that left me so unnerved, I dropped my sandwich onto my plate and nervously wiped the crumbs from my lips. "Glimmerville is no ordinary town," he continued. "And until you learn how to properly handle your gifts, I'm afraid you're a magnet for trouble."

I was vaguely aware of his mouth moving, his words flowing, but I'd mostly stopped listening. I was still stuck on the part where he'd sent Rosie Grace to babysit me, and I was horrified to think he'd actually do such a thing.

A rush of heat rose to my cheeks, and in that moment I wasn't entirely sure I wouldn't burst into flames. According to a show I once watched, spontaneous combustion could be a real thing.

"Hey—you okay?" Ramhart asked, and though he did appear genuinely concerned, unfortunately for both of us, I'd reached the end of my rope.

"You seriously sent Rosie Grace to follow me?" I cried. "Like some sort of phantom nanny?" My armpits grew damp, and my insides skipped to a jittery beat. "Do you have any idea how embarrassing that is?"

Torn between wanting to crush my hunger pangs by finishing the sandwich and not wanting to give Ramhart the satisfaction of watching me eat it, I pushed away from the table and leaped to my feet.

Ramhart tilted his head and regarded me patiently. "Come now," he said, gently patting my place mat. "You're tired, hungry. By refusing to eat, you hurt only yourself."

In the end, hunger won out, and I slumped back down in my seat, deciding to punish my grandfather by refusing all eye contact.

After a few silent beats, Ramhart said, "I'm sorry if I embarrassed you. But do you have any idea how dangerous a time slip can be?"

I frowned, polished off the rest of my meal, and reached for the platter of cookies arranged enticingly before me.

"You were lucky," he continued. "You only lost a day."

"So, it is true," I said, forgetting my vow to ignore him. "I thought for sure Crowther was messing with me."

"Crowther would never joke about something so serious." Ramhart's voice adopted a tone that bordered on scolding. "He can come off as prickly, but he's very well versed in all things supernatural. After all, I trained him myself. Which means he's all too aware of how getting lost in a time slip—or any alternate dimension, for that matter—is nothing to laugh at. It's a nasty bit of business—I should know. Though unlike you, I didn't have anyone to help guide me back. By the time I found my way out, my entire life had been turned upside down. My wife had passed on, and my son—your father—wanted nothing to do with me."

"He still doesn't believe you," I said. It wasn't something I'd planned to say, and I'm sure it wasn't news to Ramhart. But now that it had happened to me, I couldn't stop thinking how my dad had spent most of his life holding a grudge over a lie that turned out to be true. "He's convinced you made up the world's lousiest excuse to cover the fact that you abandoned your family."

Ramhart sighed and leaned toward me. "And what do you think?" he asked.

Though he kept his expression neutral, I couldn't help but notice how his hands were clasped nervously together as he fidgeted with his skull ring. I took it as a sign that he actually cared about my opinion, and honestly, it wasn't what I was expecting.

I finished my cookie, then reached for another, even though I wasn't entirely sure I wanted to eat it. I guess I was just buying some time until I figured out how to respond. "I used to believe my dad." Cautiously, I met Ramhart's gaze. He nodded encouragingly. "I mean, I had no other evidence, so what choice did I have? But now . . . well, for one misguided moment I actually considered calling him. You know, so I could explain how he'd made a mistake." I snuck a glance at Ramhart, curious to see his reaction. But whatever he might've been thinking, he kept it in check.

"And will you?" he asked. "Call him?"

I didn't even hesitate before I shook my head no. "Not about that. He wouldn't understand. He sent me here because he's hoping you can help make me normal."

"And isn't that what you're hoping for too?" Ramhart said.

I sat back in my seat, surprised to find the answer didn't come easily. I mean, here I'd survived the most terrifying two days of my life—there were moments when I was 100 percent certain I would actually die. But having come out the other side, well, it left me sort of curious to see what else might be out there.

"After all you've been through, it's perfectly understandable if you're feeling confused." Ramhart reached out to scratch Shadow between his ears, causing the beast to close his eyes and press its snout against his sleeve. "But I promised to be honest with you, so here's the truth: I can't make you 'normal,' Max." He lifted his hands to make air quotes around the word. "All I can do is help you understand that there's absolutely nothing wrong with you. But I also don't want to make light of any of this. A supernatural gift comes with its own risks. And to this day, those lost years remain the single greatest regret of my life."

From his perch on Ramhart's shoulder, Rhoven ruffled his

feathers, while Shadow let out a long, mournful howl. And while it was a lot to think about, I was too tired to try to sort it all out.

Ramhart reached across the table and briefly patted my hand. "Why not just take each day as it comes."

I nodded, started to rise from the table, only to realize Ramhart wasn't quite done.

"I feel a word of caution is in order," he said, his fingers drumming against the side of his glass.

I scrubbed a hand through my hair, gnawed the inside of my cheek. A word of caution from a man like Ramhart could mean just about anything.

"Don't go crushing on Rosie Grace." His gaze narrowed on mine as my jaw dropped open, waiting for a punch line that never arrived.

Before me, Rhoven took to flapping his wings and squawking on repeat, *"Don't go crushing on Rosie Grace! Don't go crushing on Rosie Grace!"* as my mind scrambled to make sense of the words.

For one split second, back in that alternate dimension—when I'd been teetering on the edge of *death!*—my eyes had tricked me into thinking Rosie Grace was pretty.

But surely that didn't mean that I liked her!

And it wasn't like anyone even knew that, so why would Ramhart say such a thing?

"A ghost-human romance never ends well," my grandfather continued.

"You can't be serious!" I cried, my voice pitching embarrassingly high. "I mean, clearly, I'm not the slightest bit—"

I made a gagging face, hoping to better illustrate what my frantic jumble of words never could. But judging by the way Rhoven tucked his face behind his wing, Shadow let out a terrifying growl that left his slobbery overbite on full display, and Ramhart shook his head, my attempt to convince was a fail.

"I'm sure you've heard the story about the boy who protested too much." When I didn't respond, Ramhart went on, "No one believed him." He looked at me pointedly. "You know, because he protested so much it seemed suspicious." He rose from his seat and handed me a shopping bag that contained a new blue hoodie. "Anyway," he said, his voice cheery once again. "Figured you'd need a new one, seeing as how you forfeited yours to the glowworms."

Caught between the two opposing states of shame and gratitude, I slipped my arms through the sleeves, surprised to find it fit perfectly.

"So," my grandfather said. "We okay?"

When I lifted my gaze to meet his, I found it impossible to deny him.

"Yeah," I told him, tugging the zipper. "We're good."

13
The Fundamentals of Spoon Bending

Turns out one of the side effects of getting lost in a time slip is it really wears you out. Which probably explains why I slept solidly all through the night and well into the next day. By the time I made it out of my room in search of some breakfast, I found Bex waiting for me at the bottom of the stairs.

"It's about time," she said in a huff. "You missed the last two, which makes this your last chance. So come, everyone's waiting."

She grabbed hold of my sleeve and dragged me down the hall and into a room dominated by a long table in the center, with walls of shelves filled with books and framed portraits of Ramhart and Magnus posing with various supernatural creatures and a large whiteboard resting on an easel with *The Supernaturalists* written in blue.

"Is this about the meeting?" I looked around a space that seemed specifically designed to hold paranormal board meetings.

"It is, and you're late," Bex said. "But now that you're here, I call the meeting to order." She banged a gavel onto the table and pointed me toward a vacant seat.

"Everyone—this is Max." Bex jabbed a thumb my way. "He's supposedly Ramhart's grandson, but his last name is Smith and he doesn't have a specialty, so I'm thinking we can get to the bottom of those glaring discrepancies later.

"Max, that's Krish Patel." She gestured toward the skinny boy with dark hair and eyes I'd seen the other day. Under his unzipped blue hoodie, he wore a T-shirt with a picture of Einstein sticking his tongue out. "Krish is the founding member of the Supernaturalists. But there's no hierarchy here, so he also serves as the group's secretary, recording all our experiments."

"Experiments?" I glanced between them.

"We'll get to that later." Bex quickly moved on to the girl with long brown hair and brown eyes. She wore a yellow scarf around her neck, a tie-dyed T-shirt, and a stack of beaded crystal bracelets that climbed up both wrists. "This is Julia Octavia Olivia Lucia Sanchez Medina, otherwise known as Jools Medina. Jools," Bex said. "She's like a walking Wikipedia for all things supernatural. She also provides all the cutlery for our spoon-bending parties."

"Spoon-bending?" I asked, but what I really wanted to say was: *Is that even possible?*

"It's a thing." Bex turned her attention to the pink box at the center of the table and flipped open the lid. "You'll learn all about it if we approve your membership."

"It requires a unanimous vote." Jools spoke in an apologetic tone as she helped Bex divvy up the pie.

"So . . . this is some kind of paranormal club?"

"We are dedicated to the study of paranormal and psychic phenomena, including cryptozoology, alien encounters, and many other things that fall under the definition of supernatural," Krish said, receiving a harsh look from Bex and Jools.

"So much for being a *secret* society." Bex shook her head.

"Think of it like a supernatural summer school." Jools passed me a plate of what looked to be blueberry pie. "Ramhart is our teacher, but he doesn't come every day"

"And sometimes Crowther shows up," Bex reminded her.

"Yeah, sometimes." Jools stabbed a chunk of pie with her spoon.

"But since we always begin with a snack"—Bex motioned toward the crumbled bits of the pie she'd clearly dropped at some point—"go ahead—it's Third Eye pie."

"The third eye is also known as the pineal gland, but the name isn't important," Jools said. "It's all about what the pie *does*."

"It helps you access your intuition and inner vision." Krish took a mouthful.

"It broadens your ability to see the unseen." Jools added another chunk to his plate.

"In other words, it's supposed to help you see ghosts." Bex looked right at me. "Not that *you* need any help."

I paused with my spoon halfway to my mouth.

"We saw the video," Jools explained. "Anyone with an open mind could see none of that was your fault. Clearly, you were fighting an invisible force."

I nearly choked. I was so used to kids calling me a freak,

it seemed odd to think I'd been invited to join a club simply because of my connection to Ramhart and my ability to battle against the unseen.

I stared warily at the chunk on my plate. "Are all the pies magic?"

"Miss Petunia prefers the term 'enhanced,'" Bex said between bites.

"But isn't it risky to just eat whatever?" I asked. "Shouldn't it be less random and more personalized? Like, what if the enhancement isn't one you particularly need, much less want?"

"None of the pies come with negative vibes," Jools assured me.

Figuring I had nothing to lose, I gave it a try, only to find my mouth bursting with the sweetest-tasting blueberries of my life.

"When you're finished, Krish can show you how to bend your spoon." Jools's cheeks flushed with excitement.

"Wait—so that means he's in?" Bex frowned. "Don't we at least need to vote? There are rules, guidelines. Need I remind you that membership isn't open to just anyone?"

Jools flipped her hair over her shoulder and raised her hand. "He's got my vote. I mean, he has full access to Woodbead Mansion. It seems foolish not to accept him."

Bex drummed her fingers on the table and shot me a dubious look.

"Count me in." Krish raised a hand too. "For one thing, I prefer even numbers. For another, we could really use another guy around here."

"So that's it then? Access to Woodbead and an even ratio of

guys to girls." Bex made a show of rolling her eyes, then reluctantly raised her hand. "Looks like you're in, Max. So get yourself settled and prepare to start twisting some metal."

I glanced suspiciously between Bex and my spoon. The only way it was going to bend was if I purposely forced it.

"Do you recognize this man?" Bex reached into a purple notebook and retrieved a photo of some guy with dark hair and a penetrating gaze. "He's a world-famous spoon bender." She slid the picture toward me.

"Never seen him before." I gave it right back

"His attitude is going to be our biggest obstacle." Krish spoke as though I weren't sitting right there beside him.

"Isn't it always?" Bex sighed.

"I think what they mean is, while all this may sound strange at first, with an open mind, you'll soon find that lots of strange-sounding things turn out to be real." Jools flashed a friendly grin.

"Maybe I need a demonstration. You know, so I can see how it's done." I was curious to see who'd volunteer first.

"So, here's the thing—" Krish started, but Jools talked over him.

"What he's trying to say is, we haven't exactly perfected it *yet*."

I slumped low on my seat. Just as I'd thought—spoon bending wasn't a thing.

"You're forgetting that one time!" Bex frowned at Krish and Jools before turning to me. "There was this one time when Krish's spoon bent slightly backward, and we all saw it."

"It did," Jools said. "I'll never forget it for as long as I live."

But when I looked at Krish, he just shrugged. "I've been

working on my TK." Seeing my look of confusion, he explained, "That's short for telekinesis. Anyway, while I have made progress, that was also the day we forgot to take photos of the spoons before the experiment, so there's a chance it might've started out a little bent. No way to be sure."

"Don't listen to him," Jools said. "He's just being modest. His TK skills are for real. I watched with my own eyes when he bent that spoon, and I was totally jealous. I wish I could do that."

Krish looked at me and shook his head. "Jools is ace at all the technical stuff. Next to Ramhart and Crowther, she knows more than any of us. We don't call her the Walking Supernatural Wikipedia for nothing."

"It's not the same," Jools said. "I like to read. It's hardly a gift. Also, it's not like you can't do that too."

"I do enough reading for school." Krish laughed. "I'm just waiting for the day Ramhart discovers a way to download all that data straight into my brain."

"The point is," Bex intervened, "it's a simple case of mind over matter. Intention coupled with belief is everything when it comes to supernatural powers. Did you know humans only use ten percent of their brains?"

"I don't think that's actually been proven," Jools said. "It's just one of those statements that gets quoted so much it starts to sound true."

Bex ignored her. "Just imagine what you'd be capable of if you could access thirty percent or even fifty percent of your brain and put it to use. You could bend all sorts of things!"

"You could heal yourself instantly," Krish chimed in, his face lighting into a grin.

"You wouldn't even get sick in the first place," Jools said. "Not unless you needed an excuse to stay home from school."

We all laughed.

"Maybe we should skip the spoon bending and do a séance instead." Bex shot a shrewd glance my way. "I mean, since Max can see ghosts, I'm betting it'll be a really good one."

"Are there any ghosts around now?" Jools leaned toward me.

I stared at the ball of green light bouncing just past Bex's shoulder, the same one I saw the day I first met her, but for some reason, I shook my head no.

"Guess we'll have to summon one then." In an instant, Jools was out of her seat and reaching for an old wooden box with a detailed carving of a winged dragon on top. When she lifted the lid, the hinges squealed loudly in protest. "For those of us who can't actually see ghosts, the candle gives proof."

I watched as she pulled a small white candle from the box, placed it before her, then struck a match and promptly lit the wick.

"We light the candle, and then when the ghost arrives, it blows it out," Krish explained. "When dealing with the supernatural, confirmation is everything."

"Usually it's Rosie Grace who shows up," Bex said. "She's here so often, we consider her an honorary Supernaturalist."

The mere mention of that name was enough to make my stomach lurch toward my knees as my face filled with heat.

After Ramhart's accusation, Rosie Grace was pretty much the last ghost I wanted to see.

"How can you tell it's her?" I asked. After my visit to the haunted Glimmerville Graveyard, I figured it could be just about any spook and there was no way for them to discern the difference.

"The scent of roses is strong," Krish said. "Almost over-powering. But I think she just does that as a sort of announcement, because it fades pretty quickly."

"And the best part—it's so easy!" Jools cut in. "All you have to do is call her name. Just say—"

"Rosie Grace, Rosie Grace, wherefore art thou Rosie Grace?" Bex sang, as they looked all around, on alert for some sign of the ghost girl.

The scent of roses came at me hard and fast, causing my head to grow woozy and my vision to blur as Rosie Grace's ghostly form swirled and took shape before me.

"I can smell her! Can you smell her?" Tentatively, Jools arced an arm toward her, missing Rosie Grace by a fraction, which caused the ghost girl to laugh as she floated out of Jools's reach.

"Hello, friend!" Rosie Grace swooped in to ruffle my hair. I quickly ducked away. But not quick enough to keep Bex from noticing.

"He can see her!" Bex cried. "You have to tell us everything! What is she doing? What is she saying?" She leaned forward, squinting as though it might give her spectral vision.

I bit down on my lip as I glanced between Bex and the ghost.

"She's, uh . . ." I stared at Rosie Grace, who wasn't doing much of anything other than hovering before me, waiting to hear what I'd say. "She's just sort of . . . hanging out."

"But how does she look?" Jools asked, fidgeting with the stack of crystal bracelets that circled her wrist.

My teeth gnawed at the inside of my cheek, as I watched Rosie Grace fluff her long curls and neaten the blue sash on her dress. "Uh . . . I don't know," I croaked. "She looks sort of . . . ghostly, I guess."

"Seriously?" Bex shook her head. "You're going to have to do better than that, Max. We need details. What is she wearing? Does she look like her statue? Is she as pretty as the portrait of her that hangs in the town hall? And what about—"

While Bex continued, Rosie Grace addressed me. "Please, do tell, Max," she said. "Am I as pretty as my picture?"

I gulped. A rush of blood rose high on my cheeks as I squirmed uncomfortably in my seat. "I, uh . . ." When I heard my voice crack, I coughed and tried again. "Um, I don't know about any portrait, but she's, uh . . . her dress is white, and, um . . . yeah, I guess she does look a lot like her statue."

Krish nodded and wrote it all down, seemingly satisfied with the data I'd provided. But Bex and Jools were far from pleased and didn't hesitate to demand a better, more thorough description.

"Listen, Max," Bex said. "If you want to be a Supernaturalist, then you're going to have to work on your observation skills."

I slouched my shoulders and slid to the edge of my chair, all too aware of Rosie Grace's watchful gaze. "Listen." I raised both my hands. "This is all new to me, so I'm not really sure what you want me to say."

Before me, Rosie Grace folded her arms over her chest. "Surely I'm not your first ghost sighting," she said, knowing full well that I was the only one in that room who could hear her. "So why are you lying to your friends?"

I sighed. Rubbed my hands over my eyes. After taking a deep breath, I looked at the Supernaturalists and plunged full speed ahead. "Look—here's the thing," I said. "While the ghost-seeing stuff isn't new . . ." I paused, aware of them all leaning forward, except for Rosie Grace, who remained unimpressed. "Admitting that I can see them is definitely not something I'm used to. Mainly because I've learned the hard way that it's not the sort of thing most people want to hear. There were no Supernaturalists back in Boring. The kids all thought I was weird, and I'm pretty sure the principal agreed. Not that he ever actually said that, but I spent enough time in his office to know he thought there was something seriously wrong with me. So, yeah, this is the first time anyone ever thought it was interesting or wanted me to talk about it, and I'm not entirely comfortable with it."

I snuck a look at Rosie Grace, but her reaction was impossible to read.

"Ugh." Krish rolled his eyes as he tapped his pen against his notepad. "Typical minimifidians."

"Trust me, we get it," Jools said.

Her smile was kind, but I wasn't sure I believed her. How could she possibly understand what I'd gone through?

"But I'm not sure you do," I told her. "I mean, you guys live in a place known for enchanted pies and Woodbead Mansion. You have no idea what it's like to be surrounded by a bunch of normal people who accuse you of either lying, being an attention-seeking freak, or both."

"Well, here's another thing," Bex said. "While Glimmerville is a very odd place, most people who live here are nothing like us. They go out of their way to rationalize all the strange events that happen right in front of their eyes. They're convinced Miss Petunia's pies are a marketing gimmick, and Ramhart's house and the haunted cemetery are nothing more than tourist attractions."

I thought about those bullies Rosie Grace had thrown to the ground and how quickly they blamed me despite the fact that I hadn't so much as lifted a hand.

"It's how we all became friends," Jools said, drawing me away from my thoughts and back to them. "All those silly rationalizations and explanations—they never add up. So we formed the Supernaturalists club and asked Ramhart and Crowther to guide us."

"Do you know what I'd give to be able to see what you can?" Bex leaned back in her seat, fiddling with the end of her ponytail.

I knew she was serious, but it still seemed strange to think anyone would want my ability.

"I've spent my whole life longing to be normal," I admitted. "But now that I'm here, I'm starting to think that being normal is a lot like Einstein's theory." I gestured toward Krish's T-shirt featuring a photo of the white-haired genius. "It's all relative."

Krish and Bex laughed. Jools said, "Do you think you can teach us how to see them?"

I looked at Rosie Grace. Her arms were no longer crossed, and her face was arranged into a softer expression.

"I wouldn't even know where to begin." I thought of all the ghosts that'd terrorized me through the years—the toupee stealer, the car thief, the one who served me his own severed bloody ear. But when I focused on Rosie Grace still hovering before me, I realized I might've misjudged her. After all, she had saved me from a time slip. That had to count for something. "In my experience," I said, "the majority of ghosts are real jerks." I watched Rosie Grace's eyes narrow as her lips pressed into a thin, grim line, and I knew I needed to spit out the rest before she really took offense. "But Rosie Grace is different. She's, uh . . ." I swallowed hard. "Well, turns out, she's one of the good ones."

"Is that your way of thanking me?" Rosie Grace arched an eyebrow and levitated up high toward the ceiling. "For rescuing you from the time slip?"

I looked to the overhead lights and nodded in reply. I wasn't used to having friends. And even though, technically, one of those new friends was dead, it still felt really good to be part of a group.

"You guys see that, right?" Jools gaped as the ghost girl swooped down, plucked my spoon from the table, and bent it into a half circle before mashing it against the candle, killing the flame.

"There's their confirmation." Rosie Grace grinned, her blond curls bouncing on her shoulders as she laughed. "As for you, apology accepted."

She leveled her gaze on mine, and I noticed that two streams of black gunk were, once again, flowing from her eyes. When it dripped onto the table, she looked at me in horror and instantly vanished from sight. But everyone was so focused on the mangled spoon and snuffed candle that they missed the single drop of black sludge Rosie Grace left behind.

"This is unbelievable!" Jools held the spoon before her. "Between Max and this, we finally have solid proof she was here."

As Krish reached for a camera to document the evidence, Bex looked at me and said, "Is there anything else you can tell us?"

That ball of bouncing green light continued to hover just past her shoulder, but for some reason, I shook my head no. "She's gone." I shrugged. "It's just us now."

Us. I replayed the word in my head. And though I tried to act cool, I couldn't keep the grin from overtaking my face. I was part of a club, a new group of friends. I was part of an *us*.

Bex checked her watch, then rose from her seat. "Time for the afternoon pie deliveries." She reached for her backpack and slung it over her shoulder. "I hereby pronounce this meeting adjourned." Then, looking at me, she added, "Guess we'll see you tomorrow then."

I stared at her blankly.

"During the summer, we meet every day." She'd made it halfway to the door when she turned back to say, "Oh, and welcome to the Supernaturalists, Max."

14
Memento Mori

It wasn't long before my life at Woodbead Mansion fell into an easy routine.

Every morning I'd wake up and head to the dining room, where Ramhart would drink his blue juice and I'd feast from towering platters of bacon, eggs, waffles, and donuts, while listening to my grandfather share wild stories about all his supernatural encounters.

He told of terrifying clashes with werewolves, brutal battles with trolls, and a near-fatal encounter with a particularly nasty breed of goblin known as a red cap. Ramhart was a man who'd literally seen it all, and I was beginning to understand why the Supernaturalists were so starstruck by him. I was starstruck too.

In the afternoons, I'd meet up with Bex, Krish, and Jools, and when we weren't riding our bikes around town, watching Bex deliver pies, we'd spend hours eating those enchanted pies and conducting various supernatural experiments (most of which failed). One day Crowther even tried to teach us telepathy, but other than a few random hits that seemed more like coincidence, none of us turned out to be very good.

Rosie Grace hung around too, popping in and out at all hours. And as weird as it first seemed to have a ghost for a friend, I soon realized how much I looked forward to her visits.

It went on like that until one day when I woke up to find the mansion buzzing with activity. But when I asked Ramhart about it, he told me to go outside so I wouldn't spoil the surprise. Still, judging by the balloons and streamers hanging from the ceiling, I guessed he was planning some kind of party.

So I was out on the lawn, picking up chupacabra poop (even in Glimmerville, there was still a list of chores for me to do), when a car roared past the gate, barreled up the driveway, and plowed straight through me, causing a blast of arctic wind to lift me off my feet as my entire body went numb and tingly.

By the time I righted myself, I gaped in disbelief as the phantom car (a vintage model of a Rolls-Royce known as the Ghost, I'd later learn) screeched to a stop, the driver's door swung open, and Barnabas, the chauffeur I'd snubbed in the graveyard, climbed out.

"And so we meet again." He tipped his hat and opened the passenger door with a flourish. "May I present to you the great Magnus Woodbead!"

I literally stood with my jaw hanging open as I watched my great-great-grandfather, who looked exactly like he did in the painting (minus the supernatural hunting trophies), climb out of the ghost Ghost car and bow low before me. A moment later, his faithful bloodhound Scout scampered out of the car and to Magnus's side.

"It is my greatest honor to meet you, young man." Magnus spoke in a loud, booming voice that caused his mustache to twitch with each word. "Though I must say I would recognize you anywhere, for I can see the Woodbead in you!" He presented his hand, but I was reluctant to shake it. My fingers had only just begun to thaw, and considering how it was the same hand he'd used to carry the head of the one-eyed beast in his portrait, I dreaded the whiff of cyclops I assumed would soon follow.

"Ah yes, do forgive me," he said. "It seems I've forgotten how the youngsters greet one another these days." He curled his fingers into a fist and held it out toward me. Not wanting to be rude, I sucked in a breath and bumped my knuckles with his. Instead of cyclops, I was met with a blast of damp earth odor, while the numbness I'd feared was nothing compared to getting mowed over by the phantom convertible.

"Right, there's a good lad!" He chuckled heartily. "Now tell me, I want to hear all about your adventures. Alien encounters, Sasquatch sightings, spare me no details!"

"Uh, sir." Barnabas cleared his throat. "If you'll notice, sir, the boy is lacking blue streaks."

"What's that?" Magnus cupped a hand to his ear and leaned toward the chauffeur.

"HE'S LACKING BLUE STREAKS, SIR!" the driver shouted so loudly my eardrums vibrated in protest.

"Why, that simply can't be!" From his collection of pockets,

Magnus retrieved a small magnifying glass with a curved bone handle and held it before his wire-rimmed spectacles. "Can this really be true?" he wondered aloud as his frigid fingers combed through my hair just like my mom's had the time there was an outbreak of lice at my school. "Why, I was well on my way to earning my second blue streak when I was his age!" Magnus stood back to better observe me, as his ghost dog Scout sniffed at my feet.

"I don't know about blue streaks," I said. "But I was nearly eaten by mutant glowworms, and I almost got stuck in a time—"

Before I could finish, Magnus shook his head. "And still, no blue streaks." He sighed heavily and thrust the magnifier at Barnabas, who fumbled with the handle so awkwardly he nearly dropped it. "Well, it's the sort of thing one must earn on one's own, I suppose. Not to worry. You'll get there eventually. After all, you've got Woodbead blood in you!"

With that, he marched into the house, and I couldn't help but notice how the door serpents dipped their heads in reverence as Scout and my great-great-grandfather passed.

When it was my turn, the snakes shot me a steely-eyed gaze that saw me rushing inside to where my grandfather stood with Rhoven perched on his shoulder.

"I assume you met Magnus," he said as I watched my great-great-grandfather and his chauffeur float past Ramhart and straight through a wall. "How did that go?"

I sank my hands into my pockets and shrugged. "I think he was disappointed in my hair," I said, not wanting to admit just how relieved I was that my hair hadn't spontaneously turned blue. I may have been warming up to the stranger side of life, but I still had my limits.

Ramhart laughed. "Come," he said, clapping a hand on my shoulder. "There's something I want to show you." He steered me deeper into the house, past a series of rooms I'd yet to explore, until pausing before a painting of a man on a horse.

One half of the painting portrayed the horse with wings and the man as a skeleton. The other half showed them both as flesh-and-blood beings. It was only when I noticed the monkey-tooth medallion hanging from the man's neck that I realized it was a portrait of Ramhart.

"*Memento Mori.*" He pointed toward the gold plaque at the bottom. "A daily reminder that death comes for us all. Well, let's say most of us. I have met a few immortals in my day."

"*Memento Mori! You too will croak!*" Rhoven repeatedly squawked until Ramhart told him to shush.

"Why would you want to remember that?" I asked.

"It's a reminder to live each day to its fullest!"

From what I'd seen, Ramhart packed more into a single day than anyone I'd ever met. A reminder like that hardly seemed necessary.

When he tapped the corner of the frame, the wall creaked opened to reveal an additional wing that hadn't seemed to exist just a moment before. After leading me through a mind-boggling array of secret passageways, hidden staircases, and doors masquerading as bookcases, he stopped before a surprisingly normal-looking door.

"Few are allowed inside the Wunderkammer," he said. "Even the tour group VIP ticket holders are not allowed access. To many, it's considered a privilege, but as a Woodbead, it's your birthright." With a flourish, he gestured toward the lock. "You may do the honors."

Slowly, I reached for my key and opened the door to a room that reminded me of a cross between a library and a mad scientist's lab.

The floors were made of polished white marble. The windowless walls were covered with rich wood paneling and built-in shelves so high they had sliding ladders attached. Against the far wall sat a small set of bleachers occupied by what I later learned were a carefully chosen select group of ghosts. Immediately, I recognized Rosie Grace among them.

She waved at me. I waved back. Then Magnus stood up and called from the stands, "Who is this bright young lad you've brought with you?"

At first I thought for sure he was joking, considering how we'd already met in the driveway. But when Ramhart reintroduced us, I realized Magnus's memory was as bad as his hearing.

"Who?" Magnus leaned forward and cupped a hand to his ear.

"MAX, YOUR GREAT-GREAT-GRANDSON!" Ramhart shouted.

"Very well." Magnus bowed. "I'm pleased to make your acquaintance, young man." He settled himself once again as Rosie Grace turned and giggled into her hand and Ramhart took to the podium.

"Throughout the years, you've borne witness to some of my

greatest inventions." Ramhart's gaze moved among the spectral forms. "You've witnessed the creation of the spirit spotters, the video camera that captures the past, and the soul phone, among others. And now, it is my pleasure to present to you my most exciting invention to date!"

With an introduction like that, I expected to see something truly spectacular. So when Crowther appeared with a cloth-covered tray, I couldn't help but feel disappointed when Ramhart lifted the fabric to reveal an item that looked very much like the kind of container used for storing leftovers.

"I present to you the soul keeper!" He beamed with a sort of pride that seemed completely unwarranted. His "most exciting invention to date" looked like it was seriously infringing on a Tupperware patent.

"What does it do?" A shout came from the stands.

"Why, it's all in the name," Ramhart said. "It's a soul keeper. Which is to say it keeps the soul safely preserved in this airtight container until a new body becomes available for the soul to inhabit. Thereby allowing one's consciousness—the collection of knowledge, emotions, thoughts, and experiences—to continue to exist inside a new body. What you're looking at, dear friends, is so revolutionary that you'll be begging me to try it. It's the key to immortality!"

I had to admit that it seemed like a pretty cool idea. Though it wasn't without a certain Frankenstein feel.

"Give us a demonstration!" Magnus called, gleefully clapping his hands and stomping his feet.

Immediately, Crowther stepped forward, ready to oblige. But when Ramhart gestured for me to join him instead, I couldn't help but notice the troubled glint in Crowther's eyes.

"Don't flip the latch," Ramhart whispered, handing me the device. "Not until I give you the signal."

I turned the soul keeper around in my hand. The bottom part was made from thick glass, and the top was composed of a tight plastic seal with a glass lid and a series of clasps. Inside was a sparkling ball of light that zinged back and forth.

"That's Luna, my cat." Ramhart's tone was surprisingly matter-of-fact. "You'd be surprised how hard it is to locate a vacant cat body in usable condition." Then, turning to Rhoven, he said, "Please forgive me, old pal. I promise to make it up to you later."

At Ramhart's instruction, I lifted the remaining latches. Then, with shaking hands and eyes that could hardly believe what they were seeing, I tipped the container toward the bird and watched as the cat soul slipped inside Rhoven's beak.

At first the raven appeared unchanged, leaving me to assume he'd merely gulped a bunch of air that would end up making him fart a few minutes later.

But then, I watched in astonishment when a battle for domination between the two mortal enemies began.

Rhoven started meowing and squawking.

His smooth bird body shifted and bulged, morphing into a strange lumpy shape.

His wings flapped wildly, as his clawed feet shot out from under him as though prodded by an invisible force.

After what felt like an eternity of flying feathers and terrible, shrieking, feline cries, Rhoven gained the upper hand and belched the cat soul right out just as Ramhart pushed me forward to capture the glimmering ball of light and trap it inside the soul keeper.

I stood frozen, covered in layers of feathers and sweat. I'd seen some strange stuff since my arrival at the mansion, but nothing came close to that. After what I'd just witnessed, I knew there was no going back. I'd never experience the world the same way again.

And, more importantly, I was no longer sure why I'd want to.

I looked at my grandfather and grinned. While I still had no interest in taking over the grave-minding duties, much less inheriting the mansion, it wasn't like I had to worry about that anytime soon.

"What else can you show me?" I asked, having no way of knowing I'd just sealed my fate.

From that moment on, my life would never be the same.

15
Dead Man's Party

After the presentation in the Wunderkammer, the doorbell started ringing nonstop, so Ramhart promptly steered me into the room we used for our Supernaturalist meetings and told me to stay put.

"Surprise!" Jools said, leaping from her seat and waving her hands in the air as Bex and Krish looked on and laughed.

"What's going on?" I glanced between them, wondering if maybe Ramhart had mistakenly thought it was my birthday.

"Today's the Annual Summit of Interdimensional Leaders," Krish said. "It's kind of like a UN for the multiverse."

I must've looked confused, because Jools was quick to explain, "Once a year, the leaders of the favored dimensions meet. Only this year, since the meeting falls on the night of the Black Moon, Ramhart's also throwing a party."

"Okay . . . ," I said, still not getting why everyone was in on the surprise except me.

"Also, Ramhart agreed to let us stay over," Bex told me.

"Which means it's pretty much destined to be the coolest slumber party ever." Jools laughed.

"But staring is strictly forbidden," Krish said. "As Ramhart says, 'They may look strange to us, but we look just as strange to them.'"

"Just try to keep chill." Bex looked me over like she doubted I could. "You're going to see some really weird stuff."

I was about to tell her I couldn't possibly see anything weirder than what I already had, when she led us out the door, down the hall, and into a scene so strange it seemed straight out of a movie.

Ghostly waiters dressed in tailcoats and bow ties floated around with flutes of champagne for the living and bottles of bubbles for the deceased. (You seriously haven't lived until you've heard a ghost fart after consuming too many bubbles too quickly.)

There were long tables lined with towering cakes at least forty tiers high, and a giant ice sculpture carved into a three-headed fire-breathing dragon with flames shooting out of each mouth (I still don't know how they managed to keep the ice from melting).

I passed a row of air misters bearing labels like CHEESE-BURGER, PEPPERONI PIZZA, TRUFFLE FRIES, TACOS, and FRESHLY BAKED BROWNIES (Rosie Grace later explained that they allow ghosts to reexperience some of their favorite flavors from when they were living), before wandering into a room where a band of skeletons wearing sugar skull masks played before a crowd of spirits waving glow sticks around and slam dancing in a way that sent sparks zinging into the air every time their energies merged.

A clique of witches with yellow eyes and hairless winged cats perched on their shoulders cackled and squealed and tried to pluck a hair from my head when I passed.

I saw a man with a mask for a face.

A creature with a woman's head and a leopard's body.

When a wolf with glowing eyes trotted by with a pixie clinging to its back, I'd nearly convinced myself I was dreaming until a hand clamped onto my shoulder and spun me around.

"So, tell me." Crowther's eyes glinted. "What do you make of all this?"

I ventured another look around the room, cringing as two nearby ghosts, obviously drunk on bubbles, tried to out-burp each other. "It's . . . uh, interesting," I said, when clearly it was much more than that.

Crowther continued to study me with a laser-like gaze. "Yes, I suppose it is." He raised his glass and took a long sip. Then, almost as an afterthought, he tipped his head toward the pretty girl beside him and said, "Max, meet Heather. Heather, Max."

Her hair was the color of sunshine. Her T-shirt was bright pink with the words CLASS OF '78 scrawled across the front. Other than the matching roller skates on her feet, she was the most normal-looking person there, besides me.

"Heather's visiting from an alternate dimension that's stuck in the seventies."

The moment I heard *alternate dimension*, the color drained from my face.

"What's wrong with him?" Heather asked.

"Still to be determined." Crowther laughed.

Next thing I knew, she tossed her hair over her shoulder and rolled away.

"Not your best move." Crowther watched as she glided toward the opposite side of the room. Then he gestured toward a mermaid sitting sidesaddle on a shiny black horse and the man beside her, who transformed from a fox to a frog and then a moose solely for her amusement. "Recognize him? That's the famous Robin Goodfellow."

I squinted at the odd-looking man. His face was weathered, his hair straight as straw. And though I racked my brain trying to place him, he didn't look the least bit familiar.

"Well, famous in certain circles, anyway. In addition to being immortal, he's half fairy, half human. He's always chasing the mermaids. Though not very successfully."

In the background, the band switched to a song called "No One Lives Forever." As the crowd of ghosts danced and sang, Robin Goodfellow shouted, "Some of us do!"

"You don't have a clue what this is about, do you?" Crowther asked.

I tore my gaze away from the spectacle and focused on Crowther. "That pretty much sums up my entire Glimmerville experience."

"This party is for you."

I blinked. Swallowed. But mostly just stood there looking confused.

Crowther switched his old glass of champagne for a new one he grabbed from a passing tray and lifted his flute to the room at large. "It's a golden triangle—a perfect convergence of events. Turns out, your summer at the mansion has perfectly coincided with the rising of the Black Moon and the Annual Summit of Interdimensional Leaders, just as the prophecy stated."

"Prophecy? There's a prophecy—about *me*?"

"You mean, Ramhart hasn't told you?"

I shook my head.

"Then it's probably not my place to fill in the blanks. But I wouldn't get too worked up if I were you. There's a prophecy for just about everything now, isn't there? Still, the thing about prophecies is they're subject to free will."

I thought about what Ramhart had said about destinies and free will. According to Crowther, prophecies worked the same way. But then what was the point of even calling it that when it was really more like a wild guess or a vague possibility?

"It's said that the rise of the Black Moon causes one's long-held intentions and wishes to manifest," Crowther continued. "Which makes it a perfect time for spell casting and rituals. Though it can also bring out one's hidden darkness." The way his eyes peered into mine left me squirming uncomfortably.

"What does any of this have to do with me?" I asked.

Crowther nodded toward the stage. "Looks like you're about to find out."

When the song ended, Ramhart took the mic and scanned the assembled crowd. "How wonderful to see so many old friends—many of whom traveled through multiple dimensions just to celebrate this moment. I am honored by your presence."

From his place on Ramhart's shoulder, Rhoven squawked enthusiastically as the crowd erupted into catcalls and applause.

"For those who were forced to endure last week's salting, I hope you'll accept my sincerest apology for curbing your freedom, no matter how briefly."

A few grumbles could be heard, but they were soon silenced by Ramhart.

"In addition, I'm pleased to announce that on this night of the Black Moon, I've just received word that our corpse flower has recently bloomed—another fortuitous event, as you know!"

He gestured toward a marble pedestal displaying a large potted plant with green and red petals and a greenish-yellow spike jutting up from the middle.

Even from halfway across the room, the plant's putrid scent made me want to puke. The corpse flower smelled like a bucket of dead fish left to rot in the sun, and I couldn't understand what all the fuss was about.

Beside me, Crowther clapped with the kind of enthusiasm that couldn't be faked. "The plant takes over a decade to bloom." He spoke from the side of his mouth. "Show some respect."

Dutifully, I put my hands together, but the effort was half-hearted at best.

"And now," Ramhart continued, "it's my pleasure to introduce you to the youngest member of the Woodbead family—my grandson, Max, who will be spending the summer here at the mansion and thereby completing a set of auspicious omens for the future of Glimmerville!"

From seemingly out of nowhere, a single spotlight landed on me as the room erupted into loud whoops and cheers. Frantic, I turned to Crowther for help, but his expression was guarded, impossible to read.

"Max, come on up and join me!" Ramhart called.

I spun around, looking for my friends, Rosie Grace, *anyone* who might be able and willing to save me. But the crowd was too large, and next thing I knew, I was hoisted into the air and crowd-surfed to the stage, where Ramhart thrust the mic into my hands and the audience broke into a chorus of "Speech! Speech! Speech!"

Of all the scary things I'd confronted, you'd think addressing a crowd of interdimensional beings would be no big thing. Turns out, public speaking was back on the list of my Top Five Terrifying Things.

A film of sweat spread across my face. And when I accidentally held the mic too close to my mouth, an embarrassing screech shot out.

"Um . . . hey, everyone." My voice was scratchy and dull. "Uh, thanks for coming . . . you know, to Ramhart's party, and stuff . . . so . . . ." I finished with a wave so awkward I was relieved when the band started playing and Ramhart rushed me backstage.

"Your presentation could use some spit and polish." My grandfather draped his arm over my shoulder as he led me past a series of rooms. "But that's nothing a little practice can't fix."

I nodded wordlessly, thankful he didn't try to pretend like I'd aced it. As I walked alongside him, I said, "Up there onstage, you said something about how my being here was part of some omens. Is there really such a thing? I mean, an actual prophecy about *me*?"

From his perch on Ramhart's shoulder, Rhoven noisily squawked, *"Prophecy! Prophecy!"* as Ramhart took a cautious look all around.

"You sure you're ready to hear it?" Ramhart spoke in a con-spiratorial whisper that left me wondering if the prophecy might be something that was better left unknown.

And yet it was like he told me that day in the graveyard: it was up to me whether I chose to honor my destiny.

"Seems like something I should probably know." I shrugged, trying to appear chill like Bex said. But my fingers nervously racing the zipper up and down the front of my hoodie surely gave me away.

Ramhart regarded me from beneath his brow, and for a moment I wondered if he was giving me time to back out. Then he lowered his mouth to my ear and had just started to speak when Crowther appeared before us, looking like a disgruntled butler as he presented an old-timey rotary phone atop a gleam-ing silver tray.

"It's for you." He frowned. "It's your dad." He thrust the receiver into my hand.

Immediately Ramhart moved away, leaving me to my pri-vacy, while Crowther, still holding the phone on the tray, moved only as far as the cord would allow, which was well within hear-ing range.

I turned my back and pressed the phone to my ear, and though I don't remember every word of our conversation, I do know it went something like this:

Me: *Uh, hello? Dad?*

My dad: *Max—you okay? What's all that racket I hear?*

Me: (raising my hood up over my head in a futile attempt to block out the background noise) *Um, nothing. What's up?*

My dad: (speaking in an increasingly alarmed tone) *Max, are you having a party? Did Ramhart leave you there on your own?*

Me: (speaking in an increasingly panicked tone) *What? No! Everything's fine and . . . totally normal. We're just, uh . . . just having a movie night.* (I involuntarily flinched at the lie.)

And then more stuff was said, mostly me trying to convince my dad I was neither acting like a delinquent nor facing some sort of mortal danger, before my dad finally got to the point.

My dad: *Do you think you can hang in there for one more week?*

Me: (Alarm bells ringing in my brain, and I was thinking: *Only a week?*)

My dad: *Because I've got great news, Max—I've landed a new job and a new home in Normal, Illinois! As soon as everything's signed and confirmed, I'll swing by the mansion to get you. You'll be out of there in no time.*

That's the last thing I remember before the whole world went black.

16
Creepy Red Room

Okay, maybe the world didn't actually go black.

It just felt like it did.

And even though the rest of my conversation with my dad is kind of a blur, what I do know is he sounded pretty happy about all his good news, so I did my best to pretend like I was happy too.

But while I'd managed to convince my dad, I couldn't fool Crowther. The second I hung up, he took one look at me and said, "Everything okay, Max? You seem pretty shaken."

I'd just received what I considered to be terrible news. And while part of me wanted to get it all off my chest, Crowther was not the kind of person I'd ever choose to confide in. From the first day we met, he'd made it abundantly clear how he didn't consider me worthy of my inheritance, much less Ramhart's attention. So I wasn't about to give him the satisfaction of knowing my time at the mansion would soon end.

"I'm fine," I told him, casually swiping a hand through my hair and lifting my chin like some cool action hero in a blockbuster movie. But the truth was, I felt shaky, unsteady, and about as far from fine as a person could be. To make matters worse, I had no one to blame but myself.

From the start I'd known my stay at the mansion was temporary. And still I'd allowed myself to get so caught up in the magic of hanging out with Ramhart and making new friends that I'd totally abandoned my original plan to get my hands on the *Field Guide* so I could rid myself of my supernatural gifts and finally blend in with the rest of the minimifidians.

I'd wasted all that time, and because of it, my days were literally numbered. I couldn't afford to delay any longer. Luckily, I knew just who could help.

Rosie Grace could literally float through walls, which meant there was a pretty good chance she'd be able to find the book. And yet, when I finally managed to lure her away from the dance floor to ask if she knew where Ramhart kept it, her reply was not at all what I expected.

"The *Field Guide*?" Her blue eyes narrowed as her fingers picked at the blue sash at her waist. "I don't know, Max. Ramhart says it's strictly off-limits. I don't think it's something you should pursue."

"That's not really your concern," I said. "All I want to know is if you know where it is. And if not, then will you help me find it?"

She continued to hover before me, making me wait. So by the time she said, "I can't do that, Max," I wasn't surprised, though I was really annoyed.

"I thought we were friends." I searched her face, noticing how her eyes grew dark and drippy while her body began to fade.

"We *are* friends." She clasped her hands before her, but her fingers quickly vanished from view. "And sometimes being a good friend means helping someone stay out of trouble."

In any other situation, her commitment to Ramhart and what she considered my personal well-being might've seemed admirable. But at that moment, I was so frustrated by her refusal to help with what was clearly the most important task of my life that I ducked my head and stormed right through her. And though the resulting blast of cold nearly knocked me off my toes, I still managed to look back and say, "I should've known better than to trust a ghost. I'm going to find my real friends. The ones who aren't dead."

Last thing I saw was a pair of dripping black eyes before Rosie Grace blinked out of sight.

When I found Bex, Krish, and Jools over by the chocolate fountain, taking turns drinking from the part that was caramel, I got right to the point. "Is there some sort of protocol to call for an emergency meeting?" I looked to Bex. Out of all of them, she was the stickler for rules.

"We're in the middle of a party!" she said, voice rising in exasperation. "Can't it wait?"

"If it could, then it wouldn't be an emergency," I snapped. I was jittery, antsy, jumping from foot to foot. After Rosie Grace's rejection, I needed them more than ever. "It's a life-or-death situation," I added, hoping that would get her attention.

"Life or death?" Bex stood before me, her skinny arms folded over her chest. "Can you be more specific?"

I looked all around, making sure no one was listening. But the music was loud, and no one was paying us the slightest notice. Still, I motioned them into a huddle and said, "What do you know about the *Field Guide?*"

"It's Ramhart's masterpiece," Krish told me, as Bex continued to glare. "It's basically the key to unlocking the supernatural universe."

"And exactly how does this qualify as an emergency?" Bex asked, but I ignored her and focused on Krish.

"Have you read it?" I asked him.

"None of us have," Jools said.

"Though we have seen it," Krish said. "Or at least the front and back covers. It's bound in leather and covered in crystals."

A slow grin crept across my face. He'd just described the same book I'd glimpsed during the glamour glitch.

"Do you have any idea where Ramhart keeps it?" I asked.

"Why not ask him?" Bex glared. "Or does he not want you to see it?" Her eyes locked on mine, but luckily, I had the perfect reply.

"If he didn't want me to see it, then he wouldn't have given me this." I retrieved the skeleton key from my pocket and dangled it before them like an old-time hypnotist. "This is the master key to the mansion. According to Ramhart, it decides which rooms I'm allowed to enter. So if it doesn't allow access, then no harm done. But if it does . . ."

I watched as they silently consulted with each other before returning to me.

"I still don't see how this qualifies as life or death." Bex regarded me for an agonizingly long while until she let out a frustrated sigh. "Fine," she said. "We'll look for it tomorrow. Do you think you can manage to live until then?" Her skeptical gaze met mine.

It wasn't what I wanted to hear, but at least they'd agreed to help, and I knew better than to argue with that. To Bex, I said, "Looks like I'll have to."

The party raged well into the morning. Which meant we didn't get a chance to go in search of the *Field Guide* until the next afternoon. And while I never thought finding it would be easy, I guess I assumed the Supernaturalists knew their way around the mansion better than I did. Turns out, I was wrong.

We'd just explored one of the first-floor hallways for a full thirty minutes only to end up right back where we'd started.

"Maybe it's a sign?" Jools said. "You know, like we're not actually supposed to be doing this, so we're getting thrown off?"

"The key is the sign." I held it up to remind them. "It either works or it doesn't." Determined to get them back on my side, I started down a different hallway, only to stop when Shadow darted in front of me and let out a menacing growl.

"Uh . . . maybe this isn't the best way to go." Keeping a wary eye on the beast, I started to backtrack, only to watch in amazement when Jools knelt down beside him and smoothed a hand down the bony ridge of his back.

"He's just being protective." She scratched the bit of leathery flesh between his short, spiky ears and laughed when he nuzzled against her. "Once you get to know him, he's just a sweet little baby. Aren't you? Aren't you just a sweet little baby?"

He responded by slobbering all over her cheek.

While she distracted him with snuggles and baby talk, the rest of us took advantage of the moment to slip past.

"Where do you think that leads?" Krish motioned toward the end of a narrow corridor, where an unmarked door shimmered in a way that made it seem like a mirage.

"Do you think it's enchanted?" Bex turned to me in alarm.

Enchanted or not, my key slipped right in, and I opened it to find a long set of stairs leading to an oversized red door at the top.

"I'm not sure about this." Bex frowned at the door, which to my eyes, with its bright red paint and unusually large frame, seemed the very definition of foreboding. "Don't you think it gives off a weird, kind of 'beware all ye who dare enter' vibe?"

"It is strange how it seems hidden from the rest of the house," Krish said as Jools came to join us with Shadow panting happily alongside her.

With shaky fingers, I slid the key into the lock, only to have it jam at the halfway mark.

"Well, I guess that's that!" Bex started to turn away just as the barrel began to vibrate, the bow clicked into place, and the door sprang wide open to reveal a short staircase that led to yet another red door slightly smaller in size.

"I did not see that coming," Krish said, as Bex laughed nervously and Shadow let out a menacing growl.

Once more, I inserted the key. After a brief hesitation, it clicked into place, and the door opened to another set of stairs that led to yet another smaller red door.

"What do you think?" Krish asked. "Four more Russian doll doors? Five?"

Behind me, Shadow began to pace. Even Jools couldn't calm him.

After going through the door, climbing more stairs, and unlocking six more doors (making a total of nine, in case you lost count), I opened the final, significantly smaller, tenth red door to reveal a very small, dim, high-ceilinged, octagon-shaped room with windowless walls covered in a deep red silk fabric, a floor of dark polished wood, and a red velvet chair beneath a stained-glass dome. In the center, a book was displayed on a pedestal. The luminous glow emanating from its pages reminded me of a halo.

"Ramhart wasn't kidding about keeping the book in a secure location." I gazed upon it in wonder.

"It's like the room was built specifically for it," Krish said, as we all gathered around, none of us brave enough to reach out and touch it.

"Seeing it like this . . . well, it's kind of spooky." Jools rubbed her hands over her arms, warding off shivers, as Shadow cowered outside, refusing to come any closer.

It was spooky, no doubt. But I hadn't gone through all that just to stare at it. So I blew past the warning bells in my head, plucked the book from the pedestal, plopped myself onto the velvet chair, smoothed a hand across the cluster of purple crystals embedded in the intricately hand-tooled leather cover, flipped to the first page, and read:

> Beware!
> This is no ordinary book.
> It is not meant for browsing, light reading, or
> MILD amusement.
> This is a dangerous book that poses great peril
> to the uninitiated reader.
> Continue at your own risk.

Below the warning was a detailed sketch of a skull and crossbones.

Bex, Jools, and Krish gathered to read over my shoulder as Shadow growled menacingly from beyond the tenth doorway.

"Uh, that's a pretty serious word of caution." Krish glanced longingly toward the exit.

"Maybe this isn't such a good idea after all." Jools fidgeted uneasily.

It wasn't like I didn't agree, but now that I'd found it, there was no turning back. "Pretty sure the warning doesn't apply to me," I said, hoping I sounded more confident than I felt. "After all, I'm a Woodbead."

"I thought you go by Smith." Bex stood over me, eyes narrowed, a random red curl falling over her cheek, but I refused to be swayed.

"We're all Supernaturalists, right?" I pressed the book hard against my knee to keep it from jiggling as I waited for them to agree. "So what better way to learn than by reading Ramhart's masterpiece?" I turned to Krish. "Or at least I think that's what you called it?"

His jaw tensed. His eyes darkened. He was conflicted, that much was clear. But he didn't try to stop me, and that was all the encouragement I needed to flip the page over and read Ramhart's messy scrawl:

Remember:
Believing is seeing.

At the time, I didn't think much of it. I just continued flipping the pages, barely making it halfway through when the book began to vibrate.

"Is the book—" Bex took a wary step back. "Is it actually . . . *moving?*"

It *was* moving.

And pulsing.

And humming.

As though it were alive.

As though it had a heart beating from somewhere deep inside.

I gripped the book harder, skimming past captions like *Phone Calls from the Dead—Table Tipping—The OZ Effect—Black-Eyed Children—Reptilians—Floating Islands—Phantom Houses—Vampires: An A–Z Glossary—Reversing the Polarity of Galactrite.*

There were pages scrawled with various spells, remedies to cure alien burn, instructions on how to handle a confrontation with a road troll, a map of the world's best phantom diners, a recipe for zombie powder, how to create a bogey, and more.

It would take days to read all the entries and even longer to make sense of them. Despite the intricate drawings, the footnotes with detailed explanations, and the bits of fur and botanical samples attached, I had no idea where to begin. There was no table of contents. The topics were arranged in a haphazard manner.

As the trembling increased, the hum grew so loud that Krish and Jools leaned closer to see what all the fuss was about.

"Is the *Field Guide . . . screaming?*" Jools cried, when the book launched into a full-blown whine as though it was coming to life.

The illustrations were yawning, stretching, transforming into something more than just a dash of ink on a page. When I came to the part titled "The Watcher," the book started wailing so loudly, I would've covered my ears if it didn't require both hands to hold the book steady.

"What is that?" Bex shouted over the noise, peering at a meticulously drawn illustration of the same dark-hooded figure I'd seen in the Woodbead family mausoleum.

"I saw this!" My finger stabbed at the sketch until the book nearly bucked out of my hand.

"It says it's a soul collector." Bex's worried tone matched her expression. "But it remains invisible to the soul it's come to collect. You said you've seen it?"

I nodded, barely able to breathe. The memory of that creepy hooded thing was practically tattooed on my brain.

"Then there's nothing to worry about, since it's clearly not coming for you."

For a moment, my body relaxed, until I remembered—I could see it, but Ramhart couldn't.

The Watcher is coming for Ramhart!

Just after I thought it, Shadow let out a bone-chilling howl, and I turned to see my grandfather looming in the doorway.

Max's List of Top Five Terrifying Things

1. Ramhart catching me in the creepy red room
2. The Watcher
3. Time slips
4. The Soul Eater
5. Mutant glowworms

17

Hornswoggled

"What on earth are you doing?"

The book slipped from my fingers as Ramhart stood before me, eyes blazing, voice thundering, monkey-tooth medallion swinging from his neck.

"All of you out! *NOW!*"

In an instant, the Supernaturalists fled for the door as Shadow yelped, his skin vanished, and he collapsed into a pile of bones.

"Jools, do you mind?" Ramhart nodded at the chupacabra heap sprawled across the floor.

"He literally gets scared out of his skin," Jools told me as I watched her pile the skeleton bits into her arms.

"Crowther is waiting at the bottom of the stairs. He'll lead you out." Ramhart watched them go before turning to me. "As for you . . ." His ring-stacked fingers caught at my sleeve. "This room is strictly off-limits!"

My knees turned to jelly, wobbly and weak.

"Locked doors remain locked for a reason. No exceptions."

"But—my key let me in." My voice was a whimper, and when he squinted as though he didn't understand, I said it again.

He snatched the key from my fingers, but of course when he tried it, the key no longer fit. "I will not be hornswoggled!" he shouted, and though I had no idea what the word meant, I knew it wasn't good.

"But it worked. I swear! How else would I have made it through all the doors?" I was desperate for him to believe me.

"How much did you see?" He plucked the book from where it had fallen and tucked it under his arm.

"I mostly just skimmed."

Ramhart closed his eyes as though counting to ten. When he opened them again, his gaze was so piercing that I was sure he could see straight through my skull.

"I need to know if you stopped on any page in particular."

I'd been handed a test I was destined to fail. So I gulped past the lump in my throat and told him the truth. "The Watcher. It's the only page I actually read. And that's only because I recognized it from the mausoleum."

Again, he closed his eyes and exhaled the sort of deeply troubled sigh that left me so on edge, I found myself sweating more than I had in the tunnel of death.

"I only read it because I was curious to know more." The words came out in a rush. "You know, after having seen it earlier and all . . . and I . . ." My voice faded. My breath sputtered out of me. I was up to my neck in shame. Fear and regret trailed close behind.

"You don't learn to run at the finish line." Ramhart slipped the book from under his arm and returned it to the pedestal. "You have to begin at the starting block and earn your way to the end. The *Field Guide* . . ." He smoothed a reverent hand over the cover. "Is the finish line. It's the last few meters of the final stretch. Do you understand?"

I did understand, but Ramhart had it all wrong. I wasn't on a quest to learn more. I'd gone back to my original quest to make it all go away.

I snuck a glance at the book where it sat on the pedestal. It was silent and still, as though it had gone into sleep mode, and the sight of it made my heart plummet. I was nearly out of time, and clearly out of luck. I'd failed myself in every conceivable way.

Ramhart squinted past me and raked a hand through his mass of feathers and blue streaks. "You have a power you can't begin to imagine," he said.

I gulped. Before the phone call with my dad, I would've celebrated the news. Now it just made my palms sweat, my heart race. "But that's the thing," I told him. "I changed my mind. I don't want to progress—I want to make it all stop. I just want to be normal."

My grandfather stood before me, regarding me with a somber expression. "It's done," he said, his tone unmistakably final. "You've set something in motion, and now there's no going back."

"But I don't—" Before I could finish, Ramhart cut in.

"The best advice I can give you at this point is to stay open to the clues."

I shifted nervously. I had no idea what he was talking about.

"There are always clues," he continued. "But you have to be present enough to spot them. You saw how Shadow refused to venture past the final door? Well, that should've been your first, second, and last clue that you shouldn't have gone any farther. His instincts are good—he knows where danger lurks because he's tuned into his surroundings. The warning you saw on the inside cover is no joke. The *Field Guide* holds great power—and in the wrong hands, it poses great danger."

"But I'm a Woodbead!" I cried. "These are Woodbead hands." As if to prove my point, I held up my hands, and honestly, I don't know what I was expecting to see, because they looked pale and scrawny and not the least bit impressive. "I guess I don't understand how a book can be dangerous."

"Merely by opening the *Field Guide* and giving it a skim, you've created a serious breach." His voice reflected the chill in his words. "As I've already mentioned, Glimmerville is a window area."

Wordlessly, I nodded. Too frightened to speak.

"Keeping the worlds perfectly contained requires great training and skill."

Again, I said nothing. I just braced against whatever horrifying truth would come next.

"Much like your encounter with the Soul Eater, simply by acknowledging the book, you risk bringing the contents to life. Do you understand?"

My head was spinning. I felt lost, confused. I didn't understand much of anything.

"We discover our true selves only when we're up to our neck in it with seemingly nowhere to turn. Someday soon, you'll be put to the test. That's when you'll discover what you're truly made of."

"But why would you even write such a dangerous book?" I cried. I didn't mean for it to sound like I was shifting the blame. It's just that it seemed really irresponsible, even for him.

"Because in the right hands, the book holds great power. But it's done, Max. And now there is much to prepare."

"Prepare for what?" My lower lip trembled as I met my grandfather's gaze.

"The supernatural storm."

At that moment, the light streaming through the glass dome dimmed in a way that left him looking ancient beyond his years, as though the weight of keeping Glimmerville safe had finally caught up with him.

A second later, the clouds shifted, and he was back to looking like the Ramhart I knew, but the memory of what I'd seen wouldn't be forgotten anytime soon.

"What can I do?" I asked, hoping to reverse at least some of the damage. "There must be some way I can help."

With his hand on my back, Ramhart guided me through the multiple doorways.

"Not a word of this to anyone, okay? Not until I have a chance to—"

Next thing I knew, Ramhart staggered forward and crumpled to the floor.

18
Blue Hair Juice

I wish I could claim that the second Ramhart fell, I switched into full-on superhero mode and did something awesome and heroic, but that's not at all how it happened.

Truth is, after screaming my head off, I froze in my tracks, gawking at the terrible thing happening before me like some inept teen in a horror movie.

By the time I got moving, Crowther had arrived, and I mostly just followed along in a state of shock as he got Ramhart into his room and settled in bed.

"He'll be okay, though, right?" I hovered nervously as Crowther tucked a blanket beneath Ramhart's feet. "Do you think I should call my dad?"

Crowther snorted derisively. "Yeah. Call your dad. That'll fix it." He shook his head and left the room, and though he didn't have to act like such a big jerk, I knew he was right.

There was no use dragging my dad into a situation that was clearly my fault.

I'd read the *Field Guide*.

I'd looked into the eyes of the Soul Eater.

Not to mention the supernatural storm I'd apparently started.

Standing there in my grandfather's oversized room with the elaborately carved canopy bed, the vast collection of masks and crystal skulls, and the shiny silver sword encased in a jeweled leather sheath that hung above the stone hearth, it struck me just how small, helpless, and dull I really was.

Ramhart's collection of artifacts was more than it seemed: it told a story of bravery and courage. It was the sort of thing you might see in a movie about a mythical king from a faraway land. Clearly, I was out of my league.

When Crowther returned, he leaned over Ramhart and made him drink an entire glass of blue juice. When he was finished, my grandfather fell into a deep sleep. "You going to tell me what happened up there?" Crowther lowered his voice to a whisper and ushered me away from the bed so as not to disturb Ramhart.

I snuck a worried glance toward my grandfather, unsure what to say. Before he collapsed, he'd warned me not to tell anyone what I'd done, but surely that didn't include Crowther? He'd worked for Ramhart for years—he'd trained him, trusted him. So it stood to reason that if anyone could help me find a way to undo what I'd done, it was him.

"I found the *Field Guide*," I said, painfully aware of my cheeks burning with shame. "And because of it, I accidentally set off a supernatural storm, and—"

At that moment, Shadow blew past me, leaped onto the bed, and howled in despair. I have no idea how he knew, but between Ramhart's blue lips and ghostly pale face, there was no mistaking that my grandfather had taken a turn for the worse.

Crowther rushed to the bed and went about checking Ramhart's vital signs. When he finally turned to me, my gut sank to my knees. "I'm sorry, Max," he said. "I'm afraid this is it." He seemed so sure, but I knew he was wrong.

"Don't be so dramatic," I snapped. Shoving Crowther aside, I tugged Ramhart's blanket higher onto his chest and tucked it snugly under his arm. "He's just a little cold, that's all."

"The end comes when it comes," Crowther said, his voice somber, but when the words replayed in my head, it sounded as though he'd been screaming. "I know this is difficult for you, but it's better for him to go quickly than to suffer unduly."

I whirled on Crowther in a fury. "Ramhart's fine! He's just sleeping! He's—"

"Max . . ." Crowther placed a hand on my shoulder as though willing me to calm down. "This is not the first time I've seen something like this. I know the signs. Whatever you have to say, I urge you to make your peace now, before it's too late."

I stared dumbly, bleary-eyed, unable to put a voice to my thoughts. All I could do was watch Crowther lean down, place his mouth over Ramhart's, and inhale a very deep breath. Then, with his cheeks puffed with air, he retrieved the vacant soul keeper from the nightstand and exhaled Ramhart's soul into the container before securing the latches and tucking it into his bag.

Returning to me, he said, "As you know, the Watcher collects souls."

I nodded mutely, my mind racing to catch up with everything my eyes had just seen.

"This ensures he'll never get Ramhart's."

I glanced between my grandfather and Crowther's bag. In theory, it made perfect sense that Crowther would take Ramhart's soul for safekeeping—Crowther was Ramhart's assistant, and the only one besides Magnus who understood the wild, upside-down world my grandfather lived in. Still, as I pored over his wispy mustache, pointy beard, and the silver snake ring with jeweled purple eyes that circled his index finger, I couldn't help but feel a deep sense of dread.

"What exactly are you planning to do with it?" I motioned toward the soul keeper tucked inside his bag.

"I'm going to keep it safe, not to worry."

The words were meant to reassure, but his icy gaze made him appear eerily detached for someone who'd just lost a long-time mentor and friend.

"We all grieve in our own way," he said, responding to what must've been a confused, if not suspicious, look on my face. "For me, it's easier to focus on the details. Rest assured I've got everything covered. I'll even handle the grave-minding duties and shut down the portal, since, as you know, Ramhart didn't have time. For now, I'll give you some room to process."

When the door closed behind him, I returned to my grandfather, and I could hardly believe what I saw. With his soul gone, it was like looking at an abandoned house—the structure was the same, but the rooms were all empty and the lights had blown out.

"He's gone," I whispered to myself as though testing the truth of those words. "He's really, truly—" I couldn't finish. My voice came out hoarse and strangled, like a lump of smoldering coal was lodged deep in my throat.

It seemed incomprehensible to think it was over—that Ramhart wouldn't leap out of bed all blue streaks, feathers, and loud, raucous laughter, ready to tackle his next supernatural adventure. I mean, here was a man who'd survived multiple encounters with yetis, Sasquatch, and countless other legendary beasts, only to go down without so much as a warning. And seeing as how Crowther had sealed up his soul, I wouldn't even get to see him in ghost form.

I'd lost more than a grandfather, I'd lost a mentor, a friend, and more importantly, the only person who truly understood what it was like to be me—a freak living in a world of minimifidians.

And now he was gone.

Just like my mom.

Never in my life had I felt so alone.

My shoulders heaved and my legs gave way, refusing to carry my weight, as heart-shattering sobs thundered through me. I'm not sure how long I stayed like that, down on my knees with Shadow beside me, the two of us howling in grief. But at some point I was caught by the sound of Rhoven's flapping wings, and

I looked up to find the bird clinging to his perch, as he repeatedly squawked, *"It's blue hair juice—drink up! It's blue hair juice—drink up!"* so many times it made my head hurt.

At first I assumed he was mimicking what he'd overheard. But as the bird continued to squawk, I couldn't help but wonder if maybe the message was a warning of sorts.

I got to my feet and inched toward his perch. "What about the blue hair juice?" I whispered, feeling foolish for trying to start a conversation with a species known more for mimicking than chatting. Still, Ramhart had told me to stay open to the clues, which left me wondering if maybe the blue juice qualified as one.

Was there something weird about it—aside from the color?

And if so, did that mean Crowther had actually been trying to harm Ramhart?

My mind raced back to all the times I'd watched Ramhart drink it, and the one time after the time-slip incident when Crowther tasked me with giving it to him.

Was there something strange about the way Crowther had looked at me when he handed it over?

I leaned closer to Rhoven, my heart squeezing tight and mean like a fist in my chest. "Go on," I coaxed. "Tell me about the blue juice."

Rhoven rocked back and forth on his perch. His tone sounding eerily like Crowther's, he croaked, *"Where's the* Field Guide? *Where's the* Field Guide?"

He cocked his head toward me. His beady blue eyes fixed on

mine. And without another thought, I spun on my heel and ran for the door, but not before catching a glimpse of the tall, broad-shouldered, shadowy figure that stood against the far wall, its face obscured by a low-hanging hood.

By the time I reached the creepy red room, *Field Guide to the Supernatural Universe* was long gone.

19
Dearly Departed

I ran out the front door and past the creepy snake guardians, only to confirm what I already knew: The gate was wide open, which meant Crowther was gone and he'd taken the *Field Guide* and Ramhart's soul with him.

I dropped to my knees. The situation was so completely over my head that I was desperately in need of someone who not only understood the ins and outs of the supernatural world but who would definitely know what to do.

And then it hit me—I knew *exactly* who to call. I mean, who better to help than a celebrated monster hunter?

Assuming that what worked to summon Rosie Grace might work for him, too, I called out my great-great-grandfather's name. After the third time, he popped into view. A moment later his dog Scout popped in too.

"Good day to you, young man!" He tugged the brim of his pith helmet and bowed low at the waist. "Allow me to introduce myself. I am Magnus Woodbead." He grinned and offered his hand as though it was the first time we'd met.

Dutifully, I got to my feet and clasped his hand in mine, and let me tell you, it was like slipping on a baseball mitt that'd been stored in deep freeze a really long time. "Actually, we've already met. I'm Max."

He stared blankly.

"Maxen Smith."

Again with the blank stare.

"Maxen Woodbead. Son of David Woodbead. Grandson of Ramhart Woodbead. Great-grandson of Roscoe Woodbead, which makes me your great-great-grandson."

Scout crept forward to sniff at my feet, as Magnus lowered his spectacles to better inspect me. Unconvinced, he propped the readers onto his forehead and frowned. "How can this be?" When he lifted his hand to have a go at my head, I ducked out of reach. I was in no mood to repeat a moment we had already lived.

"No blue streaks, I know. But I really am your great-great-grandson, and I really need your help."

He repositioned his spectacles as he and Scout took a moment to look me over again. After what felt like an eternity under their joint scrutiny, he said, "And how may I be of service?"

"It's about Ramhart." I waited for a reaction, but his face was impassive. "He's, uh, gone." I cringed. The words left a bitter taste on my tongue.

"Well, where did he go?" Magnus's gaze roamed the front yard as though he expected to find Ramhart hiding among the hedges. "Though I do recall him mentioning something about a trek through the Himalayas. Or was it Tanzania?" He twirled the tip of his mustache and squinted into the distance.

Desperate to keep him on track, I went for a more direct approach. "Magnus, Ramhart is dead." I paused, allowing plenty of time for the news to sink in, but when he failed to react, I added, "He died. He's really, truly gone."

Still nothing.

"He croaked."

Not so much as a flinch.

"He passed over."

Nada.

"Ramhart passed away. Transitioned. Flatlined. He has departed this earthly realm."

Even after I'd run out of ways to say it, Magnus still didn't believe me.

"Why, that's absolute poppycock!" He shook his head so vigorously he nearly lost his pith helmet. "Pure nonsense!" He set his hat right again and shot me an indignant look. "What sort of game are you playing, young man?" He grumbled unintelligibly and marched into the house.

I recognized the signs of denial, but now that I'd faced the horrible truth, it was time for him to face it as well. "Not a joke." I raced to keep up. "I was there when it happened, and—"

Before I could finish, he whirled on me in a blaze of khaki. "And you saw his spirit rise from his body?" His brow arched impossibly high.

Tentatively, I shook my head.

"Then he's not dead." Magnus breezed past the foyer and floated deeper into the house. "I would be the first to know, and since I've yet to see him in spectral form, he's not made the transition."

"He stopped breathing!" I huffed. "And his heart no longer beats. So you tell me what that means."

Magnus looked me square in the face. "It means that he's dead."

My mouth fell open, but nothing came out. I was literally all out of words.

"Only in this case, he's not, and that I know for sure."

"Listen," I said, finding my voice once again. "I don't know how they determine time of death in the spirit world, but in the physical world—"

"Where is he?"

Feebly, I motioned toward the staircase. "He's in his room, but—"

Before I could finish, Magnus and Scout were gliding up the stairs and into Ramhart's room, where the three of us stared at an empty canopy bed, a vacant raven perch, and a heap of chupacabra bones.

"I . . . I don't understand." I gaped at the unfathomable sight. "I specifically saw Crowther inhale Ramhart's last breath, then lock it inside the soul keeper. He said it was to protect it from the Watcher."

Magnus nodded toward the far side of the room. "The hooded figure in the corner—is this the Watcher you speak of?"

I glanced between the shadowy entity and Magnus. "Yes," I whispered, afraid of what might happen if it overheard.

"My dear boy," Magnus said. "That is not the Watcher."

I stared directly at the figure. It looked just like the one I'd seen in the mausoleum, just like the one pictured in the *Field Guide*.

"That is what you call a bogey."

"I know what a bogey is, and that—" I didn't get very far before he cut in.

"It's a sort of thought form brought to life—though that's not to say it's truly alive. And yet, given enough time, they have been known to take on a certain lifelike quality. They can also become quite unruly and hard to control once they develop a will of their own. It's said that it takes more skill to destroy a bogey than to create one. I wouldn't know, as I've never engaged in such foolishness. Though I once knew a man who conjured a bogey to fetch his slippers and pour him a scotch. A ghastly thing it was, and it did not end well, not at all. . . ."

"But if it really is a bogey, then how come we can see it but Ramhart couldn't?"

Magnus's eyes gleamed. "Well, that seems to be the whole purpose of this particular bogey. To trick you into thinking Ramhart wasn't long for this world."

The second he said it, I knew he was right. I also knew Crowther was somehow behind it, though I didn't know why.

"There's an ancient Roman tradition of inhaling the departing soul for safekeeping," Magnus said. "Which is exactly what

Crowther did with Ramhart's soul. Only in this case, I'm not convinced the keeping is safe. When was the last time you saw Crowther, anyway?"

"Just after he pronounced Ramhart dead, inhaled his soul, locked it inside the soul keeper, then stole the *Field Guide* on his way out." I hadn't exactly witnessed that last part, but he was the only possible suspect.

I watched Magnus float to the nightstand, where he lifted the glass Ramhart had drunk from, ran his finger along the rim, then brought it to his beak of a nose to take a good sniff before offering it to Scout to sniff too. The two of them reminded me of detectives in an old black-and-white movie, only their detecting was of the paranormal variety. "And did Crowther serve him this?"

I explained how he'd referred to it as blue hair juice, and how Rhoven had squawked about it like some kind of warning. "Ramhart drinks it every day."

"Maybe so," Magnus said. "Though my guess is Crowther added an extra ingredient. Possibly increasing the amount over time, which ultimately resulted in this."

"What do you mean?" My voice rang high-pitched and frantic. "Like, some kind of poison?" The thought alone was enough to make my head spin.

"It's been awhile since my last encounter with the substance," he said. "If I recall, it was sometime back in 1868. Or was it nine?"

"But what exactly *is* it?" I was in no mood for Magnus's distracted jabber, not when Ramhart was potentially poisoned and missing in action. "What did Crowther feed him? What does it mean?"

Magnus paused, then slowly turned to face me. "Well, the good news is that Ramhart's not dead."

I stared at him incredulously, wishing I'd called just about anyone else, including my dad.

"The bad news is, Ramhart is what you call 'undead.'"

That was the moment my jaw dropped to the floor and my tongue rolled onto the rug. "Wait—you mean like . . . *a zombie?*"

"Not to worry." Magnus remained strangely optimistic, considering what he'd just said. "The antidote to zombie powder is sure to be found in the *Field Guide*! What do you say we go find it and put an end to this nonsense?"

I was just about to remind him that Crowther had stolen the book when a disheveled figure with a dull, lifeless gaze and a fat glob of drool dripping from the corner of his mouth loomed in the doorway.

My first thought was one of relief: Magnus was right— Ramhart wasn't dead after all!

My second thought was . . . well, I didn't really have a second thought, because at that moment, Ramhart lunged toward me, and when I looked to Magnus and Scout for help, they'd vanished from sight, leaving me alone with a zombie!

20
Brain Eater

Someone screamed.

A horrible, high-pitched shriek that swirled through the room and throttled my ears. It was only when I couldn't bear another second that I realized it was coming from me.

I edged toward the window, trying to calculate the odds of surviving the fall should I jump versus going to battle with my zombified grandpa. Either way, it didn't look good, so I tried another approach.

"Hey, uh, Ramhart," I croaked, my throat gone so dry I nearly choked on the words. "Maybe you should . . . you know, crawl back into bed and get some rest. What do you say?"

The guttural rasp that followed was completely inhuman, and as he continued lumbering toward me, his movements robotic and stiff, it was like every scary zombie movie I'd ever seen come to life.

Whether he was after my brains or something else, I couldn't be sure, but I was determined not to find out. Deciding to take my chances on a third-story jump, I raced for the window, only to find it was stuck. And with Ramhart a mere arm's length away, there was no way to escape.

I looked to where I'd last seen the Watcher that was really a bogey, thinking maybe I could use it to distract him.

"Look!" I cried, jabbing a thumb at the creepy, black-hooded figure loitering in the corner. "I mean, what's up with that guy, am I right?"

As Ramhart's neck swiveled to where I was pointing, I frantically searched for something I could use in my defense. I briefly considered making a leap for the sword above the fireplace, but I was reluctant to hurt him even though he had every intention of hurting me.

I guess he preferred me to the bogey, because the next thing I knew, he grabbed my sleeve and started dragging me with the sort of freakish strength he definitely didn't possess in his usual state.

I swung my foot forward and nailed him in the shin as hard as I could, but other than the fresh glob of drool that dripped from his mouth, he gave no sign of having noticed the impact.

So I punched him in the side.

And when that failed, I sank my teeth deep into his arm.

Still he continued to drag me across the floor like a mop.

I yelled, screamed, thumped, whacked, showing no mercy, but it didn't make a dent. I was simply no match for the amped-up supernatural powers he had. I even tried to summon the same ninja fighting skills that'd helped me survive the bogey attack, only to discover they'd gone dormant again.

Despite the blue-streaked hair and the monkey-tooth medallion that swung from his neck, that soulless, vacant, unearthly beast was not the grandfather I knew. And yet, that still didn't stop me from trying to appeal to some small part of him that might've remained.

"Ramhart, please!" I begged. "You don't want to do this."

He responded by clenching a hand to my throat and squeezing so hard I was sure my eyeballs were about to explode.

I couldn't speak.

Couldn't breathe.

And my head grew so dizzy that the whole room went blurry.

In a last-ditch effort, I swung my arm forward and tried to push him away, but it was like trying to knock over a brick wall with a slap.

My vision narrowed and dimmed.

My body hurtled toward permanent sleep.

Calling on the last remaining thread of my strength, I grappled for the monkey-tooth medallion, yanked it off Ramhart's neck, and strung it around mine.

Like a shock wave jolting through my body, I suddenly sprang back to life. And as my grandfather swayed unsteadily before me, I seized the moment to snatch a giant net off the wall (a mermaid catcher, I'd later discover) and slam it down over his head.

He roared in outrage. Fought to claw his way free. I sped toward the door and locked it behind me, then sank to my knees as the full weight of the horrifying truth descended upon me:

My grandfather was a mouth-breathing, brain-chomping zombie who was out to kill me.

Max's List of Top Five Terrifying Things

1. Zombies

2. Ramhart catching me in the creepy red room

3. The Watcher

4. Time slips

5. The Soul Eater/Mutant glowworms

21
Zombie Squad

It didn't take long for Ramhart to fight his way out of the net, because the next thing I knew he was pounding the door so hard the frame began to crack.

I made a run for the stairs and slid down the rail, hitting the ground just as the front door sprang open and Bex stood in the entry. A second later Krish and Jools rushed up beside her.

"What is happening?" Bex cried.

"Where's Ramhart?" Krish pushed past Bex and looked all around.

"The front gate is wide open, and the red-eyed raven speaker is repeatedly squawking that Woodbead Mansion is closed forever!" Jools wailed.

At the sound of splintering wood drifting from the third floor, I was torn between begging for their help and instructing them to go. I didn't want to put them in any more danger than they already were.

"Ramhart's not . . . er . . . himself." I tried to appear calm and in control, but I was out of breath and drenched with sweat, and from the looks of their collective raised brows, I'd failed to convince them.

"Why are you wearing the monkey-tooth medallion?" Jools gestured toward the jeweled ornament that hung nearly to my waist.

I glanced down at myself, suddenly aware of just how ridiculous I must look. For one thing, the pendant was way too big for my bony frame. And yet I was committed to wearing it for no other reason than that it connected me to Ramhart—and it had helped me escape.

"Listen," Bex said. "All I know is, we were on our way home when the sky turned dark, the mist grew thicker than usual, and we were overcome with the scent of roses as our bikes all swung a U-turn and landed us here."

I knew right then that Rosie Grace had sent them, and every awful thing I'd said to her came roaring back to me like a slap in the face.

"Is she here?" Jools asked, looking around for some sign of the ghost girl. "I don't smell her."

I looked around too, but Rosie Grace was nowhere in sight, leaving me to wonder why she hadn't appeared alongside them if she knew I needed help. Was she holding a grudge, or was it something else?

I snuck a wary glance at the stairway. It was just a matter of time before Ramhart managed to break down the door. It was anyone's guess what happened then.

"The window is open." Krish wandered deeper into the house as Bex and Jools followed.

At first I thought he was talking about an actual window. But when I saw his troubled expression, I knew he meant the portal between Glimmerville and the otherworlds.

"You know about that?" It seemed a little advanced, and I was surprised Ramhart had told them.

"You mean the fact that Glimmerville Graveyard is a hot spot?" Bex wandered too close to the stairs for my comfort. "Most people think it's a myth, but we've lived through enough strange experiences to know that all is not what it seems around here."

"Soon the whole town will be in chaos." Jools's brow pinched in a way that darkened her gaze and cast an ominous shadow over her face. "And it won't be long before the otherworlds completely bleed into ours."

As if on cue, a horrible crack sounded from three stories up, causing us to turn just in time to see Shadow's skeletal form careening down the steps. When he reached the bottom, he shook himself hard, but his tail remained stuck in the middle of his spine, while his ear hung from his neck.

"Sometimes he doesn't fully reassemble." Jools gave his tail a light whack, returning it to its rightful place, before she dragged his ear up to his head. A second later, his leathery flesh reappeared.

"Uh, what's up with Ramhart?" Jools pointed a trembling finger to where my drooling, brain-craving grandfather stared at us from the top of the staircase.

"And why is he acting like a zombie?" Krish's jaw dropped, his eyes unblinking.

"He's not acting," I told them. "He really is a zombie."

"How did this happen?" Krish glanced between me and Ramhart, his expression cycling between complete terror and full-blown awe and back again.

"Krish is really into zombie movies," Jools explained, her front teeth sinking into her bottom lip as the zombie who was once my grandfather staggered toward us.

"Then he should know better than to just stand there! We need to go—now!"

I was ready to bolt when Bex grabbed my sleeve and pointed a shaky finger at a collection of portraits that had suddenly come alive. The subjects had broken free of their frames and were wandering about as all around us the house began to shift and change, much like it had on my very first morning.

The alien skull Ramhart kept on his desk started chattering madly as it floated past.

The carnivorous houseplants started snapping their leaves as the walls rearranged themselves, turning the house into a literal maze.

"What is happening?" Jools spun in fright as Shadow collapsed once more into a pile of bones.

"It freaks me out when he does that." Bex cringed as Jools collected the skeletal bits and piled them into her arms.

"Ramhart keeps an emergency stash of Chill Out pie in the freezer," Jools said. "You think it might help?" She hugged the bones to her chest and cast a nervous glance all around.

"Who are you going to feed it to?" Bex asked. "Him?" She

pointed at a skeleton climbing astride a black horse newly escaped from its frame. The horse and rider then tore a path toward the dining room, knocking down everything that stood in their way.

"If Ramhart really is a zombie," Krish said, "then the only thing that interests him is eating our brains." He looked at me with a horrified face, as though his thoughts had finally caught up with his speech.

Next thing I knew, we were running.

We fled down a newly formed hallway, spurred on by the heavy, dull thud of Ramhart's footsteps sounding behind us. He wanted to eat us, of that I was sure. And though I was desperate to keep a safe distance, I also needed him to remain inside the mansion until I could find a way to contain him. If he found his way out, I risked losing him forever.

"Where are we?" Jools cried as new walls popped up before us and others gave way.

I shook my head and drew a ragged breath, convinced my heart was seconds away from exploding in my chest.

"Do you at least have a destination in mind?" Bex skidded to the right, narrowly avoiding a door that sprang up before her.

I wanted to assure her, assure all of them, that I actually did have a plan. But I knew any attempt to explain would only result in losing their trust.

"We're going to the Wunderkammer," I told them. "It's filled with Ramhart's supernatural inventions, so there must be something in there that can help us."

From out of nowhere, a wall slammed into existence, missing

the tip of my nose by less than an inch. When I recognized the painting of Ramhart's *Memento Mori*, I exhaled in relief, until I noticed the painting had also changed. Ramhart was no longer portrayed as half-dead. In this new version, his horse was a skeleton and Ramhart resembled his zombie self, with bloodshot eyes and a glob of drool dripping from his mouth. His monkey-tooth medallion was gone as well. Art was truly imitating life.

"This is seriously creeping me out!" Jools bounced on her toes. The sound of Shadow's bones clattering together made for an ominous sound.

"It's like the house is alive!" Bex shivered. With her features so pinched and her cheeks faint to the point of translucent, she was the very definition of terrified.

I tapped the gold frame the way Ramhart had done, and we all slipped inside. When the door closed behind us, Ramhart shrieked in fury at being locked out as the pile of bones leaped from Jools's arms and onto the floor, where they reassembled (more or less) into Shadow's original form.

"Some watchdog you turned out to be." I shook my head in disdain.

Jools knelt beside him and returned his front left leg to its rightful position. "Everyone gets scared sometimes, including mythological beasts." She patted his head, and he licked her cheek.

"How long before Ramhart breaks through?" Krish shot a worried look over his shoulder as the wailing continued.

"Probably not as long as we hope." I motioned for them to

follow, and as I led the way, I caught them up on everything that had happened before they arrived.

"But why would Crowther turn Ramhart into a zombie and steal the *Field Guide*?" Jools asked.

Before I could venture a guess, Bex said, "Because Crowther's spent half his life working for Ramhart, assuming that one day all of Woodbead Mansion would be his, until Max showed up out of nowhere and stole his dream right out from under him."

I stopped dead in my tracks. It made perfect sense. Every snide look he'd given me, every verbal jab, it all came down to that.

"Um, guys, that's all fine and good, but we really need to locate the Wunderkammer." Krish gestured to the long hallway of doors, none of which looked the least bit familiar.

"Do you hear that?" Jools lifted a finger and tilted her head. "I think Ramhart's breaking through!"

With trembling hands, I slipped my key into the first lock, only to find a storage closet full of cleaning supplies and a pile of broken appliances.

The second attempt led to an elaborately tiled bathroom with a claw-foot tub that, much like the paintings, had also come to life and was scuttling around on all fours.

I slammed the door and tried another.

And then another.

Until there was only one door remaining.

With one hand, I clutched the monkey-tooth medallion for luck.

With the other, I slid the key into the lock.

When it refused entry, my heart literally sank.

But then, much like it had with the creepy red room, the key began to vibrate and shift, and the next thing I knew, we'd entered the Wunderkammer.

Bex paused just beyond the threshold to take it all in. Jools edged past us and raced toward an enormous skeleton that very much resembled a dragon, with a long, spiky tail and oversized wings. "I can't believe I'm actually inside the Wunderkammer! Not even the VIP ticket holders get access." She made a slow circle around the mythical sight as Shadow trailed closely behind.

Krish wandered to a shelf full of unidentifiable bits floating in liquid-filled jars and picked one up. "It's the toe compass." He held it up to better inspect it. "We should definitely take it. It could prove useful."

I glanced over my shoulder, watching as he shoved it into Jools's backpack. Though I was curious to finally take a look, it would have to wait. I had something far more important in mind.

"And this is the video camera that captures the past." Krish held up the sort of obsolete camcorder you might find at a garage sale. "Ramhart claims the energy from important events never fades. So, whether you point the lens at a person, place, or thing, it'll display whatever actions you most need to see."

"Anyone know where the spirit spotters are?" Bex asked. "We might need those, too."

While they picked among Ramhart's various inventions and

tools, I searched for one in particular. I knew Ramhart had made two; I just hoped Crowther hadn't taken them both.

When I found it, Bex stepped closer and asked, "What is that?"

I nodded at the luminescent ball of light captured inside. "Luna, Ramhart's cat."

Jools glanced between the bouncing orb and me. "Wait— you can't possibly . . . I mean, what exactly are you planning to do with that?"

"I'm going to feed it to Ramhart." I grinned.

22
Cat Man

"You can't put a cat soul inside a human!" Bex cried in protest. Krish and Jools were quick to agree.

"I know it sounds a little extreme." The words rushed out of me. "But Ramhart coached me through something similar when I fed Luna's soul to Rhoven. And while, granted, Rhoven wasn't thrilled, in the end he was fine."

"He does have a point," Krish said, causing Bex and Jools to stare, bug-eyed. "According to just about every zombie movie I've ever seen, right now, Ramhart's body is soulless, empty. It's the zombie juice that keeps him animated. Which also means his actions are driven purely by impulse and stimuli. He's probably hungry, and since we have brains, he looks at us like we're an all-you-can-eat buffet."

Jools shuddered at the description but reluctantly admitted that Krish was right. "It's not like Luna's soul will be in direct conflict with anything, since there's no other soul inside Ramhart to conflict with," she said. "The worst that'll happen is he coughs up a fur ball and takes a long nap."

"I hardly think that's the worst that can happen," Bex snapped. "Not to mention how it's totally unethical! You're actually suggesting we turn Ramhart into a cat!" She glared accusingly, even though Krish had done a pretty good job of making my case.

"Temporarily," I said. "Only until I get his soul back and can make the exchange."

"It sounds really dangerous." Jools chewed her nail down to nothing.

"More dangerous than letting him run around as a zombie?" I looked among them. "Right now, he's a threat to himself and everyone in his path. At least this way I can keep him safely contained."

"How?" Bex asked. "You planning to give him a ball of string and some catnip?"

I sighed. It was the only idea I'd come up with. "Do you have a better plan?"

Reluctantly, Bex shook her head.

"I'm in," Krish said. "Just tell me what to do."

"I've only done it once, but I think I have a grip on the mechanics. The hard part will be finding a way to subdue him. He's freakishly strong."

"Now would be a good time to call Rosie Grace," Jools said. "We could use a little supernatural intervention."

"Seems kinda strange she didn't show up after going to the trouble of getting us here." Bex frowned.

I wondered the same thing. But after Jools called her name three times, Rosie Grace failed to appear, which filled me with the sort of worry I didn't have time for.

With our tools gathered, we exited the Wunderkammer. By the time we found ourselves on the other side of the *Memento Mori* wall, we had definite, visual proof that the supernatural storm was officially on.

Outside, the sky crackled with electricity as buckets of something dull gray and slimy crashed onto the lawn.

"It's a fish fall!" Jools rushed to the nearest window and pushed the drapes aside as we gathered to watch the inexplicable sight of fish shooting from the sky. "It's a scientific phenomenon. There are records of this exact kind of thing going back hundreds of years all over the world."

"You mean this isn't unique to Glimmerville?" Shadow edged up beside me and growled at the scene. Like him, I didn't trust what I was seeing.

"They say it's a result of fish getting swept up in a tornado, then blown around the clouds until the wind slows and they're dumped back on the ground. But seeing as how there are no tornadoes in Glimmerville, I'm guessing this is entirely due to the supernatural storm." She turned to us. "We're lucky it's not raining snakes or frogs or even alligators, which has also been known to happen."

"Um, guys . . ." Bex pointed at Ramhart, who'd seemingly appeared out of nowhere. His hair stood on end. His eyes rolled back in his head. But there was no denying his superhuman strength when he came barreling toward us.

Someone screamed.

Shadow crouched low and bared his fangs.

It wasn't until we all scattered, taking cover behind various pieces of ever-changing furniture, that I realized Ramhart was so focused on chasing Rhoven that he hadn't even seen us, which gave us an advantage we were desperately in need of.

The poor bird squawked in terror, leaving a trail of feathers as he bounced from wall to wall, searching for shelter.

Bex peeked out from behind a lone velvet chair. "Ready?" she called.

"Not really." Jools shifted uneasily, chewing on whatever was left of her nails as she watched Rhoven seek refuge on a crystal chandelier, only to have it vanish a few seconds later.

The exhausted raven screeched in protest, his wings flapping wearily as he continued the quest for a safe place to land, while Shadow, maxed out by all the drama, shed himself of his skin and collapsed in a heap, only to pop right back up again. Like the rest of the house, he was caught in a loop.

The four of us looked at each other and began the countdown from three.

On *one*, Krish slipped from his place behind an old grandfather clock and crouched into position. "If this doesn't end well, I need you to tell people I went out fighting like a superhero."

"If you go out, you'll be screaming louder than Rhoven." Jools laughed. "But don't worry, I'll be screaming right alongside you."

I turned toward my granddad. "Hey, Ramhart!" I called, flashing him a rubber-band grin, my mouth stretched so wide I feared it might snap. "Maybe you should give the bird a rest and come hang with us instead."

His head swiveled between us and the poor, ravaged bird, who was down to his final few feathers. Settling on us, Ramhart staggered our way as I held up the monkey-tooth medallion, hoping the familiar sight might work to subdue him.

Instead, he arced his arm wide and took a swing at my head that narrowly missed smashing my jaw.

"Plan B?" Bex nodded at Krish and jumped onto Ramhart's back as Krish tackled him from the front. The two of them struggled to bring him to his knees as Jools wrapped a rope around Ramhart's chest and pinned his arms to his sides.

He didn't go easily. And to be honest, it was so hard to see him reduced to a tied-up, drooling, vacant-eyed beast that I hesitated to do what came next.

"Max, hurry!" Bex cried as Ramhart bucked and grunted and tried to fight his way free. "We can't hold him much longer."

With shaking hands, I flipped the first latch on the soul keeper as Krish reached around and tried to force Ramhart's lips apart without losing a finger.

"He's slobbering all over me!" he shrieked. "It's freaking me out!"

I flipped the second latch and was going for the third when it occurred to me that if I failed to get this right, I risked losing both my grandfather and his beloved cat.

"Max, *please!*" Jools wailed, her fingers rubbed raw from the rope.

Silently, I begged Ramhart's forgiveness, then snapped the final latch and shoved the soul keeper flush against his mouth.

"Can you see anything?" I was unable to get a good look.

Jools angled closer. "If you're asking if I saw him swallow the cat soul, the answer is no."

"But do you see a ball of light inside the container?"

She bit her lip. "Hard to say, but I think, probably . . ."

Before she could finish, Ramhart jerked back and let out a distinctly feline sound.

"Wait—was that—?" Tentatively, Krish climbed off his side. "Did Ramhart just . . . *meow*?"

We stood back and stared. He definitely seemed more docile than before. But it was only when he started licking his own shoulder that we knew for sure.

"You think it's safe to untie him?" Bex asked.

"Only one way to find out." Slowly, I unwound the rope, only to watch Ramhart spring to all fours and start batting at me with a hand he mistook for a paw.

"If we filmed this, it would totally break the internet." Krish doubled over with laughter.

"It might even get more views than Max's video." Jools giggled as we watched Ramhart stretch and yawn lazily before slinking to the couch, where he sprang onto the cushion, curled up beside a pillow, and continued grooming himself.

23
Supernatural Storm

With Ramhart more or less contained, it was time to move forward with the rest of the plan.

Problem was, there was no rest of the plan. I was making it up as I went.

Outside, the storm continued to rage as schools of fish spilled from the sky.

Inside, the mansion was in a state of complete pandemonium, with shifting walls and supernatural relics come to life.

With the video camera in hand, Krish stood in the entry, which was pretty much the only part of the house that remained unchanged. When he opened the front door, I noticed the snake guardians were no longer there, and I found myself hoping that once Glimmerville was sorted, they wouldn't return.

Bex swiped an armful of fish from the stoop and tossed them to Ramhart, who bounced off the couch and dove straight for their heads.

"He looked hungry." She pulled a sheepish grin. "And since we don't really know how much of him is zombie and how much is Luna, I didn't want to risk him going after our brains."

Jools looked on in revulsion as my grandfather tore into a still-wriggling fish. "For his sake, I really hope he doesn't remember any of this. For my sake, I hope I can find a way to forget."

"If Crowther left, it wasn't through the front door." Krish squinted through the viewfinder.

"Let me see." Bex took the video camera and fiddled with the lens. Frowning, she looked up and said, "Or maybe it doesn't think Crowther's exit is important? I mean, that's how it works, right? It only displays the stuff you most need to see?"

"Guys, just a thought, but what if Crowther's still here?" Jools hugged herself at the waist and cast a worried look around a room that was growing increasingly crowded with reanimated artifacts and newly awakened oil-painted subjects.

When she jumped to avoid a furry claw scampering across the rug, I was quick to kick it across the room, watching as it ricocheted off the pile of chupacabra bones, rousing Shadow back to his flesh-and-blood form.

"It was once attached to a yeti," I explained, as Shadow snarled at the disembodied paw. "And I'm pretty sure I know where to find Crowther."

In an instant, all eyes were on me.

"He's grave-minding." I spoke with more certainty than I owned, but when I replayed the words in my head, they made sense. "Ramhart was supposed to close up the portal, but thanks to Crowther, he never got the chance. Before he left, Crowther said he'd take care of it, but I'm pretty sure he's about to blow it wide open instead."

"But why?" Bex's voice trembled, and her body grew tense. It was what all of us were wondering.

"Do you think the Black Moon has anything to do with it?" Jools asked. "I mean, it's the perfect time for wishes, spells, and rituals, because the magick manifests quicker. Do you think Crowther is somehow utilizing that?"

"I think you're right about him being jealous." I turned to Bex. "He wants the mansion, Glimmerville, my inheritance. He got Ramhart out of the way. I must be next."

"You're really starting to scare me," Bex said.

"And that's exactly what he's hoping for," Krish said. "We can't let him win."

"But what does that actually mean?" Bex asked. "How do we even begin to get a handle on this?"

"Honestly? I'm all out of answers," I said. "What I do know is that Crowther underestimated me. He thinks I'm just some useless kid with no supernatural experience and no interest in learning."

"Well, aside from the useless part, is he really so wrong?" Bex twisted her lips, and cocked her head to the side.

"I admit, I'm light on training. But you guys have been at it a lot longer, and you've been trained by the best." That was the moment I glanced toward my grandfather with pride, only to find him down on all fours, stalking a disembodied yeti claw.

"Yeah, except Ramhart never mentioned anything about

a supernatural storm," Bex said. "Much less what to do if we found ourselves in one."

I fell silent. The room was in chaos. My celebrated monster-hunter great-great-grandfather was missing. Even Rosie Grace had failed to appear. And outside, the yard was blanketed with flopping, wriggling fish, but those things were the least of my worries.

I needed to focus on the big goals, make a list, and stick to it. Because the longer I waited for some long-dormant superpower to kick in, the clearer it became that there was nothing all that super about me.

"Before Magnus disappeared . . ." I returned to my friends. "He said the *Field Guide* probably contained a cure to help Ramhart. Which means I need to find Crowther, get my hands on the book, and put an end to this mess."

"So just you then?" Bex placed a hand on her hip and lifted her chin. "You seriously think you can leave us alone? In here? With *that*?" She jabbed a thumb toward Ramhart—a full-grown man acting like the sort of house cat he once accused me of being. "Because for your information, Glimmerville is our home. And unlike you, we have to live here long after summer is over."

Our eyes locked. Hers defiant. Mine welcoming the help, but also afraid my friends could get hurt.

"I know this may sound weird," Jools cut in. "But I think there's a pattern."

She had our full attention.

"At first it seems really confusing, right? Like the house is just randomly shifting in no particular order. But if you watch closely, you'll see that it alternates through eight different versions before it briefly returns to the mansion we know. And even then, it only lasts a few seconds before it starts shifting again. The electrical storm is a time storm."

"Of course!" Krish rocked back on his heels and made a cartoonish display of smacking his forehead. "It makes perfect sense—the window is open, which means the past is bleeding into the present."

"Exactly!" Jools said. "Which also means every version we see is a previous version of the mansion. You know, all the various remodels and additions that happened since it was first constructed."

"Which is why the furnishings and artifacts blink in and out of existence!" Bex was catching on.

"So, what you're saying is, if we wait for it to cycle through, we'll eventually get to the familiar version so we'll know where to find the haint-blue-painted wall?" I hoped against hope it was true, though we'd have to move fast before it shifted again.

With an excited grin, Jools held up the toe compass. "And this will help lead us to it." She tossed it my way. The sight of the jar hurtling through the space was enough to get Shadow barking excitedly, as though we were playing a game.

Of all the things I'd seen so far, the toe compass really did make an impression. It was exceptionally big, and with its giant yellowing nail and collection of coarse hairs at the base, it appeared to be real.

"Isn't it just for lost objects?" I turned the jar in my hand, watching as the formaldehyde sloshed up and down the sides.

"Pretty sure we qualify as lost," Bex quipped.

I wasn't clear on how to use it, so I held it up like a regular compass and asked it to lead me to the haint-blue wall. To be honest, I felt kind of embarrassed talking to a severed big toe. But when it started thumping hard against the glass and the hallway popped into view, I didn't think twice—I raced toward it.

"Max, wait!" Bex called out.

"Run!" I yelled, but when the wall started to shift, there was no time to waste, and I instinctively dove for the other side. "Look for the cabinet with the alicorn horn and keep moving toward the blue wall and the tun—" Before I could finish, the wall slammed shut, cutting me off from my friends.

I raced for the cabinet, shoved a couple of snake eyes into my pocket, and reached for the jacket that lay abandoned on the ground (since the yeti claw it once hung from was still on the loose), along with the bag Ramhart had packed for my first grave-minding trip (which I thought I was too cool to carry), then made for the haint-blue wall and tapped my knuckles against it.

"C'mon, c'mon!" I whispered under my breath. Nervously hopping from foot to foot, I stole a glance behind me, hoping my friends would catch up but fully committed to going on without them if it came down to that. The fate of Ramhart's soul rested with me. There was no time to waste.

As I waited for the passage to open, I decided to put that Black Moon magick to use. I didn't know any spells or the first thing about magical rituals, but that didn't stop me from casting a wish to the universe. And though I don't remember exactly how it went, I do know the words *please* and *help* made up a significant part of it.

The wall opened.

I looked behind me one last time. My friends were nowhere in sight.

Then I leaped through to the other side.

When the wall slammed shut behind me, I was swallowed by darkness.

"Hurry!" I shouted as the wall began rising and, one by one, I helped them slide under.

By the time it was my turn, the door was already descending. Frantically, I dropped to the ground, twisted onto my back, and proceeded to push my way through.

I'd made it about halfway when the giant rock slab began free-falling so quickly, I was sure it would slice me in half.

Somebody screamed—the sound wild and frantic.

Another voice, most likely Krish, yelled, "Quick—help me grab hold of him!"

A blast of pain flared through my legs as two sets of hands took hold of my ankles and wrenched me to safety. I rose unsteadily and turned to thank them, only to find that the tunnel I'd expected was gone, and my friends were nowhere in sight.

Somehow, I was back at Boring Elementary, standing in the middle of locker alley as my worst, most humiliating moments played out all around me.

To my right, I saw myself at Jasmine Skink's party just moments after I'd vomited all over her dress, my face slack and pale, her eyes glinting with fury, while the ghostly figure who was solely responsible winked out of existence.

To the left was a scene from my first and last sleepover, when I was caught halfway down the street in the driver's seat of a black minivan, struggling to take the wheel from a joyriding ghost visible only to me.

I tried to move forward, push my way through the scenes, but it was like being stuck on a treadmill. My soles were pounding, knees pumping, but there was no way to outrun all the horrible memories.

The nights I woke up screaming, knowing that there truly were ghosts lurking inside my closet and under my bed. That they weren't "just bad dreams" like my dad said. Those moments unfurled much like they had then.

Only this time, a new scene was included, one I'd never seen before—a behind-the-scenes peek at my parents arguing. The two of them blaming each other for my problems at school and my lack of friends, making liberal use of these words:

> *abnormal*
> *strange*
> *maladjusted*
> *scary*

And then I saw it—the worst thing I'd always suspected, now confirmed.

As the other scenes dimmed, a single sheet of paper drifted past a long line of lockers, sailing past my jeering classmates and weary-eyed teachers.

When it paused before me, I reached out to grab it. The message proved I'd been right. Every time my dad claimed my mom hadn't left because of me was a lie.

Turns out, she left a note.

Not to me, but to him.

The truth behind her move to Australia explained in a single, devastating statement.

> ... for years now, every time I look at Max, I want
> to run far away.
> So I finally did.

There it was. Careful black script on crisp ivory paper. There was no mistaking the meaning. It was undeniable. Plain to see.

My mom had left us because of me.

My hands began to shake. My ears rang with the mocking laughter of my classmates. Even after I clamped my hands to my ears, there was no way to drown out the jeers.

Yet the words I really wanted to silence were now seared on my brain.

> ... for years now, every time I look at Max, I
> want to run far away.
> So I finally did.

Even when I closed my eyes, I could still see them carefully scripted on the back of my lids.

> ... for years now, every time I look at Max, I
> want to run far away.
> So I finally did.

I even put her voice to a soundtrack so my mind could play it on repeat.

... for years now, every time I look at Max,
I want to run far away. So I finally did. ...
for years now, every time I look at Max, I want
to run far away. So I finally did. ... for years
now, every time I look at Max, I want to run far
away. So I finally did. ... for years now, every
time I look at Max, I want to run far away.
So I finally did. ...

I crumpled to my knees, my mother's words reverberating in my skull, the unrelenting taunts and insults refusing to stop.

I'm not sure how long I sat in my grief before my mind latched onto a single, nagging detail that didn't quite fit.

My mom never called me Max.

I was named after the father she loved and lost early on, and not once in the twelve and a half years of my life did she ever call me by the shortened version of my name.

She called me Maxen. Always. Without fail.

When I peeked at the engraving on the back of my watch, I noticed something else:

Dearest Maxen,
Despite the miles between us, you are always
near to my heart.
Mom

The handwriting on the note was the same scripted font the engraver had used.

My mom hadn't written that letter.

And Crowther didn't know psychometry.

He'd merely read the inscription on the back of my watch and pretended to know something about me.

I mean, sure, he could see ghosts, and probably lots of other things as well. But he wasn't nearly as powerful as he wanted me to think.

And, more importantly, he'd never be a Woodbead like me.

I looked up to see an army of glowworms slithering along the ceiling as the Soul Eater—that big, disgusting, one-eyed freak—now free of the water, scuttled toward me.

The Soul Eater had siphoned my memories and feasted on my shame and fear. And Crowther had somehow used that knowledge to weaken my game.

Before me, the glowworms dropped from the ceiling and the Soul Eater rose up on its hairy hind legs as Ramhart's words replayed in my head:

There's power in the observation.

As I fed the note to the candle's flickering flame, refusing to give the monsters—or my memories—any more of my attention, the images faded, the laughter became muted, leaving only me, the tunnel, and—somewhere out there—a familiar evil I was ready to face.

25
Gargoyle Express

I made it all the way past the former glowworm lair, over the Soul Eater bridge, and through the mausoleum without so much as a single threat.

By the time I opened the final door that led to Glimmerville Graveyard and listened to the eerie chorus of chants and howls echoing in the distance, I knew why. The evil was no longer contained to one place.

The electrical storm had split the sky open, charring the veil of mist into crackling bits that left my eyes searing, my cheeks burning.

The only positive was that the fish fall had ceased, though the disgusting remains smeared across the wet grass really stank up the place.

As promised, Crowther had gone grave-minding. Only in his version, the hungry ghosts Ramhart had worked so hard to suppress were unleashed while the harmless ones got salted. Which explained Magnus's sudden disappearance and why Rosie Grace had failed to appear after alerting Krish, Jools, and Bex.

It was strange how quickly my friends had disappeared just after we'd finally found each other. And for a few self-pitying moments, I feared having to go it alone. But as I took in the neat rows of tombstones, it occurred to me that I had an entire graveyard at my disposal, and it was full of potential allies. All I had to do was find the graves Crowther had salted and sprinkle them with the same red substance Ramhart had used to wake Barnabas.

I rifled through my bag and searched all my pockets, but that strange glittery liquid was absent. So I went back inside the mausoleum, thinking maybe I could find a way to coax Magnus out of his coffin, when I caught sight of Shadow cowering in fright, his flesh and fur gone, literally scared to the bone.

"Max?"

I turned to find Jools, Bex, and Krish rushing through the far door.

"I thought we lost you! It's like, one minute you were there, and the next we could no longer see you. It was like a vaporous screen blocked you from sight." In a rush of relief, Bex raced forward almost as if to hug me. Then she stopped short and said, "You okay?"

I stared at her, at all of them, overcome with relief. It was a miracle they'd made it out in one piece. "Everything went dark," I said. "And then . . ." The memory that replayed in my head was not one I was willing to share. "Anyway, I'm glad you made it."

Krish looked confused. They all did. "Why wouldn't we? I mean, aside from being really hot and humid, there was nothing to see."

"You mean, no rope bridge? No mutant glowworms or Soul Eater?"

Bex shrugged. "We crossed a bridge, yeah. But I don't remember seeing any glowworms, much less a Soul Eater."

I frowned in confusion, wondering if I'd truly gotten rid of the monsters or if they'd simply escaped and gone elsewhere. Then I told them about the ghosts getting salted, about the sky breaking open, and how we could possibly have an entire army at our disposal if I could just locate the right grave-minding supplies.

"Did you bring any snake eyes?" Jools nodded at Shadow still trembling in the corner, too scared to approach any of us, including her.

Gently, so as not to startle him, I called out his name and offered the snake eye I'd pulled from my pocket. It didn't take long for his greed to take over.

He licked the eyeball down to a keyhole-shaped nub, then lapped his bristly sandpaper tongue around his snout and begged for another.

"There's one left," I told him, watching his ears perk up and his tail set to wagging. "But you're gonna have to earn it." His ears flattened. His tail stilled. "I need to wake up some ghosts. And I need your help."

In an instant, he was off, darting toward a large ceramic urn he insistently nudged with his snout until the lid popped off and a stash of grave-minding supplies tumbled out.

With a jar of iridescent red liquid clenched between his fangs, he raced straight for my great-great-grandfather's casket and doused the mound of salt Crowther had put there. When he'd finished, he went to work on Scout's.

"Is it working?" Bex leaned forward, straining to see Magnus's ghostly form.

"You still have the spirit spotters?" I asked.

She slipped the glasses from her pocket, slid them onto her face, and gaped in disbelief at the tendril of hazy vapor twisting and stretching as it morphed into the spectral form of my great-great-grandfather.

"Why, good day to you, young man." Magnus tipped the brim of his pith helmet and bowed low before me. "Allow me to introduce myself. I am—"

"You're Magnus Woodbead, celebrated monster hunter." I hurried through our usual greeting. "And I'm Max. We're related. And while I know that's hard for you to believe due to my lack of blue streaks, I'm hoping we can fast-forward to the part where you ask how you can be of service."

He twirled the tip of his mustache between his forefinger and thumb. "Very well, then." He spoke in his usual agreeable tone. "What seems to be the problem?"

As I rushed to catch him up, to his credit he didn't seem the least bit shocked by the news. Even when I got to the part about turning Ramhart into a cat, he just continued tweaking his mustache.

"If it's my advice you seek, then I must say that I am of the opinion that a cat-man zombie is preferable to a regular zombie."

I blinked, amazed by his complete lack of irony.

"Though I trust you have every intention to remedy the

situation? It's not healthy for a human to change species for too long."

"That's where you come in," I told him.

With a hand hitched on each hip, and his feet planted wide, he looked like a safari-bound action figure ready to take on all manner of villains. I only hoped he could keep his memory working long enough to follow through.

"I am at your service." He gave a brisk nod, then patted the top of Scout's head. "We both are." Then, taking notice of my friends, he gave them a thorough once-over. "Am I to assume these are the troops you've gathered?"

I rushed through a series of awkward introductions, letting him know that only Bex could see him, and only because she was wearing the spirit spotters. Then together we headed outside, where the black and broken sky spewed so much electricity that the brim of Magnus's pith helmet began to sizzle, Scout's ears lifted like wings, and my hair stood on end.

"And so it begins." Magnus looked skyward. "The supernatural storm. Just as the prophecy stated." Beside him, Scout howled into the night as Shadow rushed to his side and howled along with him—that is, when he wasn't sniffing Scout's butt, of course.

"You mean the supernatural storm is part of the prophecy—my prophecy?" I edged closer to Magnus and away from my friends. If that were true, did it also mean I wasn't actually responsible? That I'd merely played the card fate had dealt me?

Magnus's eyes narrowed. "So it really is you. My replacement is here."

I wasn't sure if he was speaking literally or metaphorically. I only knew I didn't like the sound of it. I wasn't out to replace anyone, least of all him.

But it was what he said next that really floored me.

"You will be the next great monster hunter."

From behind me, one of my friends let out a small gasp. I think it was Jools. But I just stared slack-jawed, 100 percent certain he'd gotten it wrong.

"That is, if you survive the ordeal."

If?

"I thought you said it was a prophecy." The words came out so strangled, even I was betting against me.

The triumph I'd felt after getting through the tunnel was long gone. As I stood before Magnus, it was like I saw what he saw: a scrawny, shaky, scared-out-of-his-wits kid whose hair was standing on end. The only thing I had going for me was Ramhart's monkey-tooth medallion, and I think we both knew I was hardly rocking that look.

"There is always the matter of free will," Magnus said, which was pretty much what Ramhart and Crowther had said. So, like the other times I heard it, I chose to ignore it.

Unlike Magnus or Ramhart, I hadn't survived a yeti attack or stared down a cyclops. I was merely a normal(ish) kid who'd found himself in a heck of a predicament. What I needed was for him to stop musing about some distant future and help me stay alive in the present.

"Listen—all I know is we need to start waking the dead. The

good dead. The harmless dead," I stated, just to be clear. Though I was pretty sure those were the only ones left. "Then we need to find Crowther, get the *Field Guide* along with Ramhart's soul, and save Glimmerville from falling even further into chaos." A deceivingly simple plan that seemed far more achievable than it actually was.

With a bottle of red liquid in hand and Shadow close at his heels, Magnus floated deeper into the graveyard. In my rush to join in, I forgot all about the carpet of dead fish until my heel slipped out from under me and I landed up to my eyeballs in gills.

For a potential celebrated monster hunter, I was off to a pretty poor start.

Overhead, the sky continued to flash. And as I struggled to stand, I saw Bex sliding toward me, arms spinning wildly. When I reached out to steady her, we both went down in a heap.

She scrambled up and offered a hand. "When this is over, it's going to take a month's worth of showers just to get rid of the stench."

I yanked a fish from my pocket and dared a look back. "Do you think Ramhart's okay?"

"Define 'okay.'" Bex peered at me sideways. "You know, I still can't believe that's for real." She motioned toward the army of ghosts that Magnus, Scout, and Shadow were quickly assembling, but I was too busy looking at her.

"What?" She wiped a self-conscious hand across her cheek. "Do I have a fish stuck to my face?" She made another pass before she began to understand. She'd lost the spirit spotters when she'd fallen and had forgotten to put them back on.

"You still see them." It was a fact, not a question. "Even without the spirit spotters, you still—" From somewhere behind us, Jools shrieked, and I peered past Bex's shoulder to see Jools thrusting her arm out before her to keep from falling, only to summon my bag right off my shoulder and into her hand.

Bewildered, she glanced between me and the bag. "I—I don't understand," she stammered. "How did this—"

"Telekinesis!" Bex cried. "Looks like our wishes came true— I can see ghosts and you have TK."

"But how is that even possible?" Jools lifted her other hand, only to coax a large silver fish from the ground and into her palm. "Gross!" she gasped, and immediately flung it away.

I looked to Krish, wondering what he could do now that he couldn't before. And though I'm not proud to admit it, when he looked at me and shrugged, I felt a wash of relief. At least I wasn't the only one who didn't get a supernatural upgrade.

"It's all due to the power of the Black Moon," he said, voice gaining speed. "That, combined with the electrical storm, is allowing their long-held wishes to come forth. In fact, did you know that . . ."

My body went rigid. If what Krish said was true, then I'd soon find myself at a huge disadvantage, since I'd spent the last twelve years wishing to be normal.

Krish continued the lecture, going on to recite a long string of little-known facts about time loops, alternate worlds, planetary alignment, and electrical storms like the one we found ourselves in. When he paused, it was like he awoke from a trance. Slapping a hand over his mouth, he said, "Where did that come from?"

Jools grinned. "It looks like we swapped gifts! You wanted a download of supernatural knowledge, and I wanted TK."

"And I wanted to see ghosts, like Max," Bex said. "And now I can!"

They turned to me then, waiting to see my miraculous gift.

From what I could tell, I had nothing. And worse, I feared that my longest-held wish might've come true. While Ramhart had warned that I could never rid myself of my gift, I *could* stop it from progressing. And since seeing spooks was normal for me, that was pretty much all I was good for, and in this case, it wouldn't do much to help me.

I retrieved my bag from Jools and cautiously picked my way across piles of fish. My immediate goal was to stay upright. My long-term goal was to survive. Neither of those things seemed particularly likely.

I was just about to take another step when the fish suddenly walled up on each side.

At first I thought maybe I'd done it—only to glance back and see Jools willing the fish away merely by pointing her finger.

With the path cleared, I caught up with Magnus just as he was introducing me as his great-great-grandson to the army of ghosts that he'd gathered.

I stared in astonishment, surprised that he remembered our familial bond.

Was that part of the Black Moon magic as well?

"Max will be leading this expedition," Magnus announced as Barnabas nodded and Shadow and Scout howled alongside him. "So, go on then." He swiveled on his heel and tipped his pith helmet toward me. "Tell the troops what you need."

I swallowed hard and took in the crowd. There were tall gangly ghosts, short squat ghosts, young ghosts, ancient ghosts, all of them looking to me like I was some kind of authority. The only ghost missing was Rosie Grace, and I feared to think what Crowther might've done to keep her away.

I guess I hesitated too long, because Bex jabbed me hard in the side. "Max," she whispered. "The plan? You do have one, right?"

Truth was, I didn't. Though I did have a goal, and that would have to be enough. "Crowther's the key to everything," I said, voice rising in an embarrassing way. "We need to find him."

"My dear boy." Magnus draped a frosty arm over my shoulder. "The target has been identified." He pointed toward a brilliant flash of light coming from the other side of the cemetery. "May I suggest we pursue without further delay?" He stood at attention, awaiting my approval. With my consent, the ghosts began the march across the very graves they had once been buried in.

"That is one of the freakiest things I've ever seen," Bex whispered into the crackling night. "And considering everything I've witnessed so far, that's really saying something."

We'd just started to follow when a powerful rumble sounded

from above, and I looked up to see a sight so unfathomable that my brain scrambled to keep up.

From beside me, Bex gasped. "Is that . . . ? Are those . . . ?"

"Gargoyles!" Krish cried, putting a name to the inexplicable sight.

Jools raised her palm, trying in vain to steer them off course as Krish recited everything he never knew about the mythical beasts until now. Me? I dropped to the ground. Then, remembering Bex, I yanked her down too.

"What do we do?" Her face was tense, her hand closed around a rock as though aiming it at the fleet of gargoyles would be enough to ward them off.

With a hammering heart, I shut my eyes against the sight and yanked my hood over my head. We were outwitted. Outmatched. Once again, Crowther was ten steps ahead.

The ground juddered and shook.

A small army of clawed feet smashed to the ground, splattering me with ground-up bits of dead fish.

Slowly, reluctantly, I peeked an eye open, only to see Ramhart's stone gargoyles having come to life and Rosie Grace perched on one's back.

"And here you assumed I'd abandoned you for good." Rosie Grace leaned forward to pat the gargoyle's neck like it was some kind of treasured pet.

With my heart still pounding, I rose to my feet and casually ejected a fish from my shoe. By the time I'd pulled it together, Bex, Krish, and Jools were standing there too.

"Is that really Rosie Grace?" Bex stared in awe at the ghost she'd summoned to countless séances but had never seen in real life. "She's even prettier than her statue. How come you never mentioned that?"

A rush of blood rolled up my cheeks. With the exception of that one time when I was nearly dead, I never, ever thought of her like that.

"Is your friend all right?" Rosie Grace tipped her head toward Bex, who continued to gawk like she was meeting some A-list celebrity.

"She can see ghosts now," I explained, watching Rosie Grace smile and run a hand through her curls as though wanting Bex to see the very best version of her.

Then, pointing at the gargoyle, she said, "They guard Woodbead Mansion." The beast rolled its beady eyes and gnashed its long, jagged teeth. "And since you're a Woodbead, they're willing to guard you, too."

I blinked at the broken chains that hung from their collars, not entirely convinced I could trust them.

"They're not really chained to the roof. Ramhart would never be so cruel. It's part of their personal mythology."

I remembered when Ramhart had used that same phrase in relation to me, back when part of my personal mythology included not believing in things like stone gargoyles coming to life. It was amazing to think how much had changed.

"Does that mean the door serpents are real too?" I found myself voicing the suspicion I'd had from the start.

In place of an answer, Rosie Grace said, "Time to pick a ride. Though one of you will need to share with me. There aren't enough to go around."

It was like choosing a horse on a crowded carousel. Bex, Krish, and Jools raced toward the unoccupied gargoyles, leaving me to ride with Rosie Grace.

She motioned toward the beast, but before I climbed on, I had something to say. "Hey—um, I'm sorry about, you know . . . all that stuff I said earlier." Tentatively, I forced my gaze to meet hers. And though I have no idea what I was expecting to find, I'm sure it was the opposite of what I saw.

Rosie Grace stood before me, eyes shining clear and bright. "While I won't pretend to agree with your choice to act against Ramhart's wishes and go in search of the *Field Guide*, you're in deep now. We all are. The least I can do is help."

"So we're still friends, then?" I asked. For some reason, I needed her to confirm it.

"Water under the bridge," she said, and when she grinned, for one split second she looked as real as she had in that time slip. "I'm afraid the ride's a little bumpy." She motioned toward the gargoyle. "But you should be fine."

Determined to ignore her use of the word *should*, I climbed on behind her. Then, with flashing blue eyes and arched bony spines, the four beasts spread their wings wide and rose into the sky.

"This. Is. Awesome!" Krish shouted as Jools broke into a wide, toothy grin and Bex leaned into the wind, flame-red ponytail streaming behind her.

We flew in formation, Rosie Grace and I in the lead, the others making up the rest of the V. We soared high above the graveyard and through the crackling mist, blazing a direct path toward the flashes of light, which grew brighter and brighter as though guiding us to them.

"You'll want to ready yourself for this next part," Rosie Grace called. "The landing can be . . . a bit of a challenge."

As the fleet of gargoyles dropped from the sky, I braced for the impact, and still the jolt that followed sent me sailing right over the gargoyle's head to land smack on my butt as everyone else gently touched down.

Despite the awkward bit at the end, it was without a doubt the most impressive entrance I'd ever made in my life. I was already imagining a future version of me retelling the story when a voice drifted toward me.

"Hello, Max."

There, just a few feet away, Crowther sat astride a gleaming black stallion.

"I see you brought friends." He nodded toward the army of ghosts at my back. "It's a decent attempt, I'll grant you that. But what you don't understand is that you're in way over your head."

He was bluffing. Of that I was sure. Clearly, he could see he was outnumbered.

I was just about to say something to that effect when Magnus stepped forward and tipped the brim of his pith helmet. "Greetings, dear sir." He gave a curt bow. "Allow me to introduce myself. I am . . ."

Before he could finish, Crowther was howling with laughter. "Is this the best you could do?" He snorted so hard his shoulders shook. "An old has-been with memory issues, a dead hound who's gone nose blind, some paranormal groupies, a chupacabra who collapses into a pile of bones at the first hint of danger, and a leaky-eyed little ghost girl?"

Scout howled. Shadow bared his teeth. Magnus consulted with Barnabas, both of them equally flustered, while my friends glared indignantly and Rosie Grace stared into the distance, a steady stream of black gunk dripping down her cheeks.

"Don't listen to him," Krish whispered. "Keep your eye on the *bag*."

He emphasized the word *bag* in a way I couldn't miss.

Jools didn't miss it either. She lifted her hand to summon it to her.

I held my breath, watching the bag begin to quiver and rise, only to have Crowther slap it back to his side.

"Don't worry." Crowther smirked. "I'm sure you'll get the hang of it someday. Just not today."

"Why are you doing this?" she shouted. "Why are you acting like such a big—"

"You can blame him." He nodded my way. "None of this would've happened if you'd just stayed in Boring. Though I suppose it's not entirely your fault, seeing how eager your dad was to get rid of you. Not to mention that *sad* bit of business with your mom." He clucked his tongue in a show of false pity. "And considering what happened to Ramhart, looks like your next stop is foster care. Just like your dad after Ramhart got stuck in the time loop and his mom passed away. Funny how history has a way of repeating itself."

There was a time when those words would've stung.

Those days were dead and gone.

"I'm not going anywhere until I get what I came for." I moved forward, fully expecting the ghosts to move with me.

Instead, Rosie Grace gasped, and I looked down to find the earth falling away, as the lake bubbled up from the ground and expanded and flooded all around me. My eyes met hers for one startled moment, and next thing I knew, she winked out of sight.

"What in carnation is this?" Magnus thundered as Scout yelped and the water continued to rise.

Barnabas paled, growing increasingly translucent at the sight. "Sir, if you don't mind my saying, it seems Skeleton Lake is rising again."

"Why, I contained that over a century ago!" With a look of regret, Magnus turned to me. "I'm sorry, Max. I—" He was gone in a flash, taking the army of shrieking ghosts with him. Once again, Ramhart was right: ghosts and water don't mix.

"As above, so below." Crowther leered.

I watched his horse rear up on its hind legs, sending a wailing shriek through the night, as the earth cracked as wide as the sky, allowing the bone-infested waters to bubble up through the soil and muddy our feet.

The same waters that, according to Ramhart, served as a conduit to the otherworlds.

No wonder Crowther hadn't seemed concerned by my army of ghosts.

And yet, I still had the gargoyles.

They charged for the ever-expanding shoreline, buried their snouts in the water, and began to drink deep gulps.

"Traditionally, they're used as waterspouts," Krish explained. "Which means, in addition to warding off evil, they ward off water." Glaring at Crowther, he moved to stand beside me, ready to claim his place in what was sure to be our joint victory.

Only the water was proving too much for the gargoyles.

They couldn't keep up.

And I watched in horror as Crowther dug his heels into his mount's side, causing the stallion's mouth to stretch wide and shoot a blast of fire across the water that instantly turned the gargoyles to stone.

"They turn to stone when they need to regenerate," Krish said. "And for the record, that's no horse." He stared wide-eyed at the fire-breathing stallion. "That's a kelpie!"

Before I could ask, the stallion leaped forward and disappeared under the water.

With no time to debate, I sucked in a lungful of air and followed them into the depths.

Max's List of Top Five Terrifying Things

1. Supernatural storms
2. Skeleton Lake
3. Time storms
4. Fish falls
5. Zombies

26
Build-a-Bogey Workshop

It was like diving into a mud puddle.

The water was murky and thick, filled with knotted tree roots, tangled clumps of algae, and an army of hollow-eyed skeletons, their bony fingers grasping and clutching.

But Crowther was nowhere in sight.

As though driven by an invisible force, I continued to plunge. When I reached the point that my lungs were about to burst from holding my breath for too long, I shot through the sludgy crust at the bottom and entered a whole other world, with a sky so dark and air so squelchy, it felt like I was still underwater.

I staggered to shore, hoping for a chance to catch my breath and decide my next move, when I was surprised by the sight of Bex, Krish, Jools, and Shadow slogging their way through the eerie bone stew.

"That was hands down the grossest, scariest, most disgusting thing I've ever done in my life." Bex twisted the front of her T-shirt, trying to wring out the filth. "Who would've thought Skeleton Lake would actually live up to its name?"

"Where are we?" Jools squinted into the distance as Shadow gave himself a good shake that left us covered in yet another layer of muck.

"An alternate dimension." Krish spoke with authority. "Also known as an alternate reality or parallel universe. Which is to say that it's part of the multiverse. Which, according to string theory, and M theory as well, means—"

"I think what she meant was *which* alternate universe?" Bex said. "What are the rules? Who lives here? How does it work?"

We all looked to him for the answers, but Krish shrugged. "How should I know? I just landed."

"Well, it can't be all bad if you can do this." Jools used her finger to squiggle a series of figure eights onto the atmosphere. The markings left a definite imprint until the soggy air washed it away.

We all took a turn scratching our initials onto the ether, then wandered up the bank until we found our way to a run-down town square with abandoned, burned-out buildings and crooked roads with deep potholes where water had collected too long.

We passed a row of boarded-up shops. The warped wooden signs hanging over the misshapen doors had names like MEDUSA'S LAIR, HEMLOCK HIDEAWAY, and SNAKEROOT TAVERN. When I spotted a girl with hair the color of sunshine wearing a pair of hot-pink roller skates, I immediately recognized her as the seventies time-loop girl I'd met at the party.

"Hey!" I went after her. "Heather, right?" I raced to catch up. "Um, I'm wondering if you've seen Crowther?"

Slowly, she rolled to a stop. When she tipped onto her front wheels and spun toward me, I knew in an instant I'd made a mistake. This girl must've been an alternate-dimension version of the one I'd met. She had a wretch of a face, blotted-out eyes, and rotten teeth with no lips.

I screamed. (You would've screamed too.) And when I noticed the cluster of shadowy figures that came out to join her, I looked at my friends, they looked at me, and we did the only thing we could think of—we bolted down the first alley we could find and ran for our lives.

At the end of the alley was an old, abandoned nightclub. The sign over the sealed-up door read DISCO INFERNO, while DEATH TO DISCO was spray-painted across the front wall.

"The window!" Bex gasped. "Do you think we can squeeze through?"

With just a few steps remaining, my foot landed wrong. My ankle went one way, my body another, and my face broke the fall.

By the time my friends scooped me up and shoved me through the broken panes, I knew that while my ankle was sore and my chin was smarting from the blow, it was my ego that had suffered the most.

Maybe Ramhart was right.

Maybe I really was a house cat—coddled, overprotected, and completely dependent on others for survival.

Shadow set about sniffing and inspecting the place, though there wasn't much to see. It mostly consisted of a long, rectangular room with a bar running along one side, some tables and booths on the other, and a raised dance floor in the center with a bunch of mirrored disco balls hanging overhead. In the corner was a DJ booth with a turntable and several tall stacks of old vinyl.

As Bex drew the threadbare red velvet curtain to cover the broken panes of glass, Jools hugged herself at the waist and cast a worried look all around. "How long before they catch up?"

It was the question we were all thinking.

Bex moved away from the window, her sneakers squeaking against the cracked tile floors, she made her way behind the bar, searching for something—*anything*—we could use to arm ourselves. "You think they're connected to Crowther?" she asked.

"Even if they're not, we can assume they're not friendly." Inwardly, I rolled my eyes at myself. Nothing like stating the obvious.

"Well, we can't hide here forever," Jools said. Having chewed her nails to the quick, she began to fidget with the end of her braid. "We need a plan."

She was right, of course. Problem was, I didn't even know where to start.

"Is your telekinesis still working?" Krish turned to Jools, watching as she took a steadying breath, turned toward the DJ booth, and raised her right hand. A moment later, an album slipped from the top of the stack and onto her palm.

Stayin' Alive. She flashed a cover featuring three strange-looking creatures dressed in silky white shirts and too-tight pants. I guess they were the rock stars of whatever weird dimension we'd found ourselves in. "Do you think it's a sign?"

"I think it's a goal." Bex folded her arms over her chest as Jools discarded the record onto a nearby table.

"And can you still see ghosts?" Krish looked to Bex.

"Are there any ghosts present?" She looked all around, then to me, but just because I didn't see any didn't mean they weren't there. I was no longer sure I could trust my abilities.

I shrugged. "I don't *think* so."

"And you? Still a walking supernatural encyclopedia?" She nodded at Krish.

"Ask me something," he said. "Anything."

As he fielded her various questions about a wide range of paranormal phenomena, my gaze found the mirror behind the bar—or rather, our reflections in the mirror, and let's just say it didn't exactly inspire confidence. Our clothes were caked with mud, and though our gifts might be impressive in the regular world, there was no denying they wouldn't do much for us here.

We needed an extra edge—something bigger, stronger, more powerful than us. Without taking time to properly vet the idea, I blurted, "Tell me what you know about making a bogey. Only the edited version. Like a quick, step-by-step tutorial."

Krish, who was still spouting facts to Bex, barely took a breath before he switched tracks. It was like having Siri or Alexa for a friend. I listened carefully while he went on, though it was pretty much the same thing both Crowther and Ramhart had said. A bogey is basically born of the imagination. It's a thought-form come to life. Matter made from mind.

"I say we make one. Only, you know, like a bodyguard bogey."
I expected enthusiasm. What I got was the opposite.

"I don't know, Max." Jools fiddled with the collection of crystal bracelets that circled her wrists. "It sounds dangerous, and what if we lose control of it?"

"Jools is right." Bex nodded. "What's to keep the monster from turning on us? I mean, that's what it is, right? An imaginary monster made real?"

It was a sobering thought, but since no one had a better idea, I called for a vote.

My hand went up. Krish's, too. Though he was quick to explain, "I'm only voting in favor because I can't think of a better alternative."

Bex was reluctant, but ultimately she was in, which left only Jools.

"Fine." Jools sighed in defeat. "Desperate times, desperate measures, whatever. But just so you know, I'm mostly agreeing because I doubt it'll work."

Bex rolled her eyes. "We need a show of hands. Verbals don't count."

Jools groaned and thrust a careless hand toward the ceiling. A second later, a mirrored disco ball broke away and crashed to the floor.

With a look of absolute panic, she glanced between the shiny silver shards scattered about and her own shaking fingers as though she could no longer trust them. "These things are like weapons—one of you could've been hurt!"

"I'm more worried someone might've heard." Bex cast a nervous look at the window, where a muted shuffling drifted through the panes. It reminded me of the sound of someone—or more likely, some*thing*—trying not to be heard.

"About that bogey . . . ," I whispered, and immediately we set to work.

We determined how it would look: Big. Strong. Scary.

How it would act: like a bodyguard bent on keeping us from harm.

Then we closed our eyes, joined hands, conjured the corresponding image in our heads, and wished the creature into the world—much like making a wish on a birthday candle, only a lot more sinister.

I'm not sure who opened their eyes first, but I do know we all felt kind of foolish when we found ourselves blinking at each other.

"How long is it supposed to take?" Jools hugged Shadow as Krish droned on about all the possible time constraints that went into the actual manifestation of a bogey, while I got to my feet, flinching at the stab of pain that shot through my ankle.

"Forget it," I said. "If the bogey appears, great. If not . . ." I made a flopping gesture with my hands. "All I know is it's just a matter of time before they find us."

"Uh, Max . . . pretty sure they already have." Bex nodded toward the window, where we could just make out the shadowy outline of something decidedly human.

27
The Girl with Reptile Eyes

A small, slim figure climbed through the window and made its way toward us. With its back to the light, its face was so obscured that it took me a moment to realize exactly who I'd come face-to-face with. And even then, I had to blink a bunch of times just to make sure.

"Hello, Max." Jasmine Skink, my sixth-grade nemesis, smirked, looking just like she had on the last day of school.

I stood before her, gaping, stammering, failing to convince my tongue to play well with my brain. All I could think was how just before the battle with the bogeys broke out, I'd watched her eyes flash yellow and her tongue flicker blue. At the time, I assumed I'd imagined it, but now I wondered if there might be more to it.

"Did—did you follow me here?" Finally I was able to form an actual sentence, but she just rolled her eyes and strode deeper into the room.

"Max, do you know her?" Bex shot a wary look between us.

Jasmine laughed, picked up the album Jools had discarded,

and flung it over her shoulder, where it cracked against the door. "Max and I go way back. In fact, I'm not sure he knows this, but our families share a . . . unique history." She lifted a hand to fidget with the purple crystal choker clasped at her neck. "Sorry about your grandfather. What *was* his name?" She tilted her head as though trying to remember. "Reinhart?"

"It's Ramhart. And it's *still* Ramhart!" Jools snapped, but Jasmine just laughed.

"You kids are cute." Her award-winning grin stretched double wide. "What do you say I give you ten seconds to clear out? Everyone except Max. He and I need to catch up."

I turned to my friends, silently urging them to go. But they shook their heads firmly, refusing to budge.

"What do you want?" I demanded. It seemed as good a place to start as any.

"You know, Max . . ." She plucked a jagged shard of mirror from a nearby table and used it to file her nails. The move reminded me of the bogey that had gone after me in the classroom, and how it had sharpened its claw just after licking it clean of my blood. As if she sensed my thoughts, her eyes blazed on mine. "Yes, Einstein, we used your blood to track you. We couldn't just let you roam free. Not after what happened in that classroom."

She indulged in a long pause, and I found myself leaning in, desperate to hear what came next—who was this *we* she referred to.

"None of this had to happen, you know. I've been watching

you since birth, and honestly, your life was so pathetic and dull that there were times I literally thought I would die of boredom. That last day of school was just another test I was sure you would fail. But when I called in the demons and realized you could see them . . ." She drew a long breath. "Well, the game was on, and I've been tracking you ever since."

Demons?

Was it possible Ramhart had been wrong and those creatures in the classroom *hadn't* been bogeys?

And if so, what else was he wrong about?

"Anyway," she went on, "I brought along a few friends. Remember them? Pretty sure they remember you."

Through burning eyes, I looked past her shoulder to see a horde of ~~bogeys~~ blood-tracking demons spilling through the window. As I watched them form a half circle around us, all I could think was that if that bell hadn't rung, I would've slayed them all too.

I gulped past the lump in my throat and took a careful step back, hoping that in the alternate world we found ourselves in, demons were visible to everyone. I wasn't so sure I could take them down on my own. The super-slaying powers I'd had on the last day of school were beginning to seem like a one-time deal.

"Uh, guys, you can see those things, right?" My voice was so shaky, I'm sure it failed to inspire anyone's confidence, including my own.

My answer came in the sound of Shadow's bones collapsing.

Bex crashing into a table in an attempt to distance herself.

And Krish quoting from a long list of demon facts that could possibly come in handy at some future point, but not at that moment.

Jools was the only one left, and I glanced over my shoulder to see her raise her right hand and direct one of the barstools at Jasmine.

It was a relief to know I didn't have to fight them alone. But when Jasmine lifted her hand and steered the barstool off course, sending it sailing all the way past the DJ booth until it crashed through the back wall, I grew anxious again.

"So, you stayed to play?" Jasmine rasped, pulling a grin so wide her face began peeling away like a snake shedding its skin.

Her pupils narrowed to slits. The whites turned the color of urine. And the rest of her split down the middle, revealing a bizarre-looking creature covered in gray-green scales from her head to her feet.

Still convinced she owned the cutest grin in the room, she stood before us like some kind of egomaniacal lizard girl.

Or, as Krish was quick to pronounce—

"You're a Reptilian!"

The second he said it, the demons made sense. According to Ramhart, Reptilians used them as pets.

Though clearly he was wrong about expelling them all. From what I could see, at least one had slipped through.

My first instinct was to run, but I was caught in the quick-sand of memory, stuck on all the times I'd sat behind her in school, having no idea that under that bratty exterior, Jasmine

Skink actually looked like an oversized gecko.

Too bad I hadn't known that back then.

She lunged.

I countered with a punch to that repulsive lizard jaw.

With my blood roaring in my ears and a surge of adrenaline blasting through my limbs, I waited for the satisfying throb of impact, the thrill of my dormant demon-slaying powers to kick in.

She caught my fist before it could land. Squeezing it in a vise-like grip, she lifted me toward the ceiling as though I weighed less than air.

"This is for puking on my dress," she said.

I fought hard. Kicked with everything I had. The toes of my sludge-covered sneakers pounded into her disgusting green scales, but it didn't make a difference. Jasmine Skink was freakishly strong.

"You know how long I've waited to do this?" she shrieked. "Do you have any idea how much I hated hiding behind that sugary-sweet little-girl face? It's the worst assignment I've ever had. But now, Max, it's finally over."

"If it makes you feel any better," I croaked, "I always thought you were annoying as—"

She smacked me across the cheek, sending my head whipping hard to the side. With a constellation of stars dancing before my eyes, I told my friends to run. To save themselves while they still had a chance. But Jools wasn't having it. She lifted a hand and sent another mirrored disco ball plunging from the ceiling and crashing onto Jasmine's scaly gray-green head.

A fountain of lime-green gunk spewed from a spot just north of Jasmine's ear. And though it didn't cause any real damage, Krish was quick to inform us that the green color was due to the way Reptilians recycle hemoglobin. Then he grabbed hold of my hood and dragged me toward the big gaping hole in the wall.

As we fled, I took one last look at the fang-faced, bug-eyed, rotting-fleshed demons and appealed to whatever was left of the Black Moon energy to help see us through.

To restore the sort of demon-slaying superpowers I'd had in the classroom.

Or, at the very least, to make that bogey appear.

Bex was the first to exit, and I'd just started to follow when she stumbled back and crashed into me, causing me to crash into Krish, who crashed into Jools. In a tangle of arms and limbs, we watched in horror as a terrifying beast *blasted* through the wall and let out a thunderous roar that shook the whole building.

"You think that's our bogey?" Krish wore an expression that could only be described as half curiosity, half terror as I gaped at the beast's massive clawed feet, then craned my head all the way back to take in its block of a head.

The creature was as tall as a skyscraper, with school-bus shoulders and a torso so bulky it seemed made of concrete. And though its slab of a face was arranged in the usual way, the features were so blunt they appeared almost concave.

At first glance, the creature, beast, *whatever* it was, definitely qualified as big, strong, and scary. But who it would attack and who it would protect was anyone's guess.

With the floor buckling and popping beneath it, the beast crossed the room, aiming straight for us.

"Omigod-ohno-omigod-Ican'tlook!" Jools buried her face in Krish's back, but it was too late. The beast zeroed in and seized hold of her braid.

I froze. We all did, watching as the creature plucked a single hair from Jools's head and ran it under its pinhole of a nose.

When Jools started to raise her hand, Krish reached back and clasped it in his. "Don't," he whispered. "It just needs to sniff out the enemy."

So many screams piled up in my throat that I had to bite my own tongue to keep them from escaping. There was no use making it worse. On the off chance that my mad demon-slaying skills did reappear, there was no way I could take down a behemoth like that.

And yet I refused to make the transition to lights-out without at least taking a shot.

With the beast still grunting and now smelling Krish's hair, I slipped free of the pile, only to find Jasmine's pee-colored eyes searching for mine.

"What've you done?" she cried. It was the first time I'd ever seen her look scared. "What foolish thing have you done?"

No sooner had she said it than the creature grabbed me by the shoulder and shoved me so hard, I flew clear across the room, smashed into the wall, and crumpled to the floor.

It was only when I dared to look up that I noticed the beast had moved on, plucked a demon by its tail, and slammed it repeatedly between the floor and the ceiling.

The next demon was hurled into the DJ booth, causing a record to drop, the needle to set, and a blast of the wildly off-key, Reptilian version of "Y.M.C.A." to reverberate through the room.

Another was stomped so hard the lighted dance floor clicked on, the colored squares blinking shades of red, yellow, and blue, as the demon's insides spewed from its mouth like spilled soup.

Bex tugged my arm, urging me to go. And though a sick part of me wanted to stick around long enough to watch my former nemesis-turned-Reptilian meet the same grisly ending she'd intended for me, I didn't hesitate to follow.

If our bogey could take down an army of demons that quickly, Jasmine would go down just as easily.

One by one we slipped through the hole. It was only once we'd made it outside and Shadow reassembled his bones that we realized he was missing a few.

"I must've dropped them!" Jools spun around in a panic and ran back toward the opening. Returning with chupacabra bones in hand and a deeply disturbed expression, she said, "Krish, how do you deconstruct a bogey?"

We looked past her to see the monster we'd made barreling toward us.

28
Black Moon Rising

We'd accomplished nothing.

If anything, we'd just made it worse.

Sure, Jasmine was gone. But since I hadn't realized she was an issue until I saw her face peel apart, she wasn't exactly on my list of things to do.

As for the bogey, I felt 100 percent responsible. I mean, it wasn't like Magnus hadn't warned me, but I'd refused to take him seriously. Which was how I found myself in my very own "kids, don't try this at home" nightmarish scenario.

According to Krish, since the attention (and intention) that created the bogey also served to keep it alive, the best and only way to destroy it was to steadfastly ignore it, put it right out of our minds.

Easier said than done when you're staring down a bogey the size of the Statue of Liberty who wants nothing more than to thrash you around like a rag doll until your guts leak out of your mouth.

"What do you see?" Bex asked as Krish poked his head around

the side of the tall hedge we were using for cover. "Any sign of Shadow or . . . well, *anything* we should know about?"

The second the chupacabra had reassembled, he'd run off like a shot, proving once again that he was no guard dog. His appearance was the most terrifying thing about him.

"I figure Shadow's off hiding somewhere. As for the bogey, it got distracted by one of the demons and is giving chase," Krish reported.

"I don't get it," Jools said. "We specifically created that bogey to protect us. So why did it turn on us instead?"

"Monster turning on master. It's so . . . Frankenstein." Bex shivered and hugged herself at the waist.

I was about to chime in when Shadow returned, head hung low, refusing all eye contact. When I spotted Crowther, still astride the black kelpie, following close on his tail, I understood the source of Shadow's shame. He'd led the enemy right to us.

Shadow crouched at our side, growling and baring his teeth at Crowther in a delayed show of ferocity.

Crowther laughed, reached into his bag, and lured Shadow away with the offer of a snake eye.

"It's almost too easy." Crowther smirked, and I wasn't sure if he was referring to Shadow's shaky sense of loyalty or how easy it had been to find us. Either way, he was right. "You should've fled when you had the chance." He held the kelpie's reins in his left hand and used the right to wag a scolding finger at Krish, Jools, and Bex.

For a moment, I was so captured by the glimmer and wink of the iridescent purple stones in his snake eye ring, it took a few beats for his words to fully resonate.

How could he possibly know about Jasmine's offer to release them?

Did Crowther and Jasmine know each other?

Sitting up high on the kelpie with his over-groomed hair and theatrical three-piece suit, Crowther appeared calm, confident, in complete control of the situation he found himself in.

The kelpie, on the other hand, wasn't nearly as pleased.

According to what I remembered from a short stint I did at a horse camp (before I was sent home due to an unfortunate roping mishap caused by a cowboy ghost in my cabin), widened eyes, flattened ears, an elevated neck, and an incessantly swishing tail were all signs of a horse that was extremely displeased with either its rider, its surroundings, or both.

The kelpie was doing all those things.

"We're happy to go." I arranged my face into a mildly agreeable expression. "Just hand over the soul keeper and the book, and we'll be on our way."

Crowther snorted. "I've wasted more than half my life serving the old man. Catering to his outrageous eccentricities, running his pointless errands, covering for him whenever one of his pathetic inventions blew up in his face, which was more times than he'd ever admit. And what did I get for my efforts?" He paused as though expecting a reply, but I just stared back with blank eyes. "Everyone thinks he's some supernatural genius."

He shook his head. "Well, now he's a zombie, so there goes that theory."

"He's a zombie because he trusted you and you tricked him!" Jools shouted.

"Ramhart tricked *me!*" He shot her a withering look. "*I* was supposed to be the heir! He promised it all to me. And then *you*—" An accusatory finger jabbed toward my face. "You showed up and wrecked everything."

"I didn't even want to come here." I gestured widely, indicating Glimmerville, the strange dimension, the particular clearing we found ourselves in, all of it, but mostly in hopes that the sudden move would unsettle the horse even further. "You know that better than anyone. I'm just waiting out the summer so I can return to my normally scheduled life." I spoke with such sincerity I nearly convinced myself.

Crowther lifted his chin and stared down his nose. "I saw the look on your face after the soul keeper demo; you were all in—hungry for more. Why do you think Ramhart invited you to partake? But just because you were born to the Woodbead name doesn't mean you deserve the estate. Which is why you'll never get your hands on the *Field Guide*. For one thing, you're too much like the old man. You'll just squander the power."

"And this is what *you* choose to do with it?" I gestured toward the wet, water-damaged streets and whatever soggy hellscape lay beyond. "Use the power of the Black Moon to crack open the worlds and destroy Glimmerville? *That's* your big move?"

He pulled a slow, mocking grin, resulting in a slick display of narrowed eyes and white teeth that set me on edge. "While I appreciate the credit, this one's on you."

I opened my mouth to respond, but the words never got past my tongue.

"*You* read the *Field Guide* on a day when the portal was partially opened. *You* skimmed the contents, which not only brought them to life, but allowed the shadow worlds to bleed into Glimmerville. It's your prophecy, Max. I'm just seizing the opportunity I've been handed."

There it was again, the prophecy. Though I was no closer to knowing what it actually said. As Crowther gloated before me, I knew there had to be more to all this—more than him wanting control of the mansion and graveyard.

Be open to the clues, Ramhart had said.

My gaze lit on Crowther's crystal-eyed snake ring.

It was the same iridescent purple crystal that lined the walls of the tunnel.

The one Glimmerville was built on.

The one Jasmine wore on her choker.

The one I'd pretended not to take after Ramhart had warned me against it.

The same powerful crystal that, according to Ramhart, allowed someone to build their own portal.

And it reminded me of something I'd once heard Crowther say that I hadn't fully understood at the time.

"The mineral rights!" My gaze burned on his. "You want

to control all the galactrite!" I cried like I'd just won the final round in a game show.

The way Crowther's eyebrows drew together and his shoulders stiffened proved I was right.

"Fine," I said, trying to come off as reasonable. "The mineral rights for the book and the soul keeper." Seemed like a good deal to me.

He grinned cheerily. "Why would I make a deal with you when I intend to have everything?" He shot me a pitying look. "Here's how it's going to happen. You're going to die right here in this dump, where your soul and Ramhart's will be trapped forever. Bit of a shame, really, considering how you're both going to miss the part where I use the power of galactrite along with the *Field Guide* to claim dominion over everything, both living and dead. And just so we're clear, Rosie Grace *will* suffer. Thought you might like to know that, seeing how you feel about her."

His taunting gaze met mine, and I watched as he withdrew the soul keeper from his bag and flipped the first latch.

In an instant, Jools shot a hand forward, but she was no match for Crowther. With a show of great delight, he flipped the second latch.

"Max," Bex whispered. "We have to do something! We can't just stand here and watch."

I didn't disagree, but I also knew that one false move on our part could prove catastrophic.

I glanced at Shadow, annoyed to see him enjoying the last remains of his snake eye.

I looked at Crowther. With only one latch left between Ramhart's glimmering soul and an eternity in a burned-out oblivion, Crowther made a show of repeatedly tipping the lock with his finger before letting it go. He was enjoying himself, that much was clear, but it was just a matter of time before he grew bored of the game and finished the job.

Ramhart had told me my true gift would appear when I was up to my neck in it with nowhere to turn.

Problem was, I *was* up to my neck in it, and so far I hadn't had a single discernable sign that there was anything all that special about me.

Crowther smirked, held the soul keeper high. "Say goodbye to Ramhart!" he sang.

At the sound of his human's name, Shadow abandoned the snake eye. When his glowing yellow eyes caught sight of that glimmering ball of light, he lunged straight for the container, knocking it from Crowther's grip and taking his right index finger along with it.

Crowther howled.

The kelpie, spooked by the sight of the angry chupacabra, started bucking so hard that Crowther was flung from its back and tossed to the ground, where he lay with a geyser of lime-green blood shooting from the stump where his finger once was.

Lime-green blood.

Just. Like. Jasmine.

Were they both the sort of Reptilian hybrids Ramhart had mentioned that had tried to take over the human world?

With rolling eyes, the kelpie continued to buck, its hind leg nailing Shadow so hard that the chupacabra crashed into a nearby tree, where he collapsed into a pile of bones.

From the corner of my eye, I caught sight of Crowther's snake ring glinting among all the skeletal bits. I figured Shadow must've swallowed it when he bit off Crowther's finger.

Cautiously, I snatched hold of the ring, slipped it into my pocket, then inched to where the soul keeper had fallen, praying the mythical horse wouldn't smash it under its hoof before I could reach it. Relying on the few skills I remembered from horse camp, I murmured softly, kept my eye on the prize, and did my best to calm the beast before it did the sort of damage that could never be reversed.

"Whoa," I cooed, trying to ignore the fact that this was no average horse but rather a fabled beast that outmatched me in strength, size, fire-breathing abilities, and just about everything else.

"Tell me what you know about kelpies," I whisper-yelled to Krish.

"They're shape-shifters," he said without missing a beat. "They lure you onto their backs and into the water, where they eat you."

None of that sounded good. The only thing I had going for me was that we were far away from the lake.

"Something maybe more useful?" I croaked, keeping an eye on the beast. Its glowing eyes flashed wildly. Its tail snapped and thrashed through the air, roaring like thunder, as fiery flames shot from its mouth.

"Control the bridle, control the kelpie!" Krish cried.

It seemed like good advice, but the kelpie was so high-strung that I wasn't sure I could get close enough to seize hold of the reins without getting trampled, scorched, or both.

"Everything's going to be all right," I sang, tentatively reaching for the bridle. My fingers just grazed the leather when the kelpie skittered backward, kicking a hind leg against the soul keeper and sending it soaring out of reach.

With a furious grunt and a burst of fire shooting from its muzzle, the horse spun around and ran off like a shot. When its hooves nearly crashed down on the soul keeper, I thought for sure it was over, only to watch the container rise from the ground and whiz past my head.

Jools.

A flood of relief washed over me.

Jools had come through after all.

"Hey, Max."

I spun around to find Crowther back on his feet, using his good hand to flip through the *Field Guide*. "Look what I managed to summon—straight from the pages of the book!" With three fingers, a thumb, and a bloody green stump, he pointed to where an army of demons and beasts, including Sasquatch, Yeti, and another giant, hairy, ape-like creature with enormous feet that I instantly recognized as a Yowie, surrounded my friends.

Jasmine stood off to the side, soul keeper in hand. "Looks like my TK is stronger than yours." Her mocking gaze landed on Jools.

The beasts looked just like the pictures Ramhart had sketched, only now they were living, breathing, flesh-and-blood beings. And I knew without being told that with one word from Crowther or Jasmine, my friends would be destroyed.

I set my sights on Jasmine and fought to keep cool. "Last time I saw you, you were about to be dead."

"Do I look dead?" She sneered.

I ran a scrutinizing gaze down the whole repulsive length of her. "Maybe a little green around the . . ." I gestured to her face. "And speaking of green . . ." I swung toward Crowther, who was now fully transformed into his true Reptilian form. "You two related? Twins, maybe? Because there's a startling resemblance."

"Funny, Max." Crowther glared. "How come I never knew you were so funny?"

"Guess you failed to bring out that side of me." I shrugged, my stomach a jumble of nerves, but I refused to let on. "Hey, I have a question. If you really are a Lizard Man, then where do you keep your tail? Is that why you always wear those fancy *tail*-coats?" I laughed in spite of myself.

"We share a common interest." Jasmine spoke in the bratty tone she used on me at school, and while I hate to admit it, I found it intimidating.

"Yeah? And what's that?" I was working on a plan. And that plan was to keep them talking for as long as I could so I could use that time to figure out an actual plan.

"To claim dominion over all the dimensions, beginning with

yours," Jasmine stated, as though that were a completely reasonable goal. The kind of thing you might say at a job interview when asked to describe where you see yourself in five years. "And in the interest of complete transparency, Crowther and I are siblings. Half-siblings."

I looked between them. "Transparency? You do realize that everything up to this moment has been a long game of lies."

"And now the game is over." Her scaly gray-green features pulled taut. "Crowther and I not only share the same father, we now share control of the book, Glimmerville, the portal, all the dimensions within those dimensions, and most importantly, the galactrite that makes it all possible. The Age of Reptilian Rule is finally here, and it's long overdue."

That was when it all became clear. This boggy, soggy, burned-out hellhole was the Reptilian world Ramhart had told me about. The one they'd single-handedly wrecked before they set out to take over ours.

From the corner of my eye, I could just make out the sight of Crowther's finger slogging through the muck. Where it was going or why, I couldn't so much as guess. Instinctively, I pinched Ramhart's monkey-tooth medallion between my fingers in an attempt to steady myself.

"Anyway, enough of all that. What do you say we finish this already?" Jasmine slipped a claw under the final latch, ready to release Ramhart's soul, when Jools shouted.

"Hey, Crowther, how 'bout we make a deal? A finger"—Jools held up Crowther's gruesome bloody stub—"for the soul keeper and the *Field Guide*. If you hurry, you can probably give this thing a good rinse and stitch it back on."

But Crowther's ugly green head bobbed with laughter as he lifted his hand. True to his Reptilian nature, he'd regenerated a new finger and was using it to draw a series of symbols onto the atmosphere that sent the air rippling and pulsing in an intricate display of angles and arcs.

Whatever he was doing, I assumed it was responsible for my feet going numb, for the way the boggy air began to crystallize into thick blocks of ice that imprisoned our bodies and rendered us frozen, immobile, unable to do anything more than watch our undoing.

"Face it, Smith, you were never cut out for this." Crowther grinned as I toppled first to my knees, then to my side. My frigid fingers were stuck to Ramhart's monkey-tooth medallion as Jasmine came to kneel before me, soul keeper in hand, wanting me to see up close and personal exactly what would become of my grandfather.

Her claw scraped hard against the glass . . .

The metal latch let out a horrible screech as it began to lift . . .

It was over.

Done.

Everything I'd grown to care about, gone.

Ramhart's soul would be lost while his body continued on as a cat zombie.

My friends would never live long enough to realize the future goals they'd set for themselves, much less pursue them.

And I'd never discover my prophecy, never become a celebrated monster hunter like Magnus proclaimed.

I'd never become much of anything.

I wondered if my dad had been right—if I should've tried harder to live under the radar.

Considering the circumstance, it made sense. And yet it still didn't feel right.

I'd spent the last twelve years wishing to be normal. Or at least that was what I'd been telling myself.

But my real wish had always been to fit in—to be accepted for who I truly was and not some made-up, minimifidian version of me.

And in Glimmerville, I *did* fit in. For the first time ever, I had an awesome group of true friends.

The realization was like a lightning bolt striking my brain.

My deepest wish *had* come true!

I fit in. I have friends.

I was a Woodbead, not a Smith. I'd been born to a supernatural legacy.

All that was left was to claim my destiny.

I glanced between Jasmine and Crowther, then over to the army of creatures surrounding my friends. My grandfather had studied those beasts. He'd tracked them. Drawn them. And, more importantly, he'd believed in their existence long before he had proof.

Believing is seeing.

Finally, I understood what it meant.

Those creatures belonged to Ramhart. They were his to command. And, as a Woodbead with a supernatural destiny, they belonged to me, too.

I settled my gaze on Yeti. Even from a distance, with his enormous paws and thick, matted fur, he looked like the most terrifying beast in the world.

Ramhart once told me that the monsters we meet in our heads are much scarier than the ones we meet in real life, but one look at Yeti left me unsure.

I closed my eyes, only this time, instead of making a wish on the Black Moon energy, I gave thanks for making my wish come true.

"Oh, Max!" Jasmine sang in a syrupy tone. "Open your eyes. You don't want to miss this."

In the two years I'd known her, I'd never seen her so happy. I guess the idea of obliterating two Woodbeads in one day seemed almost too good to be true. Then again, she had no way of knowing that the monkey-tooth medallion once frozen to my fingers was beginning to warm so rapidly my hands were soon steaming.

As I watched her tilt her scaly green face toward the sky, sending a cackling laugh into the night, waves of warmth raced through my body until I became so hot, so feverish, that the ice prison encasing me began to liquefy.

I punched an arm through the remaining crust of ice and made a grab for the soul keeper, only to find it was gone. Somehow, it'd vanished right out of sight.

I leveled my gaze on Jasmine only to find her mirroring my

surprise. Not only had I melted my own ice prison, but I'd also managed to release my friends and Shadow.

Frozen with her arm raised before her, the second Jools had thawed, she'd summoned the soul keeper. "Turns out, I did stay to play." She grinned.

"Run!" I told Jools. "Go back to Glimmerville while you can."

Instead she tilted her palm, ripped a tree from its roots, and sent it crashing down on a horde of demons. With a path now cleared for their escape, she placed the container in Shadow's mouth and ordered him, Krish, and Bex to make a run for the lake.

Jools's powers were back. And judging by the way my body jolted and pulsed like an electrical current igniting my veins, mine were back too. It was the same feeling I had on the last day of sixth grade, moments before I slayed my first demon.

And that was when I knew: I was living my destiny.

I really was born to be the next great monster hunter, just like Magnus had told me.

Still, there was no way to be sure until I put my legacy to use.

I leveled my gaze on Jasmine. I couldn't think of a better place to begin.

"You can run around for a bit, if you want," I told her. "But I gotta warn you, you'll only be delaying the inevitable."

She looked to Crowther. He still had control of the book.

"Command them!" She pointed frantically at Ramhart's creatures. "*Do* something!"

Crowther flipped through the pages, shouting for Yeti, Sasquatch, and Yowie to attack.

From somewhere behind sounded a terrible roar.

Turns out, it came from a demon, and I wasn't afraid of those anymore.

I advanced on the creepy half-siblings. They'd already started to run. And though the sight of them fleeing was pleasing, I knew it wasn't because they were afraid of me. They were more interested in saving the book.

I set off after them, running faster than I ever had in my life, as Jools continued doing battle with the demons, crashing them into trees and into each other. I hoped she could keep it up long enough for me to get hold of the book and do away with the lizard sibs once and for all.

I was gaining on them, my fingers grasping at Jasmine's scaly elbow, but her flesh was slimy and slick, and it was hard to get a good grip.

My arm fell away, so I reached out again. Only this time, a bat-faced demon crawled onto her shoulder and hissed in my face. I grabbed that instead and squeezed its pointy head until it exploded in my hand.

I was just wiping a mess of disgusting gray ooze from my fingers when Jasmine came at me with a face full of rage.

Only she'd shed her Reptilian face and was back to wearing her old face again. The one that got voted cutest smile. The face that had terrorized me since fourth grade.

My hand closed into a fist, but I couldn't quite bring myself to swing.

I guess it's true what they say about old habits and beliefs dying hard. And despite what you may have heard about me, I'm not in the habit of thrashing my classmates.

Unluckily for her, there was a glitch in the system, and I watched as Jasmine's face peeled away, once again exposing the scaly green Reptilian one underneath.

"You killed my f—"

Whether she was going to say I killed her *friend*, *family*, *fiend*, or something else entirely remains a mystery to this day. Before she could spit out the word, I landed a left hook that saw her jaw separating from the rest of her face.

When I was done, I pushed up the sleeves of my hoodie and went looking for Crowther.

Max's List of Top Five Terrifying Things

1. Reptilians disguised as classmates
2. Fire-breathing kelpies
3. DIY bogeys
4. Supernatural storms
5. Skeleton Lake

29
Calling All Yetis

I found Crowther trapped beneath a fallen tree branch, courtesy of Jools.

"You know, it didn't have to come to this." I loomed over him and planted a foot on his chest.

"It was always going to come to this." He spat. Tried to claw his way out from under the branch, but I pushed down even harder.

"Are you referring to the prophecy?" I asked, realizing Crowther might be my last chance to find out exactly what it said.

"Doesn't matter now, does it?" He attempted a laugh. "You're too far gone. There's no turning back. And just so you know, there are plenty more of us out there. This isn't over."

I have to admit, I was taken aback. It never occurred to me there might be more Reptilian hybrids just waiting to pick up where the creepy siblings left off. Still, there was no time to dwell. Crowther had the book. I could see the edge peeking out from under a tree branch, and I needed to get to it before he did something foolish.

"The Watcher is here." I gestured to a place just beyond his left shoulder. "And since I can see it, it's not here for me."

Crowther rolled his eyes. "It's a bogey, genius. Who do you think made it?"

"Only one way to be sure. Go ahead, take a look."

He gritted his teeth. Bucked hard against the tree.

"Turns out, I've been brushing up on psychometry." I flashed the snake ring he'd lost back when his finger was severed. "According to this, you're not long for this world. Or any world, really."

He shot me a baleful look, clearly annoyed with the game. I could fully relate. "Give me the ring, Max," he snapped.

I feigned like I was going to hand it to him, then lunged for the book.

Predictably, he swung it out of my reach.

So I lifted my foot, allowing him to roll out from under the branch and stand before me. "Give me the ring and walk away," he said.

I slipped the silver piece onto my thumb. "Thought I might keep it," I told him. "You know, as a sort of memento of all the fun times we spent together." I glanced up at his face just in time to catch his gaze. He had no interest in me; he was fixated on the ring. So I took a closer look too, and that was when I discovered that the jeweled eyes were both glowing as though they'd been activated.

"You have no idea what you're doing." Crowther's teeth gnashed together as he ground out the words. "That doesn't belong to you."

"You sure about that?" I raised my hand so we could both admire the gleaming silver snake adorning my thumb. Though the truth is, it was several sizes too big, and those flaring eyes were really creeping me out.

Crowther cursed under his breath. With a flick of his regenerated finger, he lit a single everlasting match and held it beneath the *Field Guide*.

My pulse pounded. The flame licked upward, seeking the pages. Was he actually willing to destroy the book for the sake of the ring, or was he just bluffing?

"You won't do it," I said, but the way my breath hitched proved I wasn't so sure.

He moved the match closer. "Are *you* sure about that?" His evil hybrid face pulled into a smirk, leaving no doubt I was looking at a Reptilian with nothing to lose, which made him more dangerous than ever.

From the corner of my eye, I caught sight of Jools. She'd finished with the demons and was heading our way, but remembering what Ramhart had once said, I signaled for her to stay put.

Never get between a yeti and a Reptilian.

They're mortal enemies.

I could only hope that held true for hybrid Reptilians too.

I flashed my palms in surrender and took a step back. "Fine," I said. "You win. The *Field Guide* is yours."

"And the ring?"

I hesitated, but only for a moment before I sighed in surrender. My gaze locked on Crowther's, his yellow eyes gleaming with victory, as I tugged the ring from my thumb, tossed it over his shoulder, and watched as he spun around to retrieve it—only to run smack into Yeti.

The book fell from his arms.

I dove to claim it as Yeti let out a terrible roar and took a powerful swing that glanced over my cheek before landing on Crowther.

Last thing I saw before I fled was Yeti diving in for the kill as the Watcher lingered nearby, waiting to claim Crowther's soul.

30

Please Don't Feed the Bogey

"Isn't the goal to always leave a place better than you found it?" Jools said.

I took in the mess of toppled trees and the scattered demon and Reptilian remains—it was the sort of apocalyptic scene you might see in a movie.

"I'm not sure that applies to burned-out Reptilian dimensions." I started to turn away when Jools pointed to the place where Yeti, Sasquatch, and Yowie were looming.

Yowie and Sasquatch scraped at the dirt, but it was Yeti who really claimed my attention. He was massive, with matted white fur, a brown face, paws as big as my head, and eyes like shiny black stones that peered straight into mine as though he wanted something I couldn't quite grasp. Until my bag began to tremble and I instinctively reached for the *Field Guide,* flipped to the first blank page I could find, and watched as Yowie vanished from sight, only to reappear as the ink sketch where I'd first seen him.

Sasquatch was next, and Jools and I watched as he disappeared in a puff of brown fur. Thankfully, the pungent scent he carried disappeared too.

But Yeti wasn't nearly as docile. Lifting his face to the sky, he let out a powerful, bloodcurdling roar. Then, setting his sights on me, he charged forward.

Instinctively, Jools lifted a hand, but I warned her against it. "I hope you know what you're doing," she said.

That made two of us.

The sight of Yeti running at full speed was as magnificent as it was terrifying.

He leaped into the air in a blaze of fury, claws scraping wildly, before he pixelated and faded to nothing, leaving Jools and me breathless and blinking.

"What *was* that?" Jools peered between the *Field Guide* and me.

"They served their purpose," I said, not knowing how I knew, but trusting that it was true. Somehow Ramhart's sketches had the ability to will the beasts into existence. Then, once their job was done, they willed themselves back into the book.

I turned to Jools. "You should go!" I told her. "Now, before it's too late."

"What about you?"

I took a look all around, then turned back to her. "I need to find a way to shut down the place," I said, hoping I sounded more confident than I felt, considering I had no idea where to begin.

"But won't it just close down on its own?" Jools said. "I mean, wasn't that Crowther's goal—to trap us all here?"

She had a point, but I had to make sure the place really did shutter for good. I couldn't risk it rising up again, and I told her as much. "Seriously," I insisted. "Go, while you still can."

She shot me an uncertain look, then turned on her heel and raced for Skeleton Lake. When I could no longer see her, I began flipping through the *Field Guide*, hoping Ramhart had included a chapter on "How to Shut Down an Alternate Dimensions in Three Easy Steps!" If he had, I was unable to find it.

Below me, the earth began to tremble, and at first I wondered if Jools might be right. Was the portal closing in on itself? And if so, how long did I have before I became trapped?

I didn't have a chance to ponder for long before a terrible scream roared through the land, and I looked up to find the bogey we'd conjured charging straight for me, causing the ground to shake under my feet.

My first instinct was to run. But as the bogey gained speed, I realized it wasn't all that different from the Soul Eater. My attention, or in that case, my fear, was what fueled it.

In our short time together, Ramhart had prepared me for nearly everything I'd encountered. It was time I trusted him with this, too. So I turned away from the rampaging beast and hoped I was right.

The scent came at me hard and fast, like rotted meat left to sit in a garbage disposal too long. When a jolt of icy-cold air blasted hard against my back, leaving me woozy, off-balance, but ultimately unharmed, I knew I'd been right—the bogey vanished on impact.

The earth grew eerily still, and I looked all around, realizing I still had no idea what to do, until a quick flash of light caught at the corner of my sight, and I knelt down to find Crowther's snake ring wedged into the dirt.

I held it before me, remembering how disturbed Crowther had looked to see it in my possession. Was it due to some kind of sentimental attachment?

Or was it because the jeweled eyes were made of galactrite—a stone that allows one to build their own portal?

Build their own portal!

Suddenly I realized that the galactrite I'd been carrying when I ran into those skateboarding bullies was what granted my wish to escape by landing me in that time slip.

And if it could build a portal, did that mean it could close one as well?

Was that why Crowther had been so upset—because he was planning to use it to destroy this whole dimension, and me along with it?

I decided that had to be it, but that didn't mean I knew how to use the ring.

I pinched it between my fingers, startled to find that the eyes were beginning to dim. I took it as a very bad sign that my time was running out, and since I'd left my own chunk of galactrite back at the mansion, Crowther's ring was my only hope left.

Last time I accidentally found my way into an alternate dimension, I'd been looking for escape. So I closed my eyes and made a wish to destroy the dimension I was in. When I opened them again, I ran for my life.

With my feet pounding the earth, I snuck another peek at the ring, dismayed to find that the eyes appeared even dimmer than before while everything around me remained completely unchanged.

Was I aiming too high—wishing for things that were over my head?

Should I shift my focus to just making it back to Glimmerville safely instead?

But as I continued to run, I remembered something Bex once said about how, when it comes to supernatural powers, intention coupled with belief is everything.

Which was a lot like Ramhart's saying: *Believing is seeing.*

I raised the ring before me, those once-glimmering jewels like a dying flame, barely so much as a flicker. With no time to waste, I doubled down on my intention to utterly destroy my surroundings as an image of that destruction bloomed in my head.

Within an instant, the sky slumped and grew increasingly darker.

The ground beneath my feet started to crumble.

I pumped my legs harder, running so fast I was sure my lungs would explode in my chest. And still Skeleton Lake was nowhere in sight.

I'd underestimated the distance.

Started too soon.

Who needed Crowther when I was more than capable of destroying myself?

With Ramhart's monkey-tooth medallion slamming hard against the front of my hoodie, I continued full speed ahead, only to have my foot catch in a crevice that sent me reeling as the earth collapsed all around me.

My heart slammed.

My ears roared with the frantic rush of my own breath.

I was seriously doubting my ability to find my way out when, for one brief glorious moment, the sky broke open, a tremendous howl rang out from overhead, and I looked up in astonishment to see a brilliant golden vision of the monkey king himself lighting up the land just long enough to guide me to the lake before it fell dark once again.

31
Personal Mythology

Before me, Skeleton Lake bubbled and churned like bone stew.

At its edge, I could just make out the sight of Rosie Grace sitting astride a black stallion.

She tugged the reins, echoing what Krish had said. "Control the bridle, control the kelpie."

I was shocked to see the fire-breathing, child-eating, mythological beast acting so tame. But mostly, I was shocked to see Rosie Grace. After all I'd been through, I wasn't entirely sure she was real. "How'd you do it?" I asked. "Ghosts can't cross water."

"I took a leap of faith. As it turns out, it was only a myth. Probably created by the living to keep ghosts at bay. Consider it another personal mythology shattered." She grinned.

Though I was happy to see her, she didn't look like her usual self. Her face was smeared with that strange black gunk, and she seemed duller, less glowy, than I was used to. Personal mythology or not, the journey had taken a toll.

"You okay?" I motioned toward the stain on her cheek.

"Are you?" She gestured to the place where the yeti had

clawed me. Then, nodding toward the ever-shrinking sky, she said, "We should hurry."

Without a word, I climbed on behind her, dug my heel into the flank, and held tight to the reins as the kelpie raced for the water.

Only the water kept receding out of our reach as the lake began to evaporate at an alarming pace, turning into a spongy graveyard of skeleton bits that popped out of the earth and snapped and crackled under the kelpie's hooves.

"This is the only way out!" Rosie Grace cried. After all we'd been through, it was the first time I'd ever seen her afraid.

"Can't you just . . . I don't know, travel through the ether or float away?"

In a small, frightened voice, she said, "Not anymore."

I looked past her shoulder, watching with my heart in my throat as the lake continued to shrink, while behind us the earth crumbled to nothing.

"We won't make it!" she cried. "And even if we do, we won't fit! It's barely so much as a puddle!"

I tried to console myself by remembering that at least my friends had made it out with the soul keeper. Between the three of them, I trusted they'd find a way to restore Ramhart to his usual blue-haired self.

Then again, I had the *Field Guide*, and I had to do whatever it took to save it.

Never mind what might become of Rosie Grace, who'd gone to great lengths just to help me.

Beneath us, the lake bed crackled and burned, belching up a horrible sulfur-like smell.

Above, a charred and blackened sky continued shrinking in on itself.

With the ground dissolving all around us, there was no time to waste. We had one shot left, and while I had no idea if it would work, I was determined to take it.

I pressed my heel hard into the kelpie's side, tugged the ring from my thumb, and made a wish to find my way safely home to Glimmerville as I tossed the galactrite ring into the air, aiming for the tiny shimmering puddle of water, only to see it land short of the target.

My heart flatlined.

Rosie Grace gasped.

But I forced myself to hold on to the vision.

Forced myself to believe it would work despite all evidence to the contrary.

Next thing I knew, those snake eyes flashed twin beams of dazzling bright purple light as the ring went into a spin, lifted from the ground, and shot straight into the earth, causing a small spray of water to burst out.

With my eye on the prize, I urged the kelpie forward. "Hold tight," I whispered into Rosie Grace's ear. "We're going in. And if we're lucky, I'll see you on the other side."

The kelpie snorted in protest, and I was sure we were done for. Then, with a powerful arch of his back, he dove headfirst into a tiny, shimmering puddle of water barely the size of a thimble.

32
Ghost Squad

I guess I assumed the return trip would be easier.

But, once again, I found myself desperate to breathe. The kelpie had vanished, leaving me totally alone and hopelessly lost in the murky underwater graveyard.

And then I saw her.

From out of nowhere she appeared in a glorious vision of undulating, raven-colored hair, flashing green eyes, and pink lips that lifted into a grin. It was the most beautiful sight I've seen to this day.

When I caught a glimpse of her glimmering tail, I knew I was looking at the real thing.

It's how Glimmerville got its name. Because of all the mermaids that live at the bottom of the bottomless lake in Glimmerville Graveyard.

I tried to return the smile, only to swallow a mouthful of water that nearly sank me. The only reason I'm here to tell the story is because the mermaid pressed a finger to my lips, gently tugged on my sleeve, and rushed me to the place where the water turned silver.

By the time I burst to the surface, the mermaid was gone, but Rosie Grace was waiting on the lawn.

"Let me guess, saved by a Glimmer?" She shot me a look of deep scrutiny.

Embarrassed, I shrugged.

"Consider yourself lucky." She frowned. "They'll just as soon drown you as save you. She must've recognized you as a Woodbead."

I shrugged again, only vaguely aware of her words, because looking at her—well, it was like I was seeing her for the very first time.

"What?" She gazed down at her dress, her shoes, and back at me.

I tried to speak but wasn't sure how to tell her she was so radiant, she lit up the sky.

"You look—" I motioned to her face, watching as she swiped a self-conscious hand over her cheek, then gasped when her fingers came away smeared with white light.

"What is that?" I asked.

When her eyes met mine, there was something hidden in her gaze that I couldn't quite read. "It's a sign," she said.

I waited for more, but she seemed hesitant to share, so I did what I could to coax it out of her. "A sign of what?" The words hung suspended before me in cold puffs of air.

"That it's time to move on."

Her answer landed like a punch in the gut, leaving me winded and dumbstruck.

"Listen, Max—" She picked nervously at the blue sash on her dress. "I'm not sure when, or even if, I'll see you again, so . . ."

I shifted awkwardly. I didn't like where this was going.

"Anyway, I guess you weren't the only one with something to prove." Her lips pulled into a half grin, revealing a dimple that marked her right cheek. "The truth is, I've been in this graveyard for a long time—by some accounts, too long. And while it's been loads of fun, it probably wasn't the best use of my time. And, well, I was starting to show the effects."

I figured she was referring to the dark sludge that dripped from her eyes, but I asked anyway just to make sure. "What are you talking about?"

"The effects of someone wasting time. Wasting away. Taking much and giving very little in return. Truth is, Max, I was acting like one of those tramp souls I'd warned you about."

"I don't see you that way. Not even close. I—"

"You haven't known me very long. And, it's possible I've changed since I met you. Maybe even . . . because of you."

I remembered the first time I saw her, how she laughed when she saw my look of panic when we nearly plowed into her. It really did seem like something a tramp soul would do.

But she'd changed since then. We both had.

"I took a big risk back there when I dove into the lake," she said. "And while I won't pretend I wasn't scared, in the end, I suppose I was even more afraid of losing you. It's been ages since I even considered extending myself to help someone else. But now, because of it, it appears I've got my Shine back."

As if to illustrate the point, she began to glow even brighter until she was completely surrounded by a halo of light.

"You've been a good friend, Max," she said. "Possibly my only real friend. But I do have a family, and it's been far too long time since I last saw them."

"Are you—are you going into the light?" Though she continued to grow even more radiant, she was also growing increasingly faint and translucent.

"Will you miss me?" Her blue eyes went wide, her bottom lip quivered.

I gulped. Took a nervous look all around.

"You know what, never mind."

She shook her head, turned, and started floating away. The sight of her leaving was like a slap in the face.

I guess I'd spent so much time defending myself against other people's assumptions, I was no longer sure how I felt about her.

All I knew was that she was my friend, and I might never see her again.

And yeah, maybe I would miss her.

Maybe I'd even miss her a lot.

I might not even know how much until it was too late to do anything about it.

But in the meantime, the least I could do was tell her the truth. After all she'd done for me, I owed her that much.

"Wait!" I called, unable to breathe until she faced me. "Uh . . . thanks. For everything." I sincerely hoped she wouldn't notice the way my face had gone red. "You've been a good friend."

"And?" She cocked her head, sending a rush of blond curls tumbling over her cheek.

I took a deep breath. On the exhale, I said, "*And* the truth is, you've been a great friend. And yeah, I'll, uh . . . I'll miss you."

The way my throat went all hot and tight, I recognized it as the kind of "big emotions" my mom always tried to get me to open up about. Still, I'd come too far not to be honest with her. So I forced myself to move past it, to not look away.

"Truly," I told her. "I'll never forget you."

Rosie Grace smiled. Then, lifting a finger, she pointed past my shoulder. "Your friend is here."

I looked to find Bex racing toward me, that green orb bobbing just beyond her right shoulder.

When I turned back to Rosie Grace, she was gone, but she'd left a white rainbow in her place.

"Oh, look, a lunar fogbow." Bex skidded to a stop and motioned toward the phenomenon. "I haven't seen one since my grandma died. They say it's what happens when bright light shines on fog, but I'm pretty sure it's a message from beyond. Anyway . . ." She looked at me. "Krish and Jools made a run for the house." Bex skidded to a stop. "But I decided to wait." She kicked a stray fish head out of the way as I walked alongside her. Though the supernatural storm seemed to be over, signs of the wreckage remained. "The book?"

I lifted the flap of my bag and revealed the *Field Guide*. It was a bit worn, splattered in muck and splotches of lime-green Reptilian blood, but really no worse for wear.

"You look different." She ran a sharp gaze across my face.

I assumed she meant the yeti scratch on my cheek, and I self-consciously reached for it.

"No, I mean, your hair." She tugged at the bit in the front. "You have a blue streak."

My hand flew to my head. Aside from it being wet and still slightly sticky from the sorts of things I didn't want to think about, it felt the same as ever. "How does it look?" I hoped it didn't look weird, and I knew I could trust her to tell me if it did.

"It looks . . ." She stopped at the edge of the sidewalk, and between the yellowy glare of the streetlight and her piercing green gaze, I started to feel doubly self-conscious. "It makes you look like a full-fledged Woodbead," she finally said.

We were just about to cross the street that led to the mansion when the three skateboarding bullies I recognized as Beanie Boy, Acne Chin, and Mean Eyes circled before us.

Mean Eyes wore a cast on his arm, and from the menacing look on his face, he still blamed me.

"Well, if it isn't Alien Girl and Ghost Lover," Beanie Boy said.

I snuck a questioning look at Bex. I was pretty sure I knew where he got Ghost Lover, but Alien Girl?

"Move it!" Bex made a show of darting forward, but they just circled tighter.

"Make us," he said, as Mean Eyes and Acne Chin laughed alongside him.

"Don't you have something better to do?" Bex arced a disdainful brow. "Like shaving your back, or repeating a grade?"

Beanie Boy curled his hands into fists, his jaw clenching in a way that made me wish Bex had kept quiet.

"I can never seem to remember." She tapped a finger to her chin, feigning a look of deep contemplation. "Will this be your second time in seventh grade, or third?"

Acne Chin and Mean Eyes continued with the Alien Girl insults, but Beanie Boy turned his focus to me.

"Remember when I said you were dead?"

I gulped. Even though I doubted he knew the meaning of *rhetorical*, I still recognized it as that kind of question.

"Well, now, because of her big mouth"—he jabbed a thumb at Bex—"your little girlfriend is about to die too."

Inside my bag was a book that held the power to summon a beast that would send Beanie Boy, Mean Eyes, and Acne Chin running and squealing, never to be seen again. Never mind the demon-slaying power thrumming inside me.

But back at the mansion, Ramhart was waiting for a soul exchange, and he'd be really displeased to wake up as himself only to learn I'd used my powers to handle this sort of nonsense.

And yet it was hard to remember any of that when Beanie Boy raised his good arm, about to take the first swing.

Instinctively, my hands curled into fists as a jolt of electricity fizzed through my veins.

I was just about to (literally) beat him to the punch when Magnus appeared on the sidewalk, accompanied by Scout and Barnabas, and said, "What in tarnation is this?"

"It seems they're having a skirmish, sir," Barnabas replied.

Magnus leaned closer, cupping his ear.

"THE BOYS ARE PREPARING TO RUMBLE, SIR!" Barnabas shouted, causing Bex and me to double over with laughter.

"Oh, so you think this is funny?" Beanie Boy, unable to see Magnus, Barnabas, or Scout taking their nightly walk, assumed we were laughing at him. "I'll show you funny!"

He leered at me. But Bex and I couldn't help ourselves, we laughed even harder.

Beanie Boy reached for my sleeve, when at Magnus's command, Scout let out a ferocious growl and leaped onto Beanie Boy's back, clamping down hard on his pants.

"That'll teach you to harass my great-great-grandson!" Magnus shouted as Beanie Boy screamed, his fingers grabbing at his butt as he lurched and jerked and pleaded with his friends to make the pain stop.

"You're right," I told him. "That is funny."

"Like, really, really funny!" Bex howled.

Acne Chin pulled his phone from his pocket and instantly started recording.

Mean Eyes started backing away, wanting no part of it.

Beanie Boy screamed in agony. Plucking at the back of his pants, he glared at me and cried, "You're dead!" As though I was responsible for his butt being under attack.

We watched as he continued the dance, screeching and flailing about, until he finally yanked off his jeans and fled down the street in a blaze of tighty-whities as Acne Chin gave chase, recording the spectacle.

"Looks like your time in the spotlight is over," Bex said. "The internet just found a new viral video star."

When I turned back to thank them, Magnus and Barnabas were already gone.

33
Alicorn Latte

We opened the gate, raced past the red-eyed rav[en]
serpents returned to their place at the door, and [up]
stairs to Ramhart's bedroom, only to find Jools d[...]
mouse before him as Krish stood in the corner [...]
phone pressed to his ear.

They had the soul. I had the book. But I sti[ll...]
where to begin.

"So, what now?" Bex, still wound up from wat[ching the]
attack, stood before me, rubbing her hands togeth[er. "How do]
we do this?"

"I only know how to introduce a new soul." I shr[ugged.] "I'm
not sure how to remove one to make room for anoth[er."]

"Ramhart needs to invent a soul exchanger," Bex [said. "You]
know, once he's back to his normal self."

"Whatever you do"—Krish replaced the receiver an[d faced]
the group—"do it fast. Your dad's on his way."

I spun toward him. There was no way I heard that [right.]

asn't due until the end of the week. Had we lost that much in the Reptilian dimension?

Don't shoot the messenger." Krish flashed his palms in a ⌐ of surrender "But he's almost here."

Apparently he's been calling all day," Jools said. "We tried to ⌐ him off, but it only increased his suspicion."

Should be here in the next eight minutes or so, depending on ⌐ic," Krish said. "But since there is no traffic in Glimmerville..."

He didn't need to finish. I knew exactly what that meant. ⌐ce my dad set his sights on something, he always followed ⌐ough. Normally, that was considered a good thing. But for ⌐e, I wished he were more of a flake.

I stared hopelessly at Ramhart. He looked happy enough, ⌐led up on the velvet settee, entertained by a pile of cat toys, ⌐t I knew I couldn't leave him like that.

"Uh, change of plans," Krish called from the window. "Your ⌐d just arrived."

"Nooo!" Jools chewed the raw skin on her thumb.

"He's at the gate. About to punch a hole in the raven's face, he ⌐oks so angry. But even from here, you can tell he's basically an ⌐lder version of Max. Seriously, you guys need to see this. It's like ⌐ooking into the future," Krish announced.

Next thing I knew, a loud squawk shrilled through the house.

"We have to stall him!" Jools was so shaken with fear she'd ⌐resorted to jumping in place.

"There's no point," I said, willing to do just about anything to stop that horrible squawking. "Just . . . buzz him in."

"You can't be serious?" Bex cried.

"What choice do we have?" I removed the monkey-tooth medallion from my neck and returned it to Ramhart, who immediately hissed and took a swipe at it.

My grandfather looked content, and maybe that was how I'd have to remember him. Because one thing was sure: as soon as my dad discovered that not only did I have a blue streak, but I'd spent my time conjuring bogeys, visiting alternate dimensions, and hanging out with a bunch of ghosts along with a group of kids who referred to themselves as the Supernaturalists, he'd send me so far away I'd never find my way back.

"He's rolling up the drive," Krish reported. "And . . . parking . . ."

I centered my gaze on Ramhart. I could see no way out. I was destined to fail.

In the distance, the doorbell rang.

Knowing I at least had to try, I reached for the book.

The bell rang a second time. Then a third.

"Hurry!" In addition to jumping, Jools started clapping her hands.

I flipped through the pages, not exactly sure what to look for. Then, just as quickly, I stopped. I didn't have to go looking for anything. All I had to do was make the *Field Guide* do the work.

"Show me how to make a soul exchange," I stated, then stared at the book, waiting for something to happen.

Downstairs, the doorbell continued to ring, followed by the sound of angry knocking.

The book didn't respond.

I looked to Krish, the Walking Supernatural Wikipedia.

He shrugged. "There's no entry for this. You're the first."

Was it possible I hadn't made myself clear? I decided to narrow it down to the one thing I needed the most. "Show me how to help Ramhart," I said, barely finishing the thought when the book began to quiver and pulse. A moment later, the pages whipped into a fury until they landed on a recipe for Alicorn Tea.

Somehow, without knowing (or maybe he had known?), Ramhart had taught me exactly how to cure him.

"Someone get me the alicorn horn!" I shouted. "But make sure you keep it in the bell jar. Also, I need a cheese grater, nail file, whatever you can find. Oh, and a small bowl of milk!"

Outside, my dad was yelling for someone to open the door before he broke it down.

Inside, the Supernaturalists raced into a frenzied scavenger hunt.

Jools was the first to return with the bell jar stuck to her palm as though it were magnetized.

Bex had unearthed a nail file from Ramhart's bathroom.

Krish handed me a small bowl of milk.

After carefully removing the glass cover, I grasped the alicorn horn and angled it over the bowl. Remembering Ramhart's warning about the dangers of cutting myself, I gingerly shaved a bit from the tip and watched the iridescent bits blend into the milk.

"What exactly is happening?" Bex asked, as Jools cringed at the sound of breaking glass drifting up from below.

"Ramhart once told me an alicorn horn has the power to cure anything. Here's hoping he was right." I placed the bowl before Ramhart and urged him to drink.

The four of us held our collective breaths as Ramhart gave the milk a tentative sniff.

Maybe he was just thirsty after a steady diet of fish heads, but I like to think part of him understood what I was trying to do when he eagerly lapped up the milk.

Still, even after the bowl was empty, it was impossible to tell if the zombie part had vanished when he continued to act like a cat.

As my dad proceeded to break down the front door, I made a grab for the soul keeper.

"It's still hard to believe that's actually Ramhart in there." Bex peered at the glimmering orb. "Really makes you think, doesn't it?"

I didn't exactly know what she was getting at, but I didn't disagree.

One by one I flipped the latches, then pressed the soul keeper to my grandfather's mouth, hoping that as one radiant orb slipped in, the other would slip out.

But when I heard the sound of wood splintering from downstairs, I had no choice but to accept my defeat.

Despite my best efforts, Ramhart was still a cat.

The house was . . . well, let's just say my dad was about to have something to really freak out about.

I had a yeti gash on my face, and my hair was sporting a blue streak.

And I had no idea how to explain any of that.

My personal mythology may have undergone a drastic make-over, but my destiny looked bleaker than ever.

By the time I reached the entry and caught a glimpse of my dad through a broken slat, he looked the angriest I'd ever seen him.

When I opened the door and waved him inside, I saw that his clothes were disheveled, his knuckles swollen and red, and the first thing he said was, "Max, what the heck?"

As he pushed past me, I stared longingly down the drive and seriously considered making a run for it. But as the snakes stared at me with rolling red eyes, I realized there was no escaping the mess that I'd made.

"Dad," I said, too afraid to face him. "There's something I need to tell you—"

Before I could finish, a voice cut in, saying, "Why, David—what a wonderful surprise! Had I known you were coming, I would've ordered a pie." And I turned to find the mansion under a full-blown glamour spell as Ramhart stood before us, dressed in a blue button-down shirt and pressed khakis.

Max's List of Top Five Terrifying Things

1. My dad's face after he broke down the door
2. Saying goodbye to my friends
3. "Big emotions"
4. Saying goodbye to Glimmerville
5. The thought of never seeing my mom again

ONE WEEK LATER

34

Haunted House

"So, a soul exchanger, huh?" Ramhart touched his cloth napkin to his lips. "You really think it's necessary?"

"After seeing you run around like a cat zombie and fearing you might be stuck like that forever, it's not just necessary, it's imperative," I told him.

"I must admit, after surviving such an experience, I've come to think we probably shouldn't be dabbling in things like soul transfers." Ramhart twisted a long blue braid between his fingers, as Rhoven, still short of a full set of feathers, perched on his shoulder. "Might be a bit beyond our domain."

I scraped my fork across the plate, determined to capture every last pie crumb. "I just think it would be good to have one on hand," I said. "You know, just in case. Still, the good news is, you won't have to go grave minding again."

Ramhart shot me a curious look.

"I mean, now that the portal's closed. You don't have to waste your time on that grind." I paused for the gratitude I was sure was coming my way.

"Max—" Ramhart spoke in his striving-for-patience tone. "Grave minding is not a 'grind.' It's a great responsibility to keep the worlds contained, and the harmony we strive for is the result of maintaining the balance between the dark and the light. I was wrong about the Reptilians and the demons, I admit. As for Crowther, I only ever saw his human side, and he played the part so well, it never occurred to me he might be a hybrid. Still, looking back, I can see how his need for power and control ultimately got the better of him, and that's not something relegated only to Reptilians. So let that be a lesson for how easy it is to slip down that slope. It can happen to anyone, including yourself."

At first I thought for sure he was joking. Turns out, I'd never seen him so serious.

"I know you've heard a lot of talk about prophecy and destiny, but the person you ultimately become is always the result of your choices—the ones you make on a day-to-day, minute-by-minute basis. You carry a great power within you, Max. And it's how you decide to use that power that'll determine whether the light or dark side of you wins. As a wise man once said, 'Character is fate.'"

I glanced at Shadow sitting beside me, then back at Ramhart. The conversation was getting kind of heavy, and all I really wanted was to revel a little longer in my victory. "Well, at least it's over," I said.

"It's never over." The statement was simple, but it left me chilled to the bone. "There are always more Reptilians, more demons, more bogeys, and others you've yet to meet. Evil is like water: rising, falling, but always seeking an opening."

"So it's just a matter of time until the next supernatural storm?"

Ramhart settled his gaze on my blue-streaked hair. Then, turning away, he brought his napkin to his lips and quietly coughed up a small blue fur ball, the sight of which caused Rhoven to fly away in disgust.

I gazed down at what remained of the leftover Congratulations pie (Bex had dropped off a fresh one every day), doubting I'd ever grow bored of the sweet taste of victory.

"Oh, and before I forget . . . I have something for you." Ramhart fished two fingers into his shirt pocket, removing a black velvet pouch he placed between us. "Have I ever told you how I got this?" He fingered the monkey-tooth medallion.

I carved off another piece of pie, feeding some to Shadow and keeping the rest for myself.

"It was back in the early days, on a trek through Indonesia, when I stumbled upon a troop of baby monkeys whose mother had died. They were the most adorable creatures you've ever seen. They were also frightened, and I knew they risked falling victim to either predators or starvation if someone didn't look after them. So I decided to stay until they grew big enough, and experienced enough, to survive on their own. When the monkey king learned what I'd done, he presented me with this." He tugged the leather cord at his neck, and unlike the first time I'd seen it, I no longer doubted the story. "Sometimes we go looking for trophies. Other times the trophy finds us."

He nodded at the pouch and took a sip of his green juice.

(Even with Crowther gone, he'd sworn off all blue-colored drinks for good.)

I loosened the strings and dug a finger inside, only to find a large, jagged fang with a tiny spot of blood on the tip.

"Your first supernatural trophy." He beamed proudly.

"But . . . what is it?" No matter how much I squinted, I couldn't seem to place it.

"A gift from Yeti. Or, considering the scratch on your cheek, perhaps it's a peace offering?"

"So, it was a real yeti then? Not, like, the spirit of the beast?" It was a question I'd been pondering ever since I'd watched it pixelate out of existence.

"Does it matter?" Ramhart shook his head, causing a riot of feathers and blue streaks. "Believing is seeing, Max. It was your belief in the existence of Yeti that made him appear. In a world full of minimifidians, your belief is appreciated." Then, just as I was about to ask where he'd found it, he said, "It was tucked inside the pages of the *Field Guide,* same page as your prophecy."

"My prophecy's inside the book?" I looked to Ramhart in surprise. Though it made perfect sense, it was the one place I had never thought to look.

"It was revealed to Magnus long ago. We couldn't be sure it was real until you showed up and the events began to unfold."

I remembered how Magnus had referred to me as his replacement—*the next great monster hunter,* he'd said. At the time, I didn't really like the sound of it, but things had changed since then.

"But wasn't the supernatural storm also part of the prophecy?"

"It's all connected," Ramhart said. "The yin and the yang. The dark and the light. They are partners in an eternal dance."

"So . . . I set off the storm so I could prove myself?"

Ramhart grinned. "Why don't you see for yourself?" He nodded toward the velvet bag, where I dug deeper, only to find a folded square of paper tucked inside. From the frayed edges and curled corners, it had clearly been ripped straight out of the *Field Guide*.

This is what it said:

> *On the night of the lunar darken*
> *When earth and sky meld as one*
> *The youth shall be called to harken*
> *And don the crown of Seventh Son.*

I read it again. Then again. And while I don't really know what I was expecting, I can honestly say it wasn't that.

I mean, on the one hand I figured the "lunar darken" bit had something to do with the Black Moon. But what about the Seventh Son and crown stuff?

I made a list of all the male Woodbeads in my head:

Magnus

Roscoe

Ramhart

David

Me

I was only the fifth, which left me at a bit of a loss.

"So . . . it's symbolic?" I said, trying to hide my disappointment, but not doing a very good job of it.

Ramhart shrugged. "Seems pretty direct to me."

I squinted at the paper again, then back at him. "But how can I be seventh when I'm only the fifth?"

Ramhart grinned a sly grin. "Surely you don't think Magnus is the first Woodbead?" he said. "As for the crown, perhaps it refers to that blue streak you've earned."

"So you knew all along then?" I asked him.

"I didn't know everything," he said. "Only that you would be called to do something important, so I tried to prepare you the best way I could."

When I studied the prophecy again, it did seem more direct. But it also seemed just as likely we were making it fit. And maybe that was the point. I had the free will to choose whatever meaning I gave it.

I tucked the paper back into the bag, but I wasn't sure what to do with the fang.

"Keep it in your pocket," Ramhart said. "Put it on a shelf. Get your ear pierced and try a new look." Ramhart raised a single brow. "It's entirely up to you. Though you might want to get used to the blue streak before you graduate to wearing a yeti fang earring." His smile faded and he said, "You know, I can still try to find a way to make this all go away. It's highly unlikely, but I can try."

I was about to reassure him it was no longer necessary—that

while I'd have to pretend to be a minimifidian at my new school, in my heart I'd always be a Woodbead, and that was what really mattered—but before I could get to the words, the room began to tremble and shake, alerting us to my dad's arrival.

When the rumbling stopped, my dad strode in wearing a blue button-down shirt and a pair of pressed khakis. The same outfit Ramhart now wore.

"Pie for breakfast? Again?" He shot Ramhart a look of disapproval. "Good thing I'm taking you away from all this." He rumpled my hair, which to his eyes appeared an even shade of brown, then claimed the seat beside Shadow, who now resembled a labradoodle.

I watched him settle in with his coffee, remembering how upset he'd been when he first stormed into the house. But after a little coaxing and a generous slice of Ramhart's emergency stash of Chill Out pie, we managed to convince him it was all a big misunderstanding—that the electrical storm had caused the landline to fail, which was the only reason he hadn't been able to reach us.

Of course, it hadn't hurt that Ramhart found a way to glamour only the parts of the house my dad occupied, lessening the risk of another glamour glitch.

And yet, the Watcher/bogey that Crowther had made continued to lurk. Ramhart insisted that only by steadfastly ignoring it would it cease to exist. And though I knew it was true, I couldn't keep from looking at it. And every time I did, it served up a fresh new batch of the creeps.

My dad drained his coffee and pushed away from the table. "Max, you ready?"

I sighed and rose to my feet. It was the moment I'd been dreading.

My dad was determined to get an early start on the drive. We were headed to Normal, Illinois, whether I liked it or not.

It was funny to think how just a few weeks earlier, I would've been overjoyed by the news, but my time in Glimmerville had changed me.

Ramhart had changed me by introducing me to a great, big, extraordinary world where I had friends who liked me because of the very things that once made me a freak.

It was a lot to give up for the appearance of normalcy.

I excused myself from the table and made my way outside. When I passed the twin door serpents, I could've sworn they bowed their heads as I passed. But by the time I whirled around to double-check, they were back to their usual glassy-eyed stare.

Bex rode up on her bike, pulled a pink box from the basket, and gave it to me. "It's a Bon Voyage pie," she said.

I stared at the box, smiling at the memory the phrase sparked. "That's what my mom used to say instead of 'sweet dreams.' She said our dreams allow us to journey without limits." I looked past Bex, searching for the one thing I was desperate to see. "I guess she wanted to travel like that. Without limits. Now she can."

Bex regarded me with a careful gaze.

At first I hesitated to explain, but it was more out of habit than anything. The truth was getting easier to face.

I scuffed the toe of my sneaker against the ground and gave myself permission to finally say the actual words. "My mom's, uh—"

Bex cocked her head. "She's in Australia, right?"

I knew she was trying to help, but my constant denials were only making it worse.

"No," I said, my voice stronger, surer. "She passed away. In a small plane crash. In Australia."

"Oh." It was followed by the sort of long, sorry silence I once feared. But Bex was my friend, so I allowed it to stretch for as long as she needed. "I didn't know. I'm sorry. But . . . you still see her, though, right?" She pushed a stray curl away from her face, only to have it spring forward again.

She really was my friend, maybe even my best friend, and while I appreciated her willingness to listen, there were some things I still wasn't ready to share. The fact that, despite all the ghosts I'd encountered, I'd never once seen my mom was one of those things.

My gaze roamed the grounds, moving from the regenerated gargoyles to the octagonal window caught in a perpetual lightning storm, then back to Bex, watching as she picked at the end of her flame-colored ponytail, completely unaware of the bright green orb hovering just past her shoulder.

"Can you still see them?" I asked. "The ghosts?"

"You mean like them?" She pointed toward the lawn, where Magnus and Barnabas ran through the sprinklers as a crowd of skeptical ghosts looked on, and Shadow, still glamoured as a labradoodle, was forced to suffer the indignity of Scout's nose sniffing his butt.

When Magnus spotted me, he shouted, "My dear boy, have you tried this? Why, it's absolutely tremendous! You must join us at once!"

Bex and I laughed. A moment later, her expression grew serious. "But if you were asking if I can see that?" She hooked a thumb at the twinkling light just past her shoulder. "It's not for me."

With a smile and a swing of her ponytail, she returned to her bike. "Oh, I almost forgot—Jools had to babysit, and Krish's mom made him go to the mall to buy shoes, but we all agreed to FaceTime the Supernaturalists meetings from now on. So, seeing as how you're still a member, we expect you to be there. On time." With a final nod, she rolled toward the gate, but I wasn't ready for her to leave, not yet.

"Hey!" I yelled after her. "You never told me—why did they call you Alien Girl?"

Her soles skidded across the stone pathway until she came to a rest. When she looked over her shoulder, a slow grin spread across her face. "My dad owns a flying saucer repair shop."

I didn't even try to hide my surprise, which I know probably sounds weird considering Ramhart's collection of alien skulls and pictures of crash sites. I guess I still had a hard time making that leap.

Bex shook her head. "You've got a lot to learn, Max Woodbead!" A moment later, she was swallowed by mist.

By the time I headed back to the house, my dad was sitting on the front steps with his head sunk in his hands. I placed the pie box on the stoop and claimed the space beside him.

"The job fell through." He shook his head and frowned. "And if that weren't enough, the landlord just called. She rented the house to someone else. We're back to square one." His shoulders slumped.

"We can always stay here," I suggested. "You know, temporarily. Until you get sorted." I tried to act like I was just casually putting it out there and wasn't the slightest bit attached to the outcome, but he refused to even consider it.

"Listen, Max," my dad said. "Ramhart's been more than generous, don't get me wrong. And while I'm glad you two have formed a nice bond, I think it's better if we find our own place."

A moment later he was back on the phone, trying to line up a new home. Which was probably a good thing, because while he was distracted, a newspaper popped out of nowhere to land at my feet.

I looked toward the lawn, where Magnus, Barnabas, and now Scout, along with the rest of the ghosts, were enjoying the sprinklers, while Shadow lay off to the side eating a snake eye.

Clearly none of them were responsible, so where had it come from?

My dad ended his call and squinted at the copy of the *Glimmerville Oracle*. "What's this?" He peered down the drive. "I didn't see anyone deliver it."

"Maybe you were too distracted by your phone to notice your

surroundings." I laughed. It felt good to be on the other side of that.

My dad shook his head and returned to his phone, so I reached for the paper and gave it a skim. When I reached the real estate section, I noticed a listing for a house for rent circled in red.

Beside me, my dad grumbled angrily. I knew he was desperate to leave Glimmerville, but he'd be a fool to ignore the bargain I'd found.

"Listen," I said, catching him between calls. "I think I found something. 'Charming home in quiet neighborhood, within walking distance to Miss Petunia's and Glimmerville Middle School, this clean, modern gem offers three bedrooms and three and a half baths, with a large backyard including a delightful side garden, utilities included.'" I looked at my dad. "A charming, clean, modern, delightful gem! Sounds even better than the old house in Boring."

My dad wore a skeptical frown. "Yeah, how much? Castles don't come cheap, Max."

I quoted the price.

He insisted I'd read it wrong.

I handed it over for him to read.

He insisted it must be a typo.

"Only one way to find out." I punched the number into his phone and handed it over when a woman picked up on the other end.

"Not a typo?" He held the phone away and squinted at the screen as though I might've tricked him or something. "You sure?" He pressed it back to his ear. "So, what's the catch?"

Though I had to strain to hear the Realtor's reply, I'm pretty certain she mentioned something about the last tenants fleeing in the middle of the night.

"Hauntings? You mean, *ghosts*?" My dad peered at me sideways. I nodded eagerly. "Okay," he said. "We'll be right over to have a look."

"So, we're in?" My heart was thumping overtime, but I forced myself to sound neutral.

"A haunted house." He squinted at me. "You sure you're okay with that?"

After everything I'd been through, I could honestly claim with the utmost authority that ghosts really were at the bottom of the supernatural food chain.

To my dad, I said, "Pretty sure I can handle it. And if not, we can always call on Ramhart for help."

I held my breath as my dad gazed into the distance, weighing his options. "You really do like it here?" he said, speaking in a way that was somewhere between a question and a statement.

"I do," I said. "It feels like home."

My dad stared down the drive for a long, contemplative moment. When his gaze returned to me, his voice was quietly wistful. "You know, Max, while I'm not convinced I've been told the real truth of what went on before I knocked down Ramhart's door, I do know that whatever it was, it seemed to work in your favor."

I blinked at my dad, not entirely sure what he was getting at.

"I didn't send you to stay with Ramhart in hopes that he

would cure you. I sent you here so he could help you make peace with your gifts."

"But—I thought—" I started to cut in, but my dad wasn't finished.

"I know what you thought. And I'm afraid I gave you good reason. But the truth is, I never wanted you to be like anyone else. It's just . . . I was also bullied as a kid, so I know firsthand just how difficult life can be for those who stand out from the crowd, and I guess I let my fears get the best of me. You're a special kid, Max. And I wouldn't change a single thing about you. I'm enormously proud of the person you are."

From out of nowhere, the backs of my eyeballs started to sting, while my throat grew unbearably tight.

"And as for that blue streak . . ." My dad grinned. "No need to hide it. It suits you."

"Wait—" My jaw dropped. My hand flew to the top of my head. "You know about that?"

My dad laughed. "Ramhart's glamours never work as well as he thinks." Without another word, he folded the paper and used it to tap me on the shoulder. "C'mon," he said. "Let's go have a look at this haunted house."

Just then a faint breeze swept over me, and I could've sworn it carried the sweet, heady scent of night-blooming jasmine.

My mom's favorite flower.

The kind she grew on the trellis right outside my bedroom window.

I paused beside the car to see that same glimmering green

orb I associated with Bex twist and grow until I was looking at a full-blown apparition of my mom. And I knew in that instant that she'd never really left me. She'd been there all along.

The only reason I hadn't seen her was because my personal mythology told me I didn't deserve to.

The backs of my eyes started to sting, but in a good way.

And from the way she smiled and waved, I knew she wanted me to stay in Glimmerville, where I belonged. So she'd found a way to make that happen.

"Hey, Max, we need to hurry," my dad said. "We can't afford to miss out on this one."

"Coming," I told him. Settling onto the passenger seat and gazing out the window, I sent a silent thanks to my mom.

For the first time in my life, I was really, truly home.

You made it to the last page.

You are now one step closer to becoming a bona fide Supernaturalist!

But first you'll need to retake the quiz to see if any of your answers have changed. t

So grab a pen. Or, if this book doesn't belong to you, then . . . well, you know the drill.

Anyway, here goes:

Do you believe in ghosts?

YES   **NOT SURE**   **NO**

If you answered YES, you are 100 percent correct and eligible to join the Supernaturalists. Congratulations!*

---

*Bex wants to remind everyone that membership requires a unanimous vote. But seeing as how you made it this far, your membership is hereby automatically granted. But only you. No one else.

If you answered NO, please keep in mind that just because you don't believe in something doesn't mean it doesn't exist. For further proof, please return to page one and begin again.

If you're NOT SURE if you believe in ghosts, you should absolutely reread this book so the next time someone asks you that question, you can answer correctly.

Acknowledgments

No book is ever written alone, and I owe a huge debt of gratitude to the following people:

Michael Zoumas and Charles Matthau, for the inspiration and support and believing in Max from the very first draft. This book would not have been written without them.

Sarah McCabe, whose smart and insightful editorial suggestions elevated Max and company to a whole other level.

Elizabeth Bewley, as editor, took a chance on me back when she published my debut novel. Now, twenty-plus books later, she represents me as my agent. I'm forever grateful for her years of wise counsel and friendship.

Sandy, the unsung hero behind all my books who, thanks to Ramhart and Max, now knows exactly what to do should he ever get caught in a time slip.

ALYSON NOËL is a #1 *New York Times* bestselling author of many award-winning and critically acclaimed novels for readers of all ages. With nine *New York Times* bestsellers and over eight million copies in print, her books have been translated into thirty-six languages, been sold in over two hundred countries, and topped the bestseller lists of the *New York Times*, *USA Today*, the *LA Times*, *Publishers Weekly*, the *Wall Street Journal*, the NCIBA, and Walmart, as well as several international lists. She is best known for the Immortals series, the Riley Bloom series, and *Saving Zoë*, which was adapted into a movie now available on Netflix. Born and raised in Orange County, California, she's lived in both Mykonos and Manhattan and is now settled in Southern California.